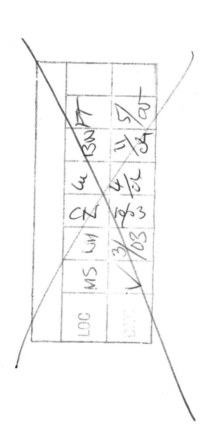

THE SEND-OFF

The sequel to A Bombay Affair

Bombay, 1959: when Monica Fernandes meets movie producer Stevie Stone, she thinks she may have found the rich husband she's been looking for. Meanwhile, Dee and Ben Carmichael are expecting their first child, but receive worrying news from the family doctor. And Dee's best friend, Anne, has found that a husband and baby don't always mean happiness.

THE SEND-OFF

THE SEND-OFF

Elisabeth McNeill

THE CITY OF EDINBURGH COUNCIL	
C0017678595	
Cypher	29.10.01
ROM	£18.99

Severn House Large Print
London & New York

This first large print edition published in Great Britain 2001 by
SEVERN HOUSE LARGE PRINT BOOKS LTD of
9-15, High Street, Sutton, Surrey, SM1 1DF.
First world regular print edition published 2000 by
Severn House Publishers, London and New York.
This first large print edition published in the USA 2001 by
SEVERN HOUSE PUBLISERS INC., of
595 Madison Avenue, New York, NY 10022

British Library Cataloguing in Publication Data

McNeill, Elisabeth
    The send off. - Large print ed.
    1.   Bombay (India) - Social life and customs - 20ᵗʰ century -
         Fiction
    2.   Love stories
    3.   Large type books
    I.   Title
    823.9'14 [F]

    ISBN 0-7278-7091-2

Printed and bound in Great Britain by
MPG Books Ltd, Bodmin, Cornwall.

Author's Note

The events and circumstances of Dee's pregnancy and her worries about her rhesus negative blood group are as they happened to the author in the 1950s in Bombay where the incidence of rhesus negative blood is much smaller than in Europe.

One

He came on board late at night, after thirty-five bright orange containers had been swung up on to the deck and the ship was preparing to sail. The din and clamour of the day had ceased and everything was uncannily silent. A sinister grey mist like witches' hair was drifting round the heads of skeletal cranes that stalked bird-like along the quay, and security lights cast pools of vivid yellow on to the matt black tarmac of the quayside.

Dee Carmichael, sleepless, staring out of her cabin window, was wondering if this journey was a mistake when her gloomy musings were interrupted by the sudden flurry of activity. A large car came swishing up to the end of the gangway where a fat little crewman in a yellow hard hat waited to open its boot and haul out four big suitcases. The man who stepped from the car was huddled in a long raincoat but his head was bare and the cruelly shadowless light from above turned his eyes into black holes and made his high forehead shine like ivory. One of the officers hurried obsequiously down the gangway and shook his hand.

He must be important, thought Dee, peering through the glass, for the officers did not normally behave like that. The newcomer was not young but somehow very formidable looking, and she guessed he was the fourth passenger on the *Selbridge Delta*. The agent had said there were to be four passengers on board and she'd already seen two of them. The last to arrive obviously knew his way around because he quickly climbed up to the metal companionway behind the officer and disappeared from sight.

There was nothing for Dee to do after that but take a shower and go to bed.

When she woke next morning the ship was cutting its way through the slate-grey waves of the Bay of Biscay, and heaving around in an unsettling way. She sat up in bed and quickly lay down again, once more filled with doubts about the wisdom of booking a twelve-day passage on a container ship carrying a crew of thirty-two seamen and four passengers to New York.

It had seemed a good idea when she booked, for she needed to be free of ringing telephones and doorbells. She was badly behind schedule in drafting the outline of her next book, a project that was getting nowhere at home.

She had been commissioned to write a novel about Eleanor of Aquitaine. All the research was finished – it had taken two years – and what she must do now was get down to planning the outline and at last start writing. Easier said than done, unfortunately.

"Take a sea trip," suggested her anxious editor, and that idea appealed to Dee. So here she was, comfortably installed in a large cabin furnished like a good hotel room with the extra bonus of the eternally fascinating sea outside her porthole. Her laptop lay open on the cabin table, her box file of notes neatly beside it. All she had to do was start working...

However, the usual deferring tactics had to be overcome and today that was even more difficult because the *Selbridge Delta* was rolling heavily and phalanxes of enormous orange containers stacked on top of each other like giants' building bricks on the deck below thudded and vibrated with terrible booming noises.

Buying time while she waited for inspiration, Dee lay in her bunk for the first day out of Le Havre, reading a mystery novel and trying to solve the puzzles in the *Daily Telegraph Book of Concise Crosswords* without turning to the clues at the back of the book. Next morning, however, though the ship was still shuddering, she felt well enough to go down to the salon for breakfast.

Seated at a round table she found the two passengers she had already seen. Though their faces were slightly greenish, they were very smart, impeccably groomed women who introduced themselves as Lucy Cavendish and Harriet Beecham.

Like her, they'd joined the ship at Tilbury. "I didn't expect such rough weather in September," said Lucy in a long-suffering voice.

"The captain says it'll clear when we're out of the Bay of Biscay," said her friend Harriet, "Besides, no matter how rough it gets, it's better than flying." She looked across at Dee and said, "We always cross the Atlantic by freighter because we're both *terrified* of flying."

Dee nodded in tacit sympathy. She avoided giving her own reason for sailing because she didn't want to sound pretentious or to get into a conversation about Queen Eleanor. Too much discussion of a subject before writing tended to kill it, she always found. Instead she said, "I understand. Anyway, it's nice and peaceful on board with only four passengers."

"I thought the fourth one missed the sailing from Tilbury," said Harriet.

"Well, I saw a man who looked like a passenger come on late at night in Le Havre just before we left," Dee told her.

Lucy, who had a halo of straw-like hair dyed to a Scandinavian shade of blonde, visibly brightened at this news. "A man? On his own? You're sure he wasn't crew?"

"I don't think so. He had lots of baggage and wasn't in uniform ... anyway, he didn't look like crew somehow. And he seemed to be alone – there was no one with him at the time," said Dee.

Lucy swiftly turned to Ray, the Filipino steward, who was lurking in the doorway between the dining room and the kitchen, openly eavesdropping on their conversation.

"How many passengers are on board now?" she asked.

"Four, ma'am. There's another one in the owner's suite," was the reply.

"In that big double cabin up on top below the bridge? Only one person?" she asked.

"Yes'm."

"What's the passenger's name?"

Ray frowned and hesitated for a moment, but, intimidated by Lucy's demanding eyes, gave in and said, "Mr Steindl."

"Steindl? Are you sure?" she asked.

"Yes. Mr Saul Steindl," affirmed Ray.

She gave a small scream like a child being tempted by a cream bun. "It can't be *the* Saul Steindl, can it?" she cried, turning so excitedly to her friend that her heavy gold jewellery jangled. "You don't think it could be *S.N. Steindl*! What luck if we're on the same ship as him!"

"It's not likely to be the same one. He'd have a private jet," replied Harriet less animatedly, carefully replacing her cup in its saucer. She was obviously used to Lucy's enthusiasm.

"I'm sure it's him. It's such an unusual name – Saul Steindl. There can't be many people around called that. It's not like Smith or Brown."

Two round red spots of excitement were shining in Lucy's immaculately made-up cheeks as she turned to Dee and asked, "You saw him. How old did he look?"

"Late fifties, sixtyish, but I only saw him in the distance and in the dark so I can't be sure," said Dee.

"That's about the right age. What luck!" carolled Lucy who was convinced of her own theory.

"Why? What's special about him? Who is he?" asked Dee, bemused, and the other two looked disappointed by her ignorance.

"Haven't you heard of Saul Steindl? He's a famous collector of Pre-Raphaelites. He has an even better collection than Andrew Lloyd Webber. It just happens that I own an art gallery in Islington, and I have a very good Holman Hunt in stock at the moment

14

that would be sure to interest him. I'm selling it for a friend – Lord Ragwood, actually," explained Lucy, her eyes glowing as if she'd glimpsed the Holy Grail.

She turned back to Harriet and added, "Isn't it lucky I brought the catalogue and transparencies with me for that New York dealer! I'll show them to Mr Steindl too."

Practical Harriet said, "Good idea, if we can get hold of him." Then she asked Ray, "Has Mr Steindl breakfasted yet?"

"He eats breakfast in his cabin," was the answer.

"But when I asked if I could have breakfast in my cabin, you said it wasn't possible!" she cried indignantly.

Ray shrugged. "He's a very important man. He can eat in his cabin if that's what he wants," he said.

The friends chorused their disapproval but Ray walked off into the kitchen, his posture telling them he'd heard many such complaints before.

In the afternoon the sun really began to shine, the pitching stopped and the ship settled down on top of the sea like a mother hen in her nest. There was still no sign of Mr Steindl, but Roman, the Polish chief engineer, who always enjoyed female company, turned up for dinner with the passengers. Beaming like a benevolent father he announced, "For you, ladies, tonight I fill the swimming pool!"

The pool was a deep, blue-painted pit, about twelve feet square, on the second deck. To swim across it would take only ten or twelve strokes but it would at least be wet and warm in the September sun and they eagerly anticipated the diversion.

Dee looked forward to having a swim, but dreaded exposing her ageing body to the critical eyes of Lucy and Harriet, who were much younger and as trim as racehorses. They looked as if they spent hours "working out" in London gymnasia.

Because of her timidity about her appearance in a swimsuit, she was out of bed early next morning, determined to swim before anyone else was around. When she emerged on deck there was a transcendentally beautiful dawn with streaks of salmon pink and pastel blue on the eastern horizon. As it rose, the sun slowly cast a sheen of silk over the aquamarine ocean and the wake behind the ship furled and frothed like a train of bridal lace.

When Dee was halfway down the companionway, her heart sank as she heard the sound of splashing from the pool below and she drew back in disappointment. Someone had beaten her to it and there was not really enough room in the pool for two, especially as the present occupier was thrashing around like a Channel swimmer out to

16

break a record.

Leaning over the rail and staring down, she saw the man who had come aboard at Le Havre ploughing powerfully up and down, turning head over heels like a fish whenever he reached the edge. His face was in the water but his arms flailed like windmills. She noticed that he was wearing an enormous watch, as big as a saucer, that glittered like a plutocrat's beacon when the sun struck it.

I'm very expensive and the man who wears me is very rich, it seemed to boast for it was the sort of watch that cautious travellers would avoid wearing when visiting crime-ridden parts of the world.

As she watched, something clicked in her brain like a switch being activated. Suddenly she was back in the past watching another man ploughing up and down in the water, another man who wore an enormous, flashy watch. He'd been the first person she'd ever seen going in to swim wearing a waterproof watch, for in those long ago days such things were rarities.

She stood hidden in the shade as the swimmer reached for the pool rail and pulled himself out of the water. Dripping, he stood on the deck. He was not tall, about five foot six or seven, skinny, sun tanned, sparse haired, with thin, almost prehensile arms. The flagrantly boastful watch and its atrociously thick metal strap – made of platinum, she guessed – adorned his left wrist.

Unaware of her presence he looked back over his shoulder, reaching for the towel he'd left on a chair, and she got a glimpse of his face – big nose, high forehead and hollow cheeks, tragic-looking deeply hollowed eyes. In spite of the passage of over thirty years, he hadn't changed much, but, she remembered, he'd always been old looking, even when he was young.

"Stevie!" she cried out without premeditation. He turned quickly towards her, his eyes alert.

"Stevie Stone," she repeated, stepping into the full sunlight, "I can hardly believe it's you. It *is* Stevie, isn't it?"

Startled, he blinked like an owl, and reached for his eyeglasses, which lay on the seat of a white plastic sunchair.

It was obvious from his expression that he had no idea who she was as he stared blankly at her across the stretch of gently lapping blue water in the pool. Why should he remember? she suddenly thought. Her once dark hair was now a grey bob and her boyish slimness long gone.

"It's Dee Carmichael," she told him, "From Bombay."

When he heard the name his jaw seemed to clench as if she'd given him an unpleasant surprise – which upset her, because she'd considered him a friend. Her disappointment disappeared, however, when he relaxed a little and smiled as he replied, "Gee, that's a name from the past. How did you recognise me?"

She laughed to put him more at ease. "Because of your watch. I remembered your penchant for big watches."

"It's not the same one. I wore a different make in Bombay," he said, looking down at his wrist as if he was buying time in this conversational exchange.

Dee said teasingly, "You were always terribly literal, Stevie! That watch may be a different one but it's just as big. Gosh, I can hardly believe it's you. I haven't seen you since the night of our big party in Bombay! Do you remember?"

Her blue eyes danced brightly in her face as she spoke and her pleasure made her look like a young woman again. Softened by this, some of his tension fell away from him and he grinned back at her as he said, "I sure do remember, but it was a long time ago."

"Yes, too true. But how amazing that we're on this ship together – after all those years! I can hardly believe it." She was still a little confused by the hostility she'd sensed in him when she first called out his name. Had she made a mistake? Was he only being polite in pretending that he knew her? Did

19

the old Stevie have a twin brother or an identical cousin?

He'd stayed in her memory as being just as defensive as this one but much more inept and somehow burned out, as if he was emotionally anaesthetised, a dry corn cob of a man. The person facing her across the pool was far more alive and vibrant, confident and immensely capable. His voice was very assured as he replied, "Yeah, it is a big surprise to meet you again, *Dee*."

The way he stressed her name strengthened her doubts and she thought again that he was only being polite and hadn't any idea who she was. In her experience, Americans were always very good at remembering names by repetition when introduced and she'd told this man hers.

But the next thing he said was, "Is Ben on board with you?"

All her doubts disappeared. He was definitely Stevie if he remembered Ben without any prompting from her.

For a long time after Ben had died, nearly twenty years ago, she'd had trouble controlling her voice, trying to stop it quavering when she spoke his name, and it was still an effort to say, "I'm afraid not. Ben's been dead for a long time."

The genuine shock on his face confirmed that he was indeed Stevie. "Gee, that's awful! He must have died young. Was it an accident?" he asked.

Though she usually avoided talking about Ben's death she suddenly wanted to tell Stevie the story. "He had a heart attack at forty-three. He dropped dead when he was on a business trip to Singapore. It was awful, Stevie. I didn't believe it when the police came to tell me, and in a funny sort of a way I still don't believe it though it happened so long ago..."

That was true. Though she'd been widowed for twenty years, she still thought about Ben every day, remembering things he said and did, the way he'd looked. To her he was forever in his prime, tall, tanned and blonde.

By the time he died, he'd given up wearing baggy old shorts and rugby shirts and had turned into an ultra sophisticate, dressed by Savile Row tailors and smelling of Trumper's hair lotion. She'd never met anyone to match him. No one else smiled the way Ben smiled, almost wolfish because of the pointed incisors at the corners of his mouth. No other man had ever been so funny either, or could fill her with such confidence and give her such reassurance. She'd truly believed nothing bad would ever happen to them while he was in charge, and they'd had a run of great success ... till, without warning, he'd died.

It was still hard to believe that someone so

vivid and alive could disappear like that in a flash. The last sight she'd had of him was his back as he bent to get into the taxi that was to take him from their London house to Heathrow. Their last conversation had been over the telephone the night before he died. He'd sounded despondent and worried; she'd told him to get on the first plane home but he'd stayed and died alone. Pain gripped her heart again and unwanted tears filled her eyes.

Stevie looked stricken when he saw how his question had affected her. "Gee, I'm sorry I asked. I'd no idea," he said. "I remember him very well. He was a great guy."

Dee fought for self-control and won, managing to smile as she replied, "Yes, wasn't he? We often wondered what happened to you, Stevie, because you vanished off the scene, just like that, after our party." She snapped her fingers sharply, a trick she'd learned from Ben.

He stared over her shoulder at the aquamarine sea and she could see he was trying to change the subject to cheer her up as he replied in a lighter tone, "Yeah, I remember the party. Tell me about the other people we knew. Do you see any of them nowadays?"

"Not many. The ones that are still alive are scattered far and wide. Most of us ended up respectable, and that's funny when you remember how wild we were... I've lost touch with lots of them but you'll remember Ralph, the doctor? He went to Australia and became a professor. Every now and again I remember somebody and wish I knew what happened to them."

What she didn't say was that the friend she thought about most frequently was Anne, who seemed to have vanished off the face of the earth. Dee hadn't heard a word from her since the day after the big party. Sometimes, when doing mundane things like hoovering or peeling potatoes, a vivid memory of Anne would pop into Dee's mind. These glimpses from the past were so real that it seemed as if there was a thought transference between them and Anne had also been thinking of Dee.

Very strange. Perhaps it means that one day I'll stumble across Anne like I've now stumbled across Stevie, she thought.

Stevie nodded at the mention of Ralph and she remembered how worked up he used to get about the Bombay health scares that were only minor annoyances to more India-hardened people. What a terrible neurotic he'd been, always attending Ralph's out-patient clinic at Breach Candy hospital, convinced he was doomed to die of some terrible tropical disease. In her memory she saw him always carrying packs of pills or wearing bandages.

The thought made her grin and she sat down on the edge of the pool, dipping her toes in the warm water as she said, "You look very prosperous. Life must have treated you well, Stevie."

"I've done OK," he said guardedly.

"Married?" she asked.

"Yeah. Same wife for nearly thirty years! That's a record among the people I know."

"You were with a film company in India, weren't you?"

"I was with Paraworld," he said.

"Are you still?"

"I'm still in the business, but not with Paraworld. I've got my own production company now. I've been over in Europe doing some deals and now I'm on my way back home. I don't fly because too many of my friends have died in plane crashes, and I always go by freighter because I hate those cruise boats like the QE2. On them you meet awful people that are always coming down with weird illnesses ... Legionnaires' Disease and things like that," he told her.

Dee thought with amusement, *Other things might have changed but you're still a raging hypochondriac.*

"It sounds as if you've a very glamorous life. Have I seen any of your films?" she asked him and he named a couple that she'd heard about though not seen. They'd been "family" films that dealt with subjects like

24

comic babysitters or chaos-causing children but they'd made a lot of money.

"Goodness!" she said in an awed tone, genuinely pleased for him because in the old days he'd seemed such a loser.

"Yeah, I'm Saul Steindl Productions," he said proudly. His evident enjoyment of this told her that the old impressionable Stevie was still there inside an apparently confident, almost brash man.

"You call yourself Saul Steindl now? In Bombay you were Stevie Stone," she said.

He shrugged. "Name, shname" said his raised shoulders. "Steindl's my real name. I used the other one in India because I didn't think people there would get to grips with Saul Steindl – the Jewish thing, you know – but Steindl's my real name and I feel better using it."

She nodded in agreement for the man facing her did not suit the old name at all. "Stevie" was the name of a buffoon, a court jester, which was the role he filled in their expatriate set. He'd been their resident fool, the guy who crashed cars, fell over at parties and broke things, ranging from his spectacles to his arm.

When someone asked, "Heard the latest about Stevie?" their listeners began grinning in anticipation of a good laugh for he was always in trouble. He'd been robbed of his wallet on Colaba Causeway and was arrested for buying bootleg gin from a fisherman at Marvi. Though everyone bought gin there, only Stevie fell into the hands of the police. It cost hundreds of rupees in bribes for him to get off.

But now, looking at rich and confident Saul Steindl, she wondered if what had been accepted as his character was actually a false impression. Had the man they knew as Stevie really been an amiable fool or was he only playing a part?

Two

Bombay, 1959

Monica Fernandes saw Stevie first.

She spotted him as a mark when he came wandering out of the Customs shed at Santa Cruz airport with two cameras hanging round his neck and an enormous, outrageously gleaming watch on his wrist.

As well as the watch he was wearing baggy shorts, a loose bush shirt with Hawaiian flowers and birds printed on it and a red baseball cap.

"I'm a rich American" everything about him said. He was also a tired American for it was two o'clock in the morning and he had been travelling for thirty-six hours.

Monica, who was reluctantly working on the Air India enquiries desk, knew in an instant that he was the miracle she'd been praying for. He could be her ticket out of Santa Cruz, but she'd have to move fast before some other girl spotted his potential. Hitching up her emerald green and purple silk sari with one hand – she hated wearing

27

saris because they made her look like a *native*, for God's sake, when she aspired to be an English memsahib – she sprinted across the floor towards him, elbowing a taxi tout out of the way as she went.

"You're the last off the plane! Were they very hard on you in Customs?" she asked in a sympathetic voice.

He blinked. "Yeah; they took all my whisky and cigars off me." His accent was pure New York.

She gasped. "That's awful. You should have bribed them."

"What the hell. All I want to do right now is sleep. I've been flying for two days," he sighed in an exhausted voice.

She looked around. "Is anyone meeting you?"

"I don't think so. They don't know I'm here. I missed my plane in London, you see. I should have arrived yesterday."

A small crowd of hopeful mendicants and thieves who blandly ignored Monica's glares gathered round them. "I get you taxi, sahib," said one man.

Monica was having none of that. She pushed the intruder away and took the American's arm. "Come with me and I'll find you a taxi. Where do you want to go?" Her accent was soft and lilting, almost like Welsh. In fact she sometimes tried to pass as being from Wales – from Cardiff, she'd say, though she'd never been there and had only the vaguest idea of where it was on a map.

"A hotel. The best hotel," he told her.

"That's the Taj," she said. She didn't add that it was very expensive – judging by his watch and cameras he could afford it.

He looked at her in open puzzlement, taking in her beautiful face and lissom figure. Then, as if he'd made a snap decision, he said, "OK. That'll do," and rendered himself up to her like a child following its mother as she cut a way through the crowd.

"Are you on holiday?" she asked.

"No. I've come to work here for a bit. I'm with Paraworld Pictures."

Her head swam.

Paraworld Pictures!

Hollywood!

Ever since she was small, Monica had heard her mother and aunt talking about one of their friends, an Anglo-Indian girl who, like them, had started her working life walking the streets of Bombay as a prostitute, but went to Hollywood and became Merle Oberon.

"She wasn't any prettier than us," they said, "Just luckier." When she became famous she had sent for her mother whom she passed off as her ayah.

Like Merle, Monica was lovely – lovelier than the film star had ever been, said her mother – but her time was running out because next spring she would be twenty-five. If a suitable quarry didn't turn up to marry her soon it would be too late. Now she was in the full blaze of her beauty, powered by desperation and a longing to cast off the stigma of being a chi-chi, touch-of-the-tar-brush girl.

The first black and yellow taxi waiting in line at the airport entrance was driven by a Sikh who gave no sign of interest when Monica stuck her head into his open window. She addressed him in Hindi. "How much to take an American to the Taj, sardarji?"

His eyes swivelled sideways and took in the bedraggled Stevie. "Two hundred and fifty," he said disdainfully.

"Arrey! The fare's only fifty!" she protested.

"For him two hundred and fifty."

"You're a robber, but I'll tell him one fifty if you give me fifty," she whispered.

The Sikh shrugged. "One seventy-five. One fifty for me and twenty-five for you."

Monica hissed like a snake but out of the corner of her eye she could see an irate-looking Mrs Bajpai, the Air India information desk supervisor, bearing down on her. There was no time to lose.

"All right, but give it to me now," she said and surreptitiously stuck out her hand to receive some grubby notes from the Sikh.

Then she told Stevie, "This man will take you to the Taj. Only pay him one hundred and fifty rupees and don't give him a tip because he is a robber."

The Sikh grinned – a streak of white teeth suddenly appearing between his dense black beard and moustache – and threw the car into gear as Stevie's bags were piled in beside him on the split upholstery of the back seat. In a second they were off, leaving Monica to face her furious boss.

"Where have you been? I go for my tea break and when I come back there is no one on the desk. Only angry passengers shouting and shouting. Where were you?" Mrs Bajpai's face and neck were mottled with red blotches like a turkey's gizzard and her kohl-rimmed eyes were flashing.

Monica managed with an effort to look meek for she needed the job. Her mother was ill, the medicines to treat her were expensive, and the money left behind by Monica's last protector, Bob, an Australian High Commission clerk, was almost all spent.

"I was helping a poor man," she said in a timid voice.

Mrs Bajpai began pushing her back into the building, saying as she went, "It is not your job to help poor men. Your job is to stand at the desk and answer questions.

31

How often am I telling you that?"

"Yes, Mrs Bajpai," whispered Monica humbly but her inner voice was shouting, *Shut up, you old cow. You hate me because I'm pretty and you look like a scabby vulture. You hate me because I look English and you're a fat, old Gujerati*. One day she hoped to be able to tell Mrs Bajpai what she could do with her job. She resolved to call at the Taj to see the American as soon as possible.

She gave him till noon, sleeping herself for only a few hours after she stopped work at six a.m. With her twenty-five-rupee bonanza from the Sikh, she bought paraffin for the cooking stove, and from the hawker on the corner got her mother a glassful of sugar cane juice which was good for sufferers of liver disease. When the sick woman was fed and settled she rushed to a Colaba hairdressing salon where a Chinese girl washed and set her luxuriant, glistening hair, expertly teasing it into girlish curls for the sum of five rupees, including tip.

There were still sixteen rupees in her handbag when she set out to walk to the Taj, wearing the white pique best dress that she shared with her cousin Carole, and a pair of high-heeled shoes that nipped her toes. On the way she gave a few annas to Maya, an old beggar woman who slept on the street beside the green-painted tea-shop, for she believed in sharing good fortune like her unexpected bonanza from the taxi driver. A dread of ending up sleeping on the street like Maya haunted her.

When she reached the massive hulk of the Taj Mahal hotel, she did not walk across the entrance court and through the imposing front door but headed for the back entrance, which, surprisingly, had a much finer outlook. It faced the sea and the Gateway of India, while the front door faced a narrow road full of hooting cars and taxis. People said the architect had inadvertently built the hotel the wrong way round and when he realised his mistake, he shot himself.

Apart from the fact that it enjoyed a better view, the less glorious entrance suited Monica's purpose because she did not want to walk past the supercilious eyes of the pair of turbaned doormen who guarded the front door. The entrance she took led through an arcade of shops – once full of luxury goods to tempt the rich, but now in more austere times either empty or occupied by photography salons and ethnic craft shops. There was also a hairdresser patronised by a few European ladies of a certain age who had been going there since the days of the Raj.

Monica hurried along the roofed passage between the shops into the gilt and marble entrance hall of the hotel. It was only when she stood before the gleaming rosewood reception desk that she realised she did not know her quarry's name. How stupid not to have found that out! The Taj reception clerks were notoriously strict in their dealings with the street girls of Colaba and guarded their guests with the same dedication as shepherds guarding flocks against predatory wolves.

Who should she ask for?

Walking up to the desk she cast her eye over the men standing behind it, trying to work out which of them would be most susceptible. There was a crafty-looking Goan with a pencil-thin moustache; a worldly-looking old man with greying hair; and a full-faced fellow, little more than a boy, with pouting lips like a greedy cherub. She almost chose the boy but something stopped her at the last minute and she directed her enquiry at the old man.

"I'm from Paraworld Pictures," she said, "And I've come to see our new gentleman from America, the one who arrived early this morning."

He regarded her gravely. "Which room number?" he asked.

"I don't know I'm afraid, but he came in this morning – about three o'clock."

"What name?" The question she dreaded. She smiled sweetly. "I don't know that either. I only work in the office, you see, and they sent me here with some papers for him – from Paraworld Pictures. I'm so *silly*. I've forgotten the name they told me to ask for and I'll be in trouble when I get back to the office if I don't see him..." Her voice trailed off with a touching little quaver.

The boy with the full mouth interrupted her. "Give us the papers and we'll send them up to him."

Her eyes filled with tears. "I was told he had to sign for them. It would be better if I spoke to him myself."

"You can't—" the young man began to say but the oldest man took control of the situation.

"You've come to see Mr Stone in room 426, miss. The bell boy will take you up."

When Monica looked into his eyes she could see they were dancing with amusement. He'd tumbled to her trick but was giving her a chance. As she walked towards the lift the clerks were talking among themselves and because she had sharp ears she heard the youngest man say to the old one, "Why did you do that?"

The other man shrugged as he replied, "Those girls have a hard time. Indians don't like them and neither do white people. They need a bit of help sometimes."

In his luxurious suite, Stevie, wearing one of the hotel's white towelling bathrobes, sat at a red lacquered table beside a window that stared out over the sun-dappled sea. On the table was a silver tray bearing a coffee-pot, bread rolls, cups and saucers and a half-finished glass of orange juice.

Facing him, in a deeply cushioned double-seated swing suspended from the ceiling by silken ropes, was a smooth Indian gentle-man called Ajay who was wearing an immaculately cut cream-coloured raw silk suit. Ajay was the Indian head of the Para-world office in Bombay and secretly he resented having to pay court to Stevie, who was more highly regarded than he was just because he was an American.

The swing was rocking gently to and fro in a motion that made Stevie slightly nauseous just watching it. He was also having trouble making conversation because Ajay's clipped English accent and strange pronounciation confused him.

"We've taken a werry nice flat for you on Malabar Hill, old boy," said the silk-suited vision, "We hope you like it. My wife Bunty chose the furnishings. She has super taste – she was educated in London at the Monkey Club."

Stevie stared at him uncomprehendingly. The Monkey Club? "What the hell is that, some sort of zoo?" he wondered.

Ajay laughed at his obvious bemusement. "Of course – you're from the States, not

London. The Monkey Club's a girls' finishing school. It teaches them how to behave in society, arrange flowers, put on dinner parties, that sort of thing. You must have places like it in the States."

"Probably; I wouldn't know," said Stevie. This joker in the swing was beginning to irritate him but he'd promised his uncle, one of the vice-presidents of Paraworld, that he wouldn't do anything to upset the local staff when he was in India.

"Just go with the flow, boy, get on with what you have to do and give me a full report when you get back," he'd been told.

A knock came to the door and he called, "Come in," half closing his eyes while he sipped his coffee. When he opened them again it was to see a vision standing beside the bell boy in the open door of his suite.

Monica in white piqué was even prettier than Monica in a sari. Her skin was the colour of cream and her enormous, dark-lashed eyes were slightly slanted in her head like the eyes of a startled deer. Her mouth was full and sweetly curved and there was a deep dimple in her left cheek.

In the silence that followed her appearance she smiled across at him and momentarily he was nonplussed. Then she said in the lilting voice he remembered, "I've popped in to make sure that Sikh taxi driver didn't kidnap you."

He stood up and said, "You're the girl at the airport! Thanks for your help. The taxi guy was OK. Brought me straight here."

"Did you tip him?" she asked, unable to disguise her practicality.

He laughed, "Yeah, I did."

"I said not to, they're all rogues those natives."

At that Ajay stood up from his cocoon of cushions, put out at having to do so because he'd placed Monica as a Colaba street girl after only one look. She was not a bit dismayed by his hostility, however.

"All the natives are rogues," she repeated, staring him in the eye, daring him to challenge her with the accusation that she was a native herself, before turning back to Stevie and adding, "I'm glad you got here safely, though."

He invited her to sit down, which she did, and offered her a cup of coffee, which she eagerly accepted, for she'd been so busy all morning that she hadn't had time to eat or drink.

Ajay watched them with a peculiar expression on his face and his mind racing. He'd thought this man Stone was a fool – one of the bosses' relatives sent out to India to get him out of the way for a while, he'd reckoned. Chaps like that came and went in foreign companies all the time and most of them were useless, which was perfectly acceptable because it left the running of the outposts of business empires to ambitious people like himself who were on the spot all the time, keeping an eye on the top jobs till Indianisation came along.

But Stone had managed to pick up this woman as soon as he got off the plane. At half-past two in the morning – and a good-looking chi-chi girl, too! How had he done it? He might be worth watching.

Tact was obviously called for, so he stood up, saying, "Well, have to dash. I've a meeting with some big cinema owners. Don't bother coming to the office today, Mr Stone. Tomorrow's soon enough. I'll send a car to take you to see your new flat this afternoon – is five thirty all right?" And he bustled away leaving a whiff of the heavy scent of patchouli behind him.

When he'd gone, Stevie and Monica looked at each other and wondered what to say. Having miraculously got into his suite, she wasn't going to leave without making an effort to seduce him but knew it would be a mistake to be too obvious, so she smiled and said, "I don't suppose you've had much of a chance to see Bombay yet?"

He shrugged. "I slept till half an hour ago."

"You poor thing, you must be exhausted. I'm sorry to have intruded on you but I was really worried about that Sikh. His kind will cut a man's throat for a few rupees, and you had those cameras. I thought if you weren't in the hotel I'd go to the police... It would've been my fault if you went missing because I put you into that taxi."

The sharp way he scrutinised her as he listened slightly disconcerted her, but in an instant he'd resumed his air of mild innocence and she wasn't sure if she'd really seen calculation in his brown eyes. She hoped he hadn't seen it in hers.

"Don't worry. I'm OK," he said. "So how'd you like to have a drink with me down in the bar? Sorry I can't offer you one up here, but the customs men took my bottles last night – and anyway, it'd be good to get out of this room and see the city."

"A drink? In the bar? Have you a permit already?" she asked.

"A permit? What sort of a permit?"

"A drinks permit. You're not allowed to drink alcohol anywhere in this city – even in a bar – without an official permit," she explained to him. Monica had a precious permit, courtesy of Bob, and she carried it with her at all times for fear that it might be stolen out of the room where she and her mother lived. She now took it from her white plastic handbag and showed it to him.

He stared at the large green double-page document in disbelieving amusement and asked, "Hey! How d'you get one of these?"

"There's an office at the docks. They issue them. You've got to pay a hundred rupees and swear or get a doctor to testify that you're an alcoholic who can't live without drink," she told him.

He laughed. "I'm not an alcoholic now but I might be when I leave here. Let's go and get me a permit. I'll make you my official guide to Bombay."

Usually the wait at the permit office was protracted and frustrating but Stevie was so prodigal with his money, distributing tips to all and sundry, that they were soon at the head of the queue and in an amazingly short time he had a pristine permit for four bottles of spirit or twelve bottles of beer a month in his hand. He looked at the intimidating document with disbelief, scrutinising the lion-on-a-pillar Government of India seals that were stamped all over it.

"You're sure this isn't a joke?" he asked Monica, but she shook her head vehemently.

"Oh no, certainly not a joke."

"But only four bottles a month! Some alcoholic! What if I give a party?"

"You buy from a bootlegger."

He laughed. "And I guess you know the bootleggers?"

"Yes, of course."

"Obviously I'm going to need you. Now

where can we use this permit? I need a beer."

Laughing gaily, she took his arm and they went to the Ritz, where Monica used to go with Bob. Thomas and Raju, the barmen, seemed glad to see her as if her reappearance was a guarantee of continuity but took care not to be too effusive in case her new escort was not aware of her past.

Stevie, in his baseball hat and another equally colourful bush shirt, was so obviously American that they treated him cautiously because they did not see many of his countrymen. Visiting Americans tended to stay safely in the protective ambience of the Taj and rarely appeared in the more downmarket Ritz.

It was cool in the darkened cavern of the bar and after Stevie and Monica had shared two bottles of beer and had them marked off on his permit, they took a taxi back to the Taj where they went to bed. Monica had caught him!

Later that afternoon, a car turned up to take Stevie to view his new apartment. He was so pleased with it that he decided to move in that evening – and a beaming Miss Monica Fernandes went with him.

Three

Stevie never took off his watch – even in the shower he kept it on his wrist, and though Monica pleaded with him to remove it in bed, he refused.

"But it has such a loud tick," she protested, "it keeps me awake."

"Then put cotton wool in your ears," he told her. The watch seemed to be welded to him and she wondered if he ever washed the strip of skin it covered.

To her surprise Stevie was not particularly amorous. They had made love on the first day they were together but when she thought about it later she realised that he seemed to do it only to establish a claim on her. It had been a swift and unerotic act which he did not seem in any hurry to repeat. Yet he did not rebuff her when she fluttered round him, stroking his hair or his cheek.

The following day, however, her practised efforts at seduction failed to excite his libido again and she began to be afraid that without sex to bind him to her, the hopes she had for him might come to nothing. The only hold she'd ever been able to establish over men in the past had been through her beauty and expertise in bed and she had never expected a man to esteem her for any other reason.

The flat that Stevie took her to on that first night was on the top of Malabar Hill with a view that took in the whole of the Queen's Necklace, the line of sparkling lights that marked Marine Drive. She walked out on to the terrace – the flat was on the top floor – and was unable to contain a gasp of admiration as she stared across the glittering city.

"It's wonderful!" she cried turning her huge eyes towards him.

He grinned, gratified at her pleasure. "If you like, we can get the driver to take us to your place to collect your stuff," he said.

It was the first sign he'd given her that he regarded her as a permanent fixture in his home and she dazzled him with her delight but shook her head at the suggestion that they fetch her things. There was no way she was going to let him see the sordid little street where she lived with her mother. "Don't let's bother tonight," she said, taking his hand, "I can fetch what I want tomorrow."

When she woke next morning she walked back on to the terrace in the bright, early morning. There was a clear view to the narrow neck of woodland that stuck out into the vast Indian Ocean like a pointing finger. That was where Government House was situated. She stood at the verandah rail and looked back towards the top of Malabar Hill. Huddling beneath some palm trees were two sinister-looking, stone-built turrets. She recoiled at the sight of them for she knew they were the Towers of Silence where Parsees laid out the bodies of their dead for vultures and crows to feast on till the bones were pecked clean.

"Don't think about them," she told herself sternly and turned back to gaze at the sea.

She was joined in her contemplation of the view by Stevie and she clung to his arm as she said to him, "Look out there. Isn't it beautiful?"

He looked, yawned and said, "Yeah, it's nice," but his tone was unenthusiastic and she wondered if he ever felt anything very deeply. He was a man that was hard to fathom.

Yet very quickly, within only a couple of days, they seemed to establish a kind of settled domesticity such as she had never known with any of her previous protectors. Every day they ate their breakfast together like a conventional married couple and then he drove off to his office.

He gave her money and never asked what

she did with it but obviously expected her to be in the flat when he returned in the evening. In his absence she went to see her mother, rearranged the furniture, ordered around the bearer, who seemed to come with the flat, and visited Crawford Market to buy huge bouquets of flowers which she used to decorate her new home. She was particularly fond of heavily scented tuberoses which filled the air in the sitting room with a heady, langorous fragrance.

While Stevie did not lust after her, he seemed to enjoy her company and they sat together on the terrace in the evenings with him questioning her about the city of Bombay – where she'd spent her entire life, though she denied that fact and fantasised about "home" – and about the people she knew there. She was a good storyteller, punctuating her narrative with little giggles, and he listened enraptured for hour after hour, plying her with questions and asking her to point out the places that she mentioned on an old city map that he'd found in a bookshop in the Fort. When their ménage was well established Monica became more confident that he was not suddenly going to throw her out, so she stopped trying to entice him physically and they settled into a wary companionship, a sort of complicity, though what it was they were meant to be planning she did not know.

Sometimes they went out together, to a cafe, a restaurant or to the cinema, and on these occasions she dressed up, acting the part of his kept woman, making herself look as desirable as possible and hanging on to his arm adoringly. Without being specifically asked to do so, she knew this was the role he wanted her to play.

At the end of her second week in his flat, she was secure enough to think of their arrangement as being at least semi-permanent and took the utmost pleasure in dressing up in a new full-skirted dress before going to Santa Cruz to tell Mrs Bajpai that she would not be returning to her job at the airline's enquiries desk.

This news did not come as a shock to her ex-employer.

"I thought you'd left anyway," said Mrs Bajpai. "You haven't been here for many days."

"I've only been absent for two weeks," said Monica.

"Have you been sick?" asked Mrs Bajpai.

"No, I have a new friend who's looking after me and he doesn't want me to work," said Monica.

"Huh; you'll be sorry giving up a good post like this one," said Mrs Bajpai darkly. "Your friend'll go home to England or wherever he comes from like all the others. You silly girls never learn."

Monica gave her head a toss. "He says he's going to take me to New York," she lied.

"So he says," retorted Mrs Bajpai. "My advice to you is don't count your turkeys."

Slightly deflated, Monica took care that Mrs Bajpai and the other curious girls on the enquiries desk saw her hiring a taxi for the return journey from the airport. She wanted them to realise there would be no more crowded buses and trains for her now because Stevie was generous with money. Only that morning he had given her a fold of hundred-rupee notes without even being asked.

The reassuring knowledge that she had crisp, clean notes in her bag gave her immense confidence. She wished she could think of some excuse for taking the money out of her handbag and brandishing it before the other women's eyes. She longed for someone to tell about her good fortune.

Suddenly she had an idea. As the taxi drew out into the main road she leaned towards the driver and changed her original instruction.

"Don't take me into the city. I want to go to Chembur instead," she said. Chembur was where her aunt Fifi lived in a little house on the side of the golf course and Fifi would be more green with envy about Monica's new stroke of luck than ten Mrs Bajpais.

Fifi was sitting in the shade of a mango tree with her Alsatian dog Sabre at her feet, sipping a glass of what looked like beer, though when her niece emerged from the taxi all she offered her was a cup of tea.

"I'd rather have a gin," said Monica grandly, producing out of her capacious handbag a full bottle of imported Gordon's which she had intended to take to her mother later. The authenticity of the gin was attested to by its wonderful yellow label decorated with juniper berries – none of that Madras-made Parry stuff for Stevie. Fifi goggled at the bottle as if it contained liquid gold but recovered herself sufficiently to call to her servant to bring some glasses.

When Leela, the old servant woman, came out with thick, ugly glasses and a bottle of soda, Monica dispensed two generous measures, then replaced the cap and put the bottle back in her bag. Her mother could have the rest, she thought. Drinking alcohol was meant to be bad for jaundice but her mother liked a gin and lime and why shouldn't she have one occasionally?

Fifi's eyes lingered maliciously over her niece's bulging handbag and pretty en-semble. "Where did you get that dress – and the new shoes?" she asked.

Monica smoothed her skirt which crack-led over a stiffly starched petticoat and said lightly, "I can give the old white dress back to Carole now. My dursi ran this one up for me yesterday. He copied it from a picture of a film star in an American magazine. Feel it, the material's good and very expensive. I got it in that shop on the corner of Grant Road."

"Huh, film star!" snapped Fifi, trying to hide the envy that gripped her. Then she asked, "How's your mother? Is this hot weather upsetting her?"

She could not let a conversation with her niece go on for very long without asking after her sister to whom she had not spoken for almost ten years.

There had been three girls in her family, all of them piously named – Eustacia, Bernadette, and Feliciana who was the youngest and soon changed her name to Fifi. After naming them and having them baptised, their father, an Irish soldier in the British army quartered in the cantonment at Deolali, had done nothing else for his girls. When his ten-year period of service was up, he had disappeared back to Britain where he took another wife, since his union with the girls' mother had only been an unofficial one.

When they grew up, his Indian family made up their own minds about what they should call themselves. Only Eustacia kept his surname which was Flynn; the other two adopted the name of their mother, Fernandes.

They all grew up pale-skinned and beautiful, with nothing in the way of inheritance except their stunning looks, so that they had no alternative but to go on the street. There was still a large army camp at Deolali and they hoped to catch a husband among the soldiers.

Eustacia, the eldest, wanted a wider horizon, however. She made enough money to travel to Calcutta but soon died of cholera, aged only seventeen. A couple of years later, when their mother died, the other two made their way to Bombay where they thrived after a fashion and still lived, conducting an unending war of jealous sibling back-biting between them. Though they never met now, each was always eager for news of the other, and they used their daughters as go-betweens.

"You should go to town and see my mother," Monica told her aunt. "It's silly to go on fighting the way you do. She'll be pleased to see you. She used to cry about you when she was sick but she's better now because she's getting the best medicines."

"Better?" snapped Fifi. "How can she be better? I heard from one of her neighbours that she has liver cancer. You don't get better from liver cancer."

Monica flinched at this for she resolutely refused to consider the possibility that her mother's illness might be fatal.

"That's not true. It's not cancer, it's only jaundice. She has a new doctor and he thinks she'll be able to go out again soon," she said firmly, for that was what she wanted to believe.

"Who is paying for this new doctor?" asked Fifi.

"I am," said Monica.

"How you are paying?" Fifi's annoyance made her forget her syntax.

"I've found a new man, a rich American, who'll give me anything I want. He's going to take me to America like Merle Oberon. He's in the film business."

Fifi snorted. "And will you take your mother as your ayah like she did with her mother? You're dreaming, Monica."

"Have another gin, Aunt Fifi," said Monica sweetly and opened her bag to take the bottle out again. She knew she had Fifi on the run and intended to pursue her advantage.

"How's Carole?" she asked when they were sipping again.

"She's in Calcutta." Fifi was obviously reluctant to discuss the circumstances or whereabouts of her beautiful but irresponsible younger daughter.

Monica was not prepared to let her off lightly however. "Who is she with now?"

"Some babu. He's got her a flat. She sent me a letter and said she's very happy there."

"He's probably a pimp who's set her up in the business. It had to happen I suppose," said Monica. Though they were all women who exchanged their favours for what they called "presents", they did not regard themselves as prostitutes – merely ladies on the hunt, because they were never involved with more than one man at a time and none of them ever used a pimp.

Fifi bridled. "She's only gone away to Calcutta for a little while because of that trouble with the Englishman."

"The one who threw her out because he found her in bed with his servant, you mean." There wasn't really any way Fifi could answer Monica's jibe and they both knew it. Carole had been guilty of a serious misjudgement and had blown what they all thought of as her big chance.

The gin helped Carole's mother to pull herself together however and she overcame her chagrin to say, "But Amy's landed lucky. She's gone to Australia. That Dennis fellow paid for her ticket. It's only for a holiday, she says, but you never can tell what's going on in Amy's life." Amy was the second of Fifi's daughters, a plain girl with a sharp tongue, and the only one of the family who did not make a living out of men. Amy had worked as a shorthand-typist in the city and was very good at her job. She openly disdained the other members of her family who regarded her with a certain amount of awe.

Monica nodded, remembering handsome Dennis who had been brought to her aunt's house as a prospective husband for Carole but who'd slipped the net. That he could be caught by the least beautiful member of the family was a surprise to them all, but no one was so stupid that they had any expectations of benefiting from Amy's good luck. They knew that when she shook the dust of Bombay off her feet it would be the last they would ever see of her. Amy, their ugly duckling, had always been the outsider in that plotting, mutually protective but feuding, improvident pack of beautiful women.

Fifi was sorry to see Monica putting her bottle of gin back into her handbag again because there was more than half of it still undrunk. "You're going? So soon?" she asked.

"Yes. I want to see my mother first and then be in the flat when my man comes back from his office."

"What's his name, this man with all the money?"

"Steven." Monica was not going to refer to him as "Stevie" to her aunt who would be sure to mock such a childish name.

"What's he like?" Fifi was sceptical about men. They all had character flaws and peculiar tastes as far as she was concerned, and she'd known many throughout her working life.

Monica looked bland and her aunt, not for the first time, noticed the beauty of her niece's brown eyes. The whites were shining and unmarked by any veining or discoloration; the lashes long and curling; the look that flashed from them completely frank and innocent, which was always a sure sign with Monica that she was not telling the truth.

"He's wonderful – handsome, very manly and generous. And he adores me. He says he couldn't go on living without me."

Fifi snorted. "They all say that at first. If he's so generous make sure you get more out of him than you got out of the last one. Where are you living?"

"At his flat – it's a penthouse actually. On Malabar Hill facing the sea."

"Hm, very nice. Next time I'm in the city I'll come to see you. Leave your address."

Monica smiled. "Yes, do come. We have a telephone but I haven't the number with me." She had to slip that in because telephones were as hard to get as snowballs in Bombay and few people had one.

Then waving her hand airily, she walked off in search of another taxi.

The woman and the dog under the mango tree watched her go with the same look of calculating malice in their golden eyes. Fifi

55

was pleased to realise that Monica didn't want her to meet this new man.

"There's something wrong with him," she said aloud, regretting that Sabre couldn't talk, and even more that her daughter Carole was not around to go over the afternoon's visit with her. For want of anyone better to talk to, she went into the kitchen where the servant Leela was shelling green peas into a colander.

"Monica has a new man," said Fifi.

"Good," said Leela. "She hasn't much time left. Her legs are getting skinny and her hips are starting to spread. Didn't you notice?"

Fifi sat herself in the kitchen chair and they settled down to a happy hour of miscalling Monica and recalling the many times in the past she'd had her heart broken by cheating, lying men.

Four

Monica had no illusions about her aunt's feelings towards her, but she was in good spirits as she trudged with difficulty in her high heels up the rutted lane towards the main road. It was late September and though it was not raining today, the heat was stifling and the atmosphere intensely humid. Flowering vines brilliant with scarlet, custard-yellow and purple flowers cascaded over the verges of the road, and leaves from low-hanging branches brushed her hair as she walked along. A city girl, she recoiled from them. *Tree snakes*, she thought, and the skin on her scalp tightened with terror.

Why does Fifi live out here in the back of nowhere? she wondered. But she already knew the answer to that question. Fifi lived in a free house provided by one of her lovers, an Indian ex-army officer who was in charge of Chembur golf course. Monica's mother Bernadette hinted that the protector of her sister had such peculiar sexual tastes

57

that Fifi was the only woman prepared to satisfy them.

Well, at least she has a free house, thought Monica, who was nothing if not practical.

Thinking about her mother, she hailed a taxi beside the police station in the main road of Chembur village. As she climbed into it, a quartet of blue-uniformed constables watched her from the verandah of the station and gave a ragged cheer as the taxi drove off. Scorning them, she turned her face away and stared out of the far window.

"Where to?" asked the taxi driver, eyeing her appreciatively in his rear view mirror. It was so hot that she considered going straight to Stevie's flat and standing under a cool shower, but Fifi's remark that people did not recover from liver cancer had made her anxious to see her mother and she decided to go to Colaba first.

"The chawl behind Cuffe Parade," she told him.

Their chawl was a narrow lane running between two major roads. At one time it had housed the stables of big bungalows that stood between it and the sea on one side, and along the main highway to the military cantonment at the end of Colaba Point on the other. Nowadays the bungalows were cut up into flats, there were no horses in the stables and a couple of hundred people lived in the ramshackle outbuildings – aged crones, harassed workers, hangdog boys and dejected young wives with dozens of children that ran around screaming and fighting while pye-dogs yapped at their heels.

Monica and her mother rented a room on the first floor of the third house on the left. It was a good room, facing the sea, which meant it got a breeze, and it also had a rickety verandah where they liked to hang out their washing, for they were scrupulously clean and always took care to turn themselves out immaculately. On the verandah Monica also grew leggy marigolds and tomato plants in old Dalda cooking oil tins filled with earth that she surreptitiously stole from the flowerbeds in the municipal gardens round the bandstand.

At the bottom of the frail wooden staircase that led up to their room, she slipped off her shoes and, carrying them in her hand, ran barefoot up the steps, joyously crying out, "Mummy, Mummy," as she ran. She always arrived home like this, glad to be reunited with the most important person in her world.

Bernadette was lying on a string bed beneath the window, her head propped up on a canvas-covered cushion. Her skin was a sickening shade of yellow and she was skeletally thin but when she heard her daughter's cries the trembling lids lifted from her pouched eyes and she beamed with joy.

"Dearest, I didn't expect you today," she said, struggling to sit up.

Monica paused in the doorway and cast a critical eye around the sparsely furnished room. How she wished she could take Bernadette back with her to the luxuries of Malabar Hill – but that was impossible.

Her eye lighted on a little table by her mother's couch. On it stood an empty pill bottle and a glass with flies crawling around inside it. She lifted the glass up and frowned. It was the one she'd used to fetch sugar cane juice the last time she had visited. The sated flies flew up into her face and she swatted them away.

"Why have you no juice and no pills? I told that woman to get them for you. Have you drunk any juice today?" she asked.

"I don't want it. I'm not thirsty," said Bernadette.

"Did you drink any yesterday?"

"I really don't want it. I only want to die." Bernadette's voice sounded so exhausted it struck a note of terror in her daughter's heart.

Angrily Monica glared around, nostrils flaring and eyes flashing. She would have hated to know that in that instant her looks changed from those of a European into those of a Rajput warrior queen.

"Where is that useless sweeper woman?" she demanded in a loud voice which she knew would be heard in all the neighbouring rooms.

Watching anxiously, Bernadette noticed the proud, savage look that suddenly transformed her daughter and knew where it came from. Though she'd always told Monica that her father was an English soldier, like her grandfather too, in fact he'd been a tall, incredibly handsome Rajput sepoy. Bernadette had given birth to her only child when she was sixteen and her family were horrified at her choice of a father because they were very proud of their European blood and always denied they had any Indian blood at all.

Behind Monica the door squeaked and a woman in a white sari came creeping in, bent almost double in an obsequious position.

"I gave you money to get my mother more pills and juice every day. Why have you not done it? You are a useless person!" Monica advanced on the cowering sweeper with her hand raised.

"She did not want anything," protested the terrified woman.

"It is not a matter of what she wants. I said she must have these things. You are working for me. Give me back my money and I'll fetch them myself. You'll get nothing more from me." She slapped furiously at the woman's hunched shoulders and drove her towards the door. "Go and fetch my money," she screamed.

The weeping woman gabbled, "I have no money. I spent it. My children's bellies were empty. I am sorry."

Monica screamed even louder, "I knew it! You are a thief. I will kill you!"

Slapping even more wildly with open palms she drove the woman from the room and only stopped screaming when she heard her mother crying out, "Monica, leave her alone. Her husband is dead and her children were hungry. A mother will always feed her children first."

Tears of frustration streaming down her face, Monica turned back to the woman on the bed and knelt by her side. "What am I to do with you? I have money, I will pay for a real ayah to look after you but you must take the medicine."

Her mother took her hand and said, "No, you mustn't waste money on me. Save it, put it in a bank. One day you will be sick and dying like me and perhaps you won't have a good daughter to look after you."

Monica sat back on her heels and said firmly, "You are not dying. The doctor said you're sick with jaundice but you're *not* dying. I won't let you die. I have plenty of money now I've got a new man. You must do as I tell you, and you must drink the sugar cane juice. It's a good cure for jaundice. Promise me you will."

Her voice was determined and her need so obvious that her mother agreed. "I promise," she said.

"Now we'll have tea and then I'll go to the doctor and fetch you more pills," said Monica before setting herself to lighting their little paraffin stove and boiling a kettle. Later she went out again and within an hour was back with a bottle of medicine and a jug of opaque juice. A sweet-faced middle-aged woman was walking in her wake.

She told her mother, "This woman is called Miriam and she is to be your nurse. She is a good woman. Maya told me about her. You must take the medicine she gives you and the food she cooks for you. I'll come back every day and see that you are doing as you are told."

Bernadette laughed almost gaily and her lined face showed traces of the beauty she'd once possessed. "You're talking to me as if I'm a baby," she teased her daughter, who laughed back, relieved to see the change in her mother whom she loved more than anyone in the world. There had only ever been the two of them, protecting each other, and the thought of Bernadette dying terrified her. The main focus of her life would be removed and she would feel totally defenceless. No husband, however devoted, could ever replace her mother, she thought.

"Tell me more about this new man you've found," said Bernadette, seeing the tears in her daughter's eyes and wanting to divert her. Just as Monica worried about her, she was even more worried about her daughter. She had accepted that she was dying – after all, her own mother had died at forty and she'd never expected to have a much longer life – but at that time she'd had her sisters with whom to share the grief. Monica had nobody. Every night Bernadette prayed that some kind man would come into her daughter's life and look after her.

"Let it happen before I die, dear Father, please let it happen," she prayed. "She's a good girl, she's a kind girl, she deserves some luck."

Monica thought about her mother's request as she looked out of the open window towards the setting sun. "My new man? He gives me money even if I don't ask for it," she said.

"That's good, but what is he like as a person?" asked her mother, taking her hand.

"He's a very secretive man. I don't know much about him. He doesn't talk about a wife or a mother or a father or his school-days like some of them do. He doesn't talk about himself at all really."

"But he must say something to you."

"He asks questions all the time – about India, about Bombay, about things he sees on the street, about the European people I know here. He asks and I talk. He likes that."

"And how does he treat you? Is he kind?"

Monica looked into her mother's face. "In bed, you mean? Yes, he's kind – but he's not very interested really. He's never said he wants to marry me or take me away with him, and I haven't asked him to. We don't pretend to each other that it's a great love affair or anything. It's more of a business arrangement somehow. It feels as if I'm working for him, acting as his lover. He's paying me so I do what he wants."

"Oh dear," sighed Bernadette.

Monica hastened to explain herself further. "I don't mean he's only using me as someone to sleep with. We share a bed but we don't make love much – hardly at all in fact. He only wants me to hold him till he falls asleep. Sometimes he wakes up shouting or throwing his arms around and I calm him down. In his sleep he shouts in a language I don't understand. One night he cried. I think he's been very unhappy and he maybe still is."

"Does he like boys, do you think?"

"I don't think so. He's not interested in men or women really."

65

"Do you mind him not making love to you?"

"No, it's a relief." A furrow appeared between Monica's finely shaped eyebrows and she gave a little smile. "It's funny, he makes me feel protective, I suppose. Maybe something terrible happened to him in the past but I daren't ask ... He might tell me what it is one day – or then again he might not."

"I think you like him," said Bernadette.

"I suppose I do, though I don't love him and I don't really know him. He's very polite to me, very correct. He makes me feel – dignified. I've never felt like that before. But I never really know what he's thinking. It's as if he's hollow inside."

"Poor man," said Bernadette.

Five

Click, click, click ... From where she was sprawled along the cane sofa with a copy of *The Eustace Diamonds* in her hands, Dee Carmichael looked up and quailed. The clicking was a sound she dreaded. It meant Bernice Budgeon was coming out armed with her Scrabble board and bag of tiles.

There was nowhere to hide. She was caught like a mouse in a trap.

Click, click, click ... Bernice was on the verandah now, brandishing the green baize bag.

"How are you feeling, my dear?" she asked in a solicitous voice as if Dee was in the grip of a terminal illness. In fact she was perfectly well though rapidly gaining in size because she was five and a half months pregnant.

"I'm fine, thanks," she replied.

Bernice swept on, "What about a game?"

Dee held out her book. "I'd like to finish this," she said feebly.

Bernice smiled. "You and your books!

You'll ruin your eyes. Put it away and let's play a game before the boys come home. You need the practice, you know. It keeps your mind active."

The boys! thought Dee, mentally gritting her teeth. Her husband Ben was thirty years old and Bernice's husband Nigel was nearer fifty than forty. They most definitely were not boys. Bernice, in her late thirties, of course referred to herself and all other women regardless of age as "girls" – she was that sort.

How did I manage to get myself lumbered with you? thought Dee, watching the Scrabble fanatic laying the chequered board and two wooden tile holders out on the coffee table.

Bernice, the bane of Dee's life, looked like the sort of woman who sold cosmetics in department stores: painstakingly enamelled, critical of less meticulous females and totally intimidating. She was tall and dark, with a coil of glossy hair twisted into an immaculate French pleat at the back of her head. Her matronly bosom was encased in a sharply peaked brassiere but she'd put on weight recently and her waxy white upper arms wobbled when she moved. She smelt of Imperial Leather talcum powder.

"What are you reading anyway?" she asked. Her voice was low toned and her accent peculiarly strangled. Dee, who had a good ear for accents, had tried to place it geographically and suspected it was Birmingham overlaid with BBC announcer-style elocution.

"*The Eustace Diamonds*," she said, laying the book down open so she did not lose her place.

"I don't like mysteries," said Bernice. "Give me a *story* every time. I loved *Peyton Place*. Did you ever read that?"

"It's not a mystery, it's by Trollope," protested Dee but she might as well have saved her breath because Bernice was preparing for battle by lining up a sharpened pencil, Collins' dictionary, and a notepad. Dee was in for another resounding defeat.

She gritted her teeth and reminded herself that if she and Ben were to go on living in their beloved bungalow, the Gulmohurs, they had to put up with their "paying guests", Bernice and Nigel Budgeon.

In early summer, when Guy, who used to share the bungalow with them, had stormed out after his mistress Carole was found in bed with the bearer Mohammed, Ben and Dee had feared they too would have to leave because they could not afford to keep up the house on their own. Ben was on a very small salary and they had no way of earning extra money. Miraculously, however, that very same week, an Indian business contact of Ben's had asked him if he knew of anyone who could offer comfortable lodgings to a

European couple who had recently arrived in Bombay.

Nigel Budgeon was the site manager overseeing the construction of a new loading jetty and deep-water harbour which was being built by an American oil company at Trombay on the other side of the island. Ben's company was also working on the refinery but in a much smaller way, though he had hopes of a bigger involvement soon.

"We can go on staying here if we take them in as PGs," Ben told his wife.

Taking PGs – paying guests – was the acknowledged way for poorly-paid Europeans to cover their expenses, by giving room and board to other poorly paid expatriates. Most young couples starting out in India either began as PGs or renting to PGs.

Though poor, the Carmichaels were reluctant to share their home with strangers and discussed the matter for quite a while.

"I don't want to leave this house," Dee said and Ben agreed.

"I don't want to go either but we've got to be realistic. We can't afford to keep it up without Guy's contribution. Sharma says this site manager guy Nigel Budgeon is a decent chap. He and his wife are living in a grotty hotel down by the docks and she hates it there. It's making her ill, apparently."

Dee, who felt more reluctant than he did to share the isolation of the Gulmohurs with anybody, realised how eager he was to follow up this opportunity, so she said, "All right, let's see them."

They met a week later on a Sunday evening when the Gulmohurs' garden was looking at its most glorious.

It was immediately obvious that the Budgeons liked the house and each couple passed the other's tests though Bernice was not the sort that Dee felt really comfortable with for she was too well groomed and ladylike – the sort who bent her little finger when drinking tea and always said, "Shall I be mother?" when pouring it out.

Dee suspected that on her part Bernice also had reservations about her new landlady because Dee tended to swear rather a lot and preferred to spend her time with her nose in books rather than have heart-to-heart chats. Nigel, however, was bluff and friendly, obviously a good sort. Ben especially took to him and the PGs moved in a week later.

That was three months ago and things had gone downhill ever since.

"It really surprises me that a girl with your education isn't better at Scrabble," said Bernice, settling down in her chair and preparing herself for the fray. She never failed to get in a jibe about Dee's university degree as opposed to her own lack of higher education. It obviously preyed on her mind.

"I'm afraid Scrabble wasn't on the curriculum when I was at university," Dee said coldly.

Bernice laughed in a tinkling way and held out the bag. "You are funny! You've such a sense of humour. Now pick your tiles, dear."

Dee glumly selected seven and found that she could make the word "puritan" out of them.

"You go first," said Bernice after having scrutinised her selection.

Dee laid out her word and prepared to be awarded fifty points as well as the tile score – but she was wrong.

"That's not allowed. Puritan has a capital letter, dear," said Bernice.

"Can't it be used as an adjective?" Dee protested but to no point. "Puritan" was not allowed by Bernice's rules which were purely arbitrary, not to be questioned and liable to be altered to suit herself. The only thing to do was to play on and pray for the sound of an arriving car – which would probably be Nigel's, for the construction site where he worked was nearer to the Gulmohurs than Ben's office in the Fort.

The two women played grimly in the still afternoon while a heat haze shimmered over the ranks of red, orange and yellow canna lilies that filled diamond-shaped flowerbeds at the sides of the lawn.

As the sun began to sink, Birbal, the gardener, came out to do the evening watering and stalked to and fro dragging his green hose. This was the time of day that Dee loved best, the time when the goatherds brought their charges along the lane from the sere fields where they had spent the day and women from the buffalo camp further up the hill came padding down barefoot in their brilliant orange and ochre cotton saris to fill their water cans at the well at the foot of the Gulmohurs' garden.

Her enjoyment of the tranquillity at the end of brilliantly sunny days spent alone in the bungalow was ruined by Bernice who clattered Scrabble tiles and talked incessantly about herself, especially about her inability to conceive a child – another reason for her dislike of Dee who was so obviously pregnant – and her distaste for the sexual demands of men.

"I'm lucky with Nigel. He wants me to have a baby because that's what I want most in the world, but he doesn't *bother* me except at the times of the month when I might be fertile. We keep a temperature chart, you see," she said, rapidly lifting out a blank that Dee had put down and substituting one of her own letters for it. According to her, this substitution was allowed by the rules providing the player had the letter which the blank represented. It was to be twenty years before Dee summoned up the nerve to play Scrabble again and then found that no such rule existed.

"What a shame," said Dee, thinking that consulting temperature charts must be a terrible passion killer.

Bernice stared at her, round eyed. "A shame? It's a blessing. I get no pleasure out of that sort of thing ... it disgusts me. Ugh."

Dee said nothing. She relished the sex she shared with Ben. It was a huge bond between them and certainly not indulged in purely for the purposes of breeding.

"I know you don't agree but you've not been married very long, and if you'd had the experience I've had you wouldn't like it either," said Bernice. Dee mentally groaned for this remark was always an introduction to Bernice's other favourite topic – the time she had been raped by an American GI during the war. In the beginning of their acquaintance, Dee had felt sympathy when she heard this tale but repetition had dulled that and the relish with which the rape was recalled made her suspect that it was the most significant sexual event in Bernice's life.

An attempt at diversion by laying down the doubtful word "didact" failed, for Bernice didn't even question it. She was too well launched into her story

74

"Rape is the most awful thing a woman can suffer. It puts her off sex for ever. Nigel is so understanding ... sometimes I wake up at night screaming and remembering that awful American. He smelt of hair oil and cigars. Nigel loves a good cigar but since we got married he never smokes them because he knows how the smell nauseates me."

Dee was spared a repetition of fuller details because a crunching of car tyres on gravel announced the arrival of Nigel who came running over the grass carrying something in his arms. Walking behind him was Jean-Paul, a stunningly handsome Frenchman, who worked as a diver on the new harbour construction.

Bounding up the verandah steps, Nigel bent over his wife and planted a kiss on her cheek. "Look what I've brought you, darling!" he cried and laid his bundle in her lap.

It was a tiny white pye-dog puppy, only a few weeks old, still fluffy and appealing to look at. When it grew older, Dee knew as she looked at it, it would become as leggy and ugly, mean spirited and growling as all the other pye-dogs that roamed and scavenged in the lanes, alleys and back streets of Bombay. A devoted dog lover, Dee could not summon up any kindly feelings towards pye-dogs for they made her think of craven, canine rats.

"Darling, how marvellous!" cooed Bernice, snuggling the dog up to her face. "It's lovely."

"I've got its mother in the car as well; the poor things are starving. I saw the mother hunting for food on the site and I just picked them up and brought them home," said Nigel, his kindly face beaming with love and benevolence. He was a sucker for animals. The week before he'd brought home a baby monkey that then ran wild in the garden and had to be caught with a fishing net before it wrecked the flowerbeds. Ben had been furious.

"Isn't it lovely?" said Bernice holding out the puppy towards Dee who drew back from it.

"Ben hates pye-dogs," she said, "He won't have them in the garden because one of the servants' wives was bitten a few years ago and died of rabies. It's a terrible death. Ben and Guy were both bitten by the rabid dog's puppy too and had to have awful injections in their bellies. It was before I came here..." Her voice trailed off because she could see that no one was listening to her.

Nigel was looking adoringly at his wife and the puppy; Jean-Paul was looking at Bernice too and she was looking up at him from cast-down lashes with undeniable coquettishness.

Gosh, is she giving him the come on? thought

Dee in surprise. Not that she blamed her really for Jean-Paul was gorgeous, especially when compared with poor balding Nigel, who was heavily built and red faced with a twisted broken nose and swollen cauliflower ears that testified to his previous career as a professional boxer.

He'd done quite well in the ring apparently, but had to retire when his injuries began to affect his performance. Not only had he been a profuse bleeder but he also began to suffer from mild brain damage which had been manifested to Ben and Dee one night when their doorbell rang as they were having dinner with their new PGs.

Immediately Nigel had sprung to his feet, tipping his chair back on to the floor, rubbing his tightly clenched fists across the base of his nose and snuffling and snorting like a terrified horse. Bernice had calmed him down and explained to the astonished couple at the table that the unexpected ringing of bells or alarm clocks always made her husband think he was back in the ring.

"What she means is the poor bugger's punchy," said Ben to Dee when they were alone and able to talk about their lodger's peculiar behaviour. They didn't mind, however, because, punchy or not, Nigel was the kindest and most pacific of men, one of the most sweet-natured people either of them had ever met. He never passed a beggar without emptying his pockets of coins; he was incapable of ignoring a sick or injured animal. The cruelties of life in India ravaged his heart.

Watching him adoring the puppy and Bernice, Dee felt a sudden rush of pity in her heart and so that they could have some privacy she rose from the sofa and left them to take their pre-dinner drinks with Jean-Paul.

Though he was incredibly handsome and very polite, there was something about that young man that repelled her. He'd been coming home with Nigel almost every night for about a fortnight now, outrageously flattering Bernice and bowing over her hand. He unashamedly drank Nigel's gin and shared their meals without ever contributing anything of his own. It was as if he felt that his physical beauty entitled him to homage as he sat nonchalantly on the verandah with one long brown leg slung over the chair arm and a miasma of Gauloise smoke hanging around his head like a halo.

Tall, deeply tanned with shining blonde hair and eyes of a distinctive hazel, Jean-Paul was woman-bait. Ben, woman-bait as well, had hated him on sight. The friendship of Bernice and Nigel with the bland Frenchman was as much a cross for him as Bernice's addiction to Scrabble was for his wife.

After leaving them, Dee lay on her bed

and listened for the sound of her husband's car coming up the lane. It drew into the parking space at seven o'clock just as darkness was falling like the dropping of a stage curtain. She jumped up and went out to meet him and warn him about the dogs and the Frenchman but she was too late.

His entry on to the verandah was precipitious. "There's a bloody pye-dog tied up in the garden," he shouted as he came up the steps.

The trio were still sitting round the drinks trolley and Bernice had the white puppy on her lap. "I brought them," said Nigel.

"Them?" asked Ben.

"There's a puppy too," was his reply.

Bernice held out the little bundle of fluff, saying, "Look. It's so cute."

Ben's face went taut and two vertical lines marked the sides of his mouth. "I told you when you came here that you couldn't keep pets, especially pye-dogs," he said.

"But its mother was starving and it's such a lovely little thing," protested Nigel.

"I'm sorry, but it can't stay. I don't want pye-dogs here any more than I wanted that monkey." Ben was angry and Dee, watching from the sitting room, saw that his cheek was twitching with the effort of maintaining calm. The experience with the rabid animal had put him off pye-dogs for life.

"It's got to go, Nigel," he said addressing

himself to the older man.

"Surely I can keep the puppy," said Bernice.

Ben didn't take his eyes off her husband. "They've both got to go," he repeated.

Nigel turned to his wife and said in a long-suffering voice, "I'm afraid if the mother goes, the pup has to go too. It's too young to be separated from her. I'll take them back to the site tomorrow and make sure the men feed it. You can come and see it there, darling."

Jean-Paul gave an exaggerated sigh and Bernice an anguished gasp, cuddling the pup closer to her, but Ben, after shooting a hard stare at the Frenchman, turned away and walked quickly to the bedroom followed by Dee. When he closed the door he leaned against it and said, "Christ, I can't stand that woman – or that bloody Jean-Paul."

"Neither can I," said Dee, "but if we're going to go on living here, we need them."

Six

Bernice never got out of bed till noon, so next morning Dee and Ben breakfasted alone and planned that she should drive with him into the city where she would spend the day and return with him at night. At least it would give her a day away from Bernice who would be sure to want to discuss the matter of the dogs.

"Which way will we go?" Dee asked as Ben turned the car into the main road at the foot of their lane. Both of them loved the crowded, chaotic jumble of hamlets, streets and alleys that lay between Chembur and their destination in the Fort, and both liked to vary their route into Bombay.

Sometimes they drove along the causeway at Sewri and past glittering salt pans where tiny fish and Bombay ducks were hung along wires to dry in the sun by raucous women with saris looped up between their knees. That route was best taken at night because when the sun beamed down the smell that came from the browning scraps of

81

fish was so pungent that it made their eyes water.

At other times their route might lead through Chembur village, taking them past Dr Bali's house with the ever-present string bed in the garden and past the market where tethered goats and chickens dolefully awaited their fate outside the butchery section. In the village, idly wandering men, out of their minds with kif even early in the morning, weaved to and fro over the road and created a driving hazard.

Or they could go through prosperous leafy suburbs where houses, painted in pastel colours like children's sweets, stood in burgeoning gardens. That way went past St Xavier's Jesuit church and the school where their neighbour Raj Kapoor's children were educated and then plunged into the industrial section, along the high, intimidating walls of a huge complex of cotton mills where the machinery was never still and kept on pounding through twenty-four hours, every day of the week. It also took them past crumbling old bungalows in Byculla that were among the first built by European settlers in Bombay, ramshackle now but still showing traces of their original glory in the wide verandas and elegant Grecian pillars holding up their roofs.

No matter which way they took, there was always something fascinating to see, and the more familiar Dee became with the teeming city, the more she loved it.

Today they went past St Xavier's church. Because it was early, the roads were fairly empty except for a few garishly painted lorries hurtling along and the straining figures of men hauling heavily loaded carts that loomed high above their bent, sweating bodies. Those coolies walked for miles pulling immense loads and few lived into their thirties but died of exhaustion at an age when men who had been dealt a better card in the lottery of life were beginning their careers.

After she dropped Ben at his office near the Maidan, Dee drove slowly through even more crowded city streets, watching, noticing, adoring and despairing of this mysterious country that was India. Her objective was the Asiatic Society Library that stood facing into Elphinstone Circle near the docks.

The library occupied a magnificent late eighteenth-century building, built as the Town House and chief administrative building by the British nabobs of the East India Company, but now deliberately being allowed to crumble away as a symbolic act of defiance on the part of the rulers of recently independent India. Louvred wooden shutters hung outside the windows, but many of the hinges had gone and they swung crazily to and fro. The paint on the façade, which once had been cream, was streaked with green mildew and badly blistered or peeling. The long flight of elegant steps that led up to the front entrance were cracked and broken and a huddle of importunate beggars were always camped out at the foot of them.

Most of the contents of the library had been left behind by the British and, though little had been added to the collection over the past fifteen years, it was still a valuable treasure trove of English books about India – memoirs of district officers, botanical and ornithological books, reminiscences of homesick memsahibs, military records, grim details of mutinies and insurrections, famines and acts of heroism.

Silverfish ran such riot through the pages that some volumes crumbled into dust when they were opened, and no effort was made to maintain a level temperature or control the humidity, so that the whole building had a strange, cellar like smell – the aroma of decay and neglect. Even the clerks behind the high wooden counter looked as if they were relics from the Raj, for they were all bespectacled, grey-haired babus who seemed surprised that anyone ever wanted to borrow anything from their shelves.

Dee had been admitted to membership of

this exclusive association through recommendation from a cultivated and charming drunk who propped up the bar at the Ritz every night. A member of a rich Parsee family, he'd been sent to study philosophy at Oxford but, after graduating, returned to a life of idleness and alcohol. One day, when she told him about her hunger for books and the impossibility of finding in Bombay the sort she enjoyed, he introduced her to the Asiatic Library and immeasurably enhanced her life.

She parked her car near Thacker's Bookshop, where the few imported books still available were too expensive for her to buy, walked past a circle of metal railings that enclosed an overgrown garden in the middle of Elphinstone Circle, and laboriously climbed twenty wide, sweeping steps to the library's pillared portico.

At the top she paused for breath and stared around, struck as always by the grandeur of the construction. The British conquerors of India had seen themselves as the inheritors of the Roman tradition, proud, superior and vainglorious. The transience of their empire was tellingly displayed in the ruined elegance of the building before her.

One of the old clerks greeted her warmly. He'd put aside for her three books of Mutiny reminiscences in faded leather bindings, which she took gratefully for he was good at knowing what she liked.

Carrying them, she went back through the entrance hall where Indian language newspapers were laid out on long wooden tables, and leaned over the head of a curving internal staircase that led down to hidden chambers at street level. Into the stairwell beneath her were crowded an amazing collection of white marble, life-size statues rounded up after Independence from various plinths in the city. They looked like a wildly excited crowd.

Glorious names out of history were represented here. British generals, politicians and administrators, the men who had carved out the British Empire in India; – Minto, Cavendish, Elphinstone, Napier, Frere, Hastings, and Wellesley, all stood in masterly poses or were casually seated on fine horses. The only statue representing a woman was one of the Queen Empress, Victoria. She sat, plump, middle aged, prim and disapproving, like a pigeon surrounded by fighting cocks. Dee loved to pay her respects to the sword-waving, gesturing figures in this collection every time she visited the library. They made her think of an elephants' graveyard.

Smiling and cheerful after bowing to them, she went back into the sunlit glare of the streets and the baking car – the steering wheel was too hot to hold without a piece of cloth to protect her hands – and headed for the house of her best friend, Anne Connor, who lived with her husband Bill and four-year-old daughter Liza in a crumbling building on Cuffe Parade, Colaba. Dee and Anne had become close after Dee's friend Baby Maling-Smith had left Bombay and gone to live in a mansion outside Helensburgh in Scotland.

Anne's house faced Back Bay and a long, curving, palm-fringed promenade where Indian families walked sedately in the evenings, the men in immaculately starched white clothes and the women with circlets of sweet-smelling jasmine flowers in their hair. When it grew dark, and they had gone home, far off to the left, the intermittent beam from the lighthouse on Colaba Point raked the sky.

The Connors' house was painted a fading dove grey, with the window frames and balcony railings picked out in cream. In the middle of the façade a large white plaster lozenge rimmed with fancy curlicues bore its name – Nirvana.

It had been built in the middle of the nineteenth century to house the family of a well-to-do box-wallah, but a hundred years later Colaba was no longer a fashionable place for Europeans to live, and the house was now divided into two flats. Beneath the

Connors lived a Parsee family called Officerwallah who kept themselves strictly to themselves and blandly ignored the frequent rows that went on above their heads.

Bill Connor was not sufficiently highly regarded by his employers to be better housed than this because he was only a tradesman – a man without background or superior education. His job was to keep the mill machinery running for a huge firm of cotton spinners. His European management colleagues regarded him as a "rude mechanical" – and he knew it.

The resentment that burned within him of the condescension with which he was treated was expressed by heavy drinking, being obstructive and uncooperative at work, and by picking fights with anyone he suspected of casting admiring eyes on his beautiful wife.

Anne was stunning – a statuesque blonde with creamy skin and a profile that would have inspired the makers of eighteenth-century cameos. She was also possessed of a low, beautifully modulated and ladylike voice that made her both look and sound like a duchess from Regency days.

The snobbish memsahibs who gathered at the Bombay Gymkhana Club every morning for coffee and to gossip and browse among the tawdry stock in the little shop there were intrigued by her. "She sounds so well bred. Why on earth did she marry that awful man?" they whispered when she passed by.

Dee had wondered that as well. Bill was strongly built, freckled and red-haired, with a tough-guy sort of sexuality, but he was difficult to put up with, especially if he had been drinking, when his tongue became cruelly sharp and he could turn violent. In a society where most of the men had been to public school – though rarely to top-rate ones – Bill boasted about his proletarian background: born illegitimate in Liverpool, so he said, and brought up by a mother who drank, he had left school at fifteen, served an apprenticeship as a printer and then began wandering the world.

He had met Anne at a tea-dance in a London hotel, to which she'd been taken by a friend of her schoolteacher father, a besotted widower twenty-five years her senior who wanted to marry her. She was only nineteen and would probably have married him if Bill hadn't cut in while she and her suitor were dancing. He literally swept her off her feet. It had been passion at first sight for both of them.

Three weeks later they were married in a registry office and went to live in a working-class Manchester street, to the horror of Anne's parents. Four years after that, when their daughter Liza was only three months old, in an attempt to better themselves and to put a distance between them and Anne's still disapproving family, Bill signed a contract to work as a maintenance engineer for another four years with a cotton-spinning company in Bombay. That contract had only a few months still to run, but he hoped to be offered another term – at more money – though he did nothing to ingratiate himself with his employers. In fact he seemed determined to alienate them.

In spite of its aspirational name the house looked dejected to Dee as she steered the nose of her grey Studebaker into the gate of its garden where nothing but a few banana trees and clumps of spiky mother-in-law's tongues fought for existence. She looked up at the glassed-in verandah of Anne's sitting room and saw that one of the panels was open. From it came the sound of piano music.

The side door was opened by the Singalese bearer Gopal who was every bit as sullen and resentful of the rest of the world as the man who employed him. When Dee said, "Good morning," he pretended not to hear her.

I'd have fired you long ago, she thought as she glared at him. He was the most recent of a long series of bad servants that the Connors had employed. Few lasted more than a month before they either ran off or were fired by Bill in one of his alcohol-fuelled rampages, but Gopal semed to have survived longer than most.

Through all the domestic chaos Anne cut her apparently tranquil way like a beautiful full-sailed galleon, seemingly unaware that her house was uncared for and her servants idle, rude and thieving. She passed her time reading, playing with Liza, cheating herself at patience, or browsing through the shoe shops that lined both sides of Colaba Causeway.

Dee suspected, however, that her friend's appearance of placidity was not genuine. There was a lot more going on beneath the surface than was at first obvious. Every now and again Anne suffered transient mini-blackouts but refused to accept they had happened. She only admitted to having them when she suffered a particularly bad attack and had to ask Dee to take over the driving of her little Fiat car in which they were taking Liza to the Botanical Gardens.

The episode upset Dee, who afterwards was ultra-sensitive to her friend's state of health. When a strange fixed expression crossed Anne's face she would ask her if she was all right but Anne always shook her head and said, "Of course. What do you mean?" The blackouts and the true state of the Connors' marriage, were both taboo subjects and Anne would never talk about them though she and Dee were close friends who discussed everything else with complete candour.

Once inside, Nirvana was much more gracious than it looked from the road because it was spacious and old-fashioned with high wooden roof beams. Slowly turning fans were suspended from them and a steeply pitched roof allowed cool breezes from the sea to cool the flat even in the hottest weather. Lured by the sound of music, Dee walked up a long passage that ran along the back of the house to the large sitting room at the far end.

It was a cheerless, utilitarian room, one half of it filled by a big dining table and eight high-backed chairs, a massive sideboard and a huge spotted mirror. In the other end facing the sea were five cane armchairs with different coloured cushions, a cane sofa, a glass-topped coffee table, and a new feature, an upright piano that stood in the middle of the floor as if a giant had dropped it down from the sky.

Anne, her golden head bent, was playing with skill and verve, perched too high on a vinyl-topped bar stool. The music that rippled from her fingers seemed to flow through the room like gentle streamers. It was not the usual sort of music that was heard in this house; when Bill was at home, he played two records over and over again –

Pat Boone's "April Love" and "They Tried To Tell Us We're Too Young". These banal pieces could move him to tears because, he said, they expressed the emotions he'd felt when he married Anne.

Dee paused by the sofa and stood listening till there was a pause. Then she clapped and said, "I'd no idea you could play like that. What was the piece? It was lovely."

"Schubert's 'Trout'. I'm not very good, I'm afraid. Lots of wrong notes."

"It sounded lovely to me. Where did the piano come from?"

"Bill hired it for me. It's out of tune but I think this climate's to blame. I love making music though I strike so many wrong notes—"

"No you don't. Play it again. I'll sit down here and listen."

Anne played a medley, bits of Bach mixed up with Schubert, and when she finished she got down from her stool with a laugh and asked, "Did you enjoy that, then?"

"Yes, very much. It's a real change from Pat Boone and it made me forget about the annoyances at home," said Dee.

"What's the trouble?" asked Anne sympathetically. She was someone you could talk to, even though she did not always fully reciprocate.

"Bloody Bernice of course. She's getting on my nerves and Nigel's getting on Ben's but we need them in order to pay the rent. Isn't that awful? Last night I wondered if it's worth it because Nigel brought home a pye-dog and its pup – and you know about Ben's horror of rabies. It's Bernice that's the real pain in the neck for me though. All she wants to do is play Scrabble for hour after hour and talk about the time she was raped by a GI." Dee grimaced.

"What's wrong with Scrabble?" asked Anne who liked parlour games.

"She cheats."

Anne laughed. "Don't take it so hard. It's only a game. You're too competitive."

"I know. That's why I came here, so you could tell me that. Now I've got it off my chest, where's Liza? Let's take her to Breach Candy for a swim."

They drove to the swimming pool with the blonde cherub of a child sitting on the front seat between them. On the way, Dee noticed that Anne had suddenly become silent, and glancing over saw the feared, fixed expression on her face.

"Anne," she said sharply, "are you feeling ill? Shouldn't you go to see Ralph?"

With an obvious effort, Anne collected herself but all colour had drained from her face.

"Of course not. I'm perfectly all right," she said, but her hands were tight on the wheel. In a few minutes, however, she had fully recovered and was not prepared to admit that anything had happened. Frowning, Dee decided that the next time she went to the Asiatic Library she would look for a medical book that could tell her about epilepsy because she suspected from past experience of acquaintances with the condition that was what was troubling her friend.

When they reached Breach Candy the lawns around the big pool were full of women slowly turning themselves in the sun like sides of meat on spits. Some of them were so bronzed that they gleamed like copper. They did nothing else, day after day, except sunbathe.

The children's pool was almost empty so they had their sunchairs and umbrella put up there in order to watch Liza splashing in and out.

Dee, who had exceptionally good long sight and was able to recognise people from a long way off, pointed out a man to Anne, who had become bright and chatty again as if nothing untoward had happened.

"D'you see that tall guy with the yellow hair and the great tan on the other side of the big pool? He's called Jean-Paul and he's French. He comes to see Nigel and Bernice a lot and she thinks he admires her so she's leading him on, but he's a philanderer. I bet if I called him over here, he'd make a play for you," said Dee.

Anne sat up and adjusted her dark glasses. "Really? For goodness' sake, don't do it, then. I can't cope with any emotional entanglements right now. But are you sure about Bernice? Didn't you say she's very strait-laced?"

"She acts as if she is but I've my suspicions because she acts like a fourteen-year-old, all sweet smiles and fluttering eyelashes, when our French friend is around."

"That I'd like to see," laughed Anne.

"Then come to lunch on Sunday."

"We can't. Bill's invited some American and his Anglo-Indian girlfriend to lunch with us. He met them in the Ritz," said Anne.

"Bring them too. I don't think I could stand another Sunday with Bernice, Nigel and Jean-Paul on their own – specially after the puppy problem," pleaded Dee.

Anne laughed, "OK, we'll come. It'll be nice for the American to see something of the countryside and people always love your house."

"Let's enjoy it while we can. I've a feeling we won't be there much longer," said Dee despondently.

Seven

Stevie's prodigality with tips quickly won round any reservations the Ritz barmen Thomas and Raju had about Americans and they greeted him with smiles and his favourite gin gimlets whenever he stepped into their dark cavern. He and Monica held court there almost every evening and were soon on chatting acquaintance with several members of the Gym rugby club, who used the bar as a rendezvous because the Gym no longer had a liquor licence. The bar there had been closed down on the orders of puritanical Hindu politicians as a way of getting at the British ex-pats.

Bill Connor did not play rugby and disdained those who did, but he used the Ritz as a hang-out after work and usually slouched alone in a corner booth drinking Lion beer until he felt drunk enough to go home for dinner. His mind was always seething with frustration at the annoyances of his job, at the high-handed attitudes of the British managers who condescended to him – at everything, in fact.

Since boyhood he had been fascinated by gangsters. Lucky Luciano, Al Capone, Bugsy Malone, and London's Jack Spot were his heroes and he could talk about their lives and exploits for hours. It was his dream to get to America and join up with a gang and he was continually dreaming up schemes for making money by illicit means, though he fortunately never got any of them off the ground.

If I got the chance I could prove I'm hard enough. I'd show those bastards, he told himself as he hunched over his beer, day-dreaming about life as a hood and scorning the bawling rugby players who were leaning on the 1930s-style chrome decorated bar in front of him.

It was when he heard a marked New York accent that Bill's attention was drawn to the stranger and, being emboldened by drink by this time, he strolled across the bar to where Stevie was sitting with Monica and introduced himself. Stevie invited him to join them and a kind of guarded acquaintanceship struck up. Bill asked Stevie questions about New York and Stevie quizzed him about life in Bombay. They chatted to and fro while Monica sat toying with her glass and looking beautiful.

Before the night ended, Bill, now in the expansive stage of drunkenness, invited them to lunch. Stevie was very pleased because it was the first time he'd been asked into any private house since he arrived in Bombay.

On the next evening, however, Bill was in the bar again and walked across to them to change his invitation. "Instead of coming to my place on Sunday, what about going out of the city with us to a place where some friends of my wife are living? They've a very nice house and they've invited all of us to have lunch with them."

"But would they want us to go?" asked Stevie.

"Oh yes, my wife has cleared that with them. Bring a bottle of gin and you'll be welcomed like Father Christmas," said Bill.

Stevie was still doubtful. "Where is it exactly?" he asked.

"At a place called Chembur," Bill told him. "You could drive out with Anne and me if you like, though our car's not very big and we'll be taking our daughter too." It was obvious from his tone that it would be preferable if they used their own car.

Monica looked up. "I know how to get to Chembur. My aunt lives there."

"In that case, you'll find the house easily. It's in the jungle on the side of Chembur hill, next door to an actor called Raj Kapoor," said Bill. "It's up a little lane that's quite difficult to see."

Stevie brightened at the prospect of

having lunch in the jungle but Monica's face went strangely still and impassive. "I know the lane quite well," she said. She did not sound very enthusiastic though neither of the men seemed to notice.

"In that case you can make your own way." Bill was relieved because he was so jealous of Anne that he did not like the idea of her travelling in a car with another man, even when he was there too. If he had his way he'd keep her in purdah.

It was arranged that Stevie and Monica should arrive at the Gulmohurs at half-past twelve on Sunday.

"And don't forget the gin," was Bill's parting shot.

At first light on Sunday, Monica rose quietly and dressed herself in her church-going clothes. She always wore a hat when she went to Mass, a round white straw one that looked like a cooking bowl and had once belonged to her mother. Stevie opened his eyes as she was perching it on top of her curls and skewering it down with a long hat-pin.

"Where are you going?" he asked, surprised at the sight of her in a hat.

"To Mass. Go back to sleep. I'll be back soon," she told him. "I haven't forgotten we've been invited out to lunch."

She took a taxi to Colaba and felt fortified by the service. Then she stayed behind for confession because that always made her feel even better, as if she was starting off in life again with a clean slate. Unfortunately, because she and Stevie led such chaste lives, she did not have much to confess and hoped that the priest, who knew her well, did not suspect her of telling lies or hiding things. Perhaps, she thought, she should make up a few sins, but she decided that would be a sin as well and it would be best to stick to the truth. When she eventually emerged from the confessional, with only a meagre penance to perform, she was feeling much better than when she had gone in.

Before she left the church she lit a candle in front of the Virgin and knelt to send up a prayer for her mother and another for herself. The request for Bernadette was to make her healthy again and for herself it was even more simple. "Get me through today. Don't let me be scared by going back there," she prayed.

Then she half ran all the way to the chawl behind Cuffe Parade, pausing only to give money to Maya.

When she reached her room, she saw with delight that the Virgin must have answered her first prayer because Bernadette was sitting up and looking fresh in a dress she'd had for a long time but hadn't worn much recently. It was a pretty pale blue with a shawl collar and a big bow under her chin which made her look particularly girlish.

"Don't you look well!" Monica exclaimed but though her mother was very bright and lively, on closer scrutiny it was not possible to ignore how thin her arms had grown. They looked like withered brown twigs, and her cheekbones were pathetically prominent with the skin stretched tight across them like transparent parchment.

"You're better, Mama!" she cried happily, hiding her disquiet. "The medicine has worked, hasn't it?"

"Yes, I'm much better. The cool weather will be here soon and that always makes me feel well. And you, my darling, are looking beautiful. What are you doing today?"

"We've been invited to lunch in Chembur. Funnily enough to that house where Carole lived with the Englishman." She smiled as she said it.

Bernadette laughed. "How funny!" Then she sobered a little and added, "But you lived near that house too, didn't you? Is the man you lived with still there?"

Monica shook her head. "I hope not. I heard he was going away. Carole's man has left too, but his friends are there. They don't know about my connection with her though. I'd rather have stayed at home today but Steven's very keen to go to Chembur because he's never been out of the city."

Bernadette took her daughter's hand.

"Don't be frightened. That's all in the past and you have your new man to look after you now."

Monica nodded solemnly. "Yes, I know. I'm not really frightened. It's just that I don't like that hillside. I was so glad to get away from there. It was a bad time of my life."

Her mother sighed and hugged her. "I wish I could be sure that your new man'll take you with him to New York when he leaves. Then I'd be able to die with peace of mind."

Monica jumped up. "Don't talk like that. You're not going to die. You're much better. I've told you that before." This sort of discussion always disturbed her so much that she sounded cross and angry.

Bernadette tried to placate her. "I know, but I'll die eventually. Everyone does. But I want you to promise that even if I'm alive when he goes, you'll go with him if he asks you."

Monica turned away, exasperated. "Of course I wouldn't go and leave you. I'd never do that so don't even ask me to. Now, where's your ayah? I want to give her money to buy you some special food today. Would you like a chicken?" Boiled chicken and rice was one of her mother's favourite dishes of the ones that she could still enjoy.

"I couldn't eat a whole chicken on my

103

own," protested Bernadette.

"Then have a party," said her daughter. "Invite some of the neighbours. I want you to have a party to celebrate the fact that you're so much better!"

When Monica got back to Malabar Hill Stevie was ready to leave, pacing across their terrace and jiggling the car keys in his fingers. Today he was driving one of his company's cars – a long green Chevrolet with silver tail fins and an air-conditioning unit that blasted out so much cold air that it made Monica shiver. He drove fast, and, once out of the city, the car took up most of the road so that when other drivers saw it coming towards them they drew into the rutted roadside and huddled there in terror.

"Where're we going? You do know the way?" he asked, turning his immense black sunglasses in Monica's direction as they drove through Worli. He seemed to be really enjoying himself on this expedition.

"Yes, I know the house we're going to. My aunt lives near it. Just follow this road," she told him, pointing ahead.

They drove past a petrol station that stood by a fork in the road where there was also an ice cream stall that sold tubs of what the vendor called "tooty prooty". The road then skirted a mound topped by a ruined fort, with a stagnant-looking pond covered with lotus leaves on the left. After that it crossed flat marshland towards Chembur village – a cluster of houses, an outdoor market, the open-air cinema, the police station, and finally the studios owned by the famous film star Raj Kapoor. A huge wooden cut-out of a sword-wielding rajah on a horse was erected beside the studio entrance.

When she saw this Monica sat forward in her seat and pointed to the right. "Take the next turning. Go more slowly, please, because it's almost hidden. You won't see it till you're almost on it." It occurred to her that the huge car might be too wide to get into the lane but then she remembered that Raj Kapoor, who lived up there too, had a white Cadillac that was even bigger than Stevie's Chevrolet.

Stevie braked suddenly when the head of the lane came into view and gave a little whistle as they turned off the main road.

"Gee, this is something!" he exclaimed, staring up at the thickly wooded hill that loomed in front of them. The surface of the lane was no longer tarmac, but bright red earth deeply rutted after the rains. Along each side ran ten-foot high hedges of cacti with spikes like the lances of medieval knights.

The lane ran straight for about 300 yards and then they saw ahead of them a sharp bend with a closed gate on the left. "Is that it?" asked Stevie.

Monica shook her head. "No, not yet, go on past the well. It's next on the left after that."

He glanced at her. "You sure know your way around here."

"Yes. I lived up this lane for a bit about six years ago."

"It's a lovely place," he said.

She shivered. "I don't like it."

He was steering the huge car around the right-angled bend when she was thrown forward in her seat by his sudden application of the brakes. The long nose of their car swerved into the cactus hedge and Stevie cursed because bearing down on them at top speed, with its horn blaring, was a large white Mercedes. Dust and little stones from the surface of the lane were thrown up in all directions by its braking wheels.

Stevie cursed again. "Hell and damnation!" he exclaimed, then, "Are you OK, Mon?"

She was lying on the floor in front of the passenger seat, crouched up like a scared child with her head on her knees.

"Are you OK?" he asked again, looking down in concern.

"Yes, yes," she whispered, but stayed huddled on the floor.

The road was too narrow for two cars to pass abreast and though the Mercedes had stopped the driver still leant on his horn. Stevie rolled down his window and yelled, "You were going too fast. Back up."

But instead of backing up, the white car started again and kept on coming, inexorably, threateningly. Though Stevie's car was large, it was tiny compared to the tanklike Mercedes which would easily be able to push them off the road and grind them into pieces. When they were fender to fender it was Stevie who had to back up, cursing and grinding the gears in his agitation. When he drew his finned tail into the fruit farm gateway, the Mercedes swept past.

Leaning out of his window Stevie saw that the driver was a yellow-haired white man who sat arrogantly behind the other car's steering wheel as if there was nothing else on the road.

"You rat!" Stevie yelled as the Mercedes swished past but at the moment they were level, the driver turned his face and stared full at him. The stare was scornful.

It had a peculiar effect on Stevie. In an instant he went pale beneath his tan and sank back in his seat with a gasp which brought Monica up from her hiding place on the floor. She put her arms round him and crooned, "Don't worry, don't worry, we're all right." He was shivering violently and she had to hold him for quite a long time till he calmed down.

Seven people were sitting on the Gulmohurs' verandah with glasses in their hands and Liza was playing in the garden with her ayah when Stevie and Monica finally arrived. The pallor which had marked him immediately after the encounter was changed to a bright red shade of agitation.

"Some guy tried to run us down out there. Didn't you hear the noise?" he asked Ben, after the introductions had been made by Bill.

"No. What kind of a car was it?"

"A white Mercedes." Stevie gladly accepted a glass of gin and soda from the hovering bearer and took a gulp.

"Oh, that's the German up the lane. He always drives too fast. One of those days he's going to hit somebody," said Dee.

Stevie turned his black spectacles towards her. "A German? You have a German living *here*? What's his name?" He sounded less scared now – almost jubilant in fact.

"I don't know. We just call him the German." Dee looked at her husband who shrugged.

"Sorry, no idea either. He was here when Guy and I first moved in so he must have been living up this lane for six years at least, maybe longer. He's not very sociable. We've invited him to a couple of parties but he's never come."

"It's just that I thought I recognised him,"

said Stevie. "You see, my family are from Germany. I was born there."

"A beautiful country, I believe," chirped a well-groomed woman with dark hair coiled round her head and folded into a French pleat at the back.

Stevie ignored her for he was still looking at Dee and saying. "Whoever he is, he's a rotten driver ... He could have killed us. Are you all right, Monica?"

She was still very pale and had slipped gratefully into a chair as if her legs were in danger of giving way. "Yes, I'm perfectly all right," she managed to say but took a large swig of her gin as she said it.

Dee already knew Monica for she had been an intermittent attender at the parties they went to for several years. Ben knew her even better because she had once been the star attraction at a party given by one of his bachelor friends with whom she'd lived for a while. He had fond memories of a younger Monica, wearing only a G-string and tassels on her nipples, jumping out of his friend's birthday cake and singing "Happy Birthday to You".

"Hi, Mon, good to see you again," he said, toasting her with his glass of beer.

Gathering himself together, Stevie looked around the party and was most impressed by Anne's spectacular beauty. It was the first time he'd met Bill's wife and was about to go over to speak to her when he saw how narrowly her husband was watching them. He recognised the devilish imp of jealousy dancing in the other man's eyes so he tactfully moved away from the lovely woman and sat down by Monica.

Bill visibly relaxed. Even little runts like his American friend, he reckoned, had to be watched, but the chi-chi girl looked capable of keeping her man satisfied and Anne did not react as though Stevie had made much of an impression on her.

Dee, who always took the fly-on-the-wall role, saw this and watched her guests with interest as they sat around drinking and chatting. There were several little dramas going on around her, and she particularly noticed the fraught exchanges between Bill and Anne. Their relationship seemed to have become more tense recently – perhaps that was the cause of Anne's blackouts. His fear of losing her could finally drive her away but there was no way you could persuade him of that.

Another drama was being enacted before her, the chief actor being the neurotically inept Stevie who never seemed to be at ease and was so jangling with nerves that she could almost see shockwaves radiating from him. What was his problem? The way he sat, folded over on himself like a moth in a chrysalis, intrigued her.

His brown eyes ranged from one member of their group to another, always searching, and she saw that there was absolutely no emotion in them. What was he looking for? He was empty, this man, as if all feelings except an underlying panic had been blocked up long ago.

His peculiar, businesslike relationship with Monica, who was clearly a girl-for-hire in spite of her pretensions to the contrary, intrigued Dee because Stevie showed little obvious carnal interest in his lovely companion. Was he impotent? Was he queer? No theory really stood up and he remained as enigmatic as the sphinx.

And there was a third grouping on the verandah. Dee was going to fetch more soda when, with a sinking heart, she saw Jean-Paul surreptitiously put a hand on Bernice's knee while he talked to the trusting Nigel. All of a sudden she hated him; and hated Bernice for allowing him to caress her like that. Nigel trusted them both so completely. Surely he was not being deceived?

I hope it's only the gin that's making them so free and easy with each other, she thought as she announced the start of lunch.

It was not a successful party for Bill was even more caustic and aggressively working class than usual. He was especially nasty about Jean-Paul who, he obviously suspected, admired Anne, and as the others saw the party collapse around them, they gradually lost any *joie de vivre* they had started with. As the afternoon progressed Bill's mood became blacker, his boasts more outrageous and by half-past three Anne announced it was time to go home. Their fight would go on in private.

Back in the city, Stevie seemed to regain the enthusiasm that had been dimmed during the lunch and was eager to discuss the other guests but Monica, normally the one who did most of the talking, was unusually subdued.

"What a surly guy that Bill is," he said in an effort to start her off.

She nodded. "He's very jealous. He's scared some man is going to take away his wife."

"Well, she is a beauty," agreed Stevie.

"She'll leave him if he keeps on behaving so badly though," said Monica.

"She might like it. You never know what goes on between people, do you?" he said, but this gamut, which would normally launch Monica into a spate of stories and speculations, fell on stony ground.

"No," she agreed and fell silent again.

He looked across at her and asked, "Are you all right, Mon? You've been very quiet. Were you hurt when you fell on to the floor of the car?"

She shook her head. "I'm not hurt."

"Then what's wrong? Something's upsetting you. I don't blame you either. The man driving that white Mercedes scared me as well."

She turned her face towards him and he saw with surprise that there were tears glistening in her huge lustrous eyes. "He scared you? He terrifies me ... I hate him, *hate* him." Her tone was vehement.

"You know him? You didn't say. Do you know what he calls himself?"

"Calls himself? I know his name. It's Hans Gelhorn."

The muscles along Stevie's jaw tightened and bunched. "Are you sure? I thought I'd seen him before but Gelhorn wasn't his name then."

She shook her head. "It's Hans Gelhorn. I lived with him for a week and he almost killed me. When I saw him behind the wheel of that car I had to hide myself. I hoped he'd moved away from there, you see, but he obviously hasn't."

"Tell me about it," said Stevie in a gentle voice and she started to talk.

Monica's story, told in tears, was a simple one. When she was nineteen and even more beautiful than she was now, she'd been picked up in the Ambassador Hotel bar by a blond-haired, handsome man in his forties who said he'd recently arrived in Bombay.

He told her he was Hans Gelhorn, a

German national, and that he worked in an import-export agency that had offices down in the docks. The young Englishman who had taken her to the Ambassador turned his back on the German and called him "a bloody Kraut", which predisposed Monica in the stranger's favour because she, as an Anglo-Indian, was used to people disdaining her.

She went off with him that night to a room in the hotel and he behaved towards her in a gentlemanly fashion, sending her home next morning with fifty rupees slipped into her purse without any attempt at bargaining.

A few days later, casually walking past the hotel, she saw him again. Both of them acted surprised at the encounter which ended up in the same room and in the same way as the previous one. They began meeting every week but always in the Ambassador – she had no idea where he lived.

Her initial hopes of making him her protector faded and almost disappeared till one morning he asked as she was leaving him, "Will you move in with me?"

She whirled round, her face showing delighted surprise. "Yes! Where do you live?"

"Out in the country. On Chembur hill."

She laughed. "My aunt lives in Chembur. It's pretty there, isn't it?"

"I've rented a bungalow. It's very quiet and lonely. Would you mind that?"

"Oh no," she said blithely. "I could walk down to the golf course to see my aunt sometimes."

"Yes, perhaps, but I don't want you bringing anyone into my house."

"All right, I won't," she promised, slightly crestfallen.

He took her out to his bungalow that weekend. The car he drove then was a Mercedes as well. The lane was much quieter in those days because the Gulmohurs was unoccupied and thickets of bamboos and neem trees shut off any sight of it. The Kapoor family were away from home too and only a watchman slept in the sentry box at the gate in the middle of the high wall that surrounded their property. The whole area seemed to brood like an enchanted forest, full of silent, watchful eyes.

At the top of the lane, where it petered out into a jungle track, was a native encampment where buffalo were kept. Early in the morning the buffalo milk was carried down to the station in metal churns on the heads of a stream of running men and taken by train into the city. The gate of the German's bungalow was almost opposite the buffalo camp and when the car drew up in that isolated place Monica felt her first stirring of disquiet. There was no one around, no

115

one to see her or notice if she disappeared. She'd told no one where she was going either because she hadn't really known herself.

The gate of his bungalow was padlocked and on the other side of it a huge, snarling dog stared through the bars with black lips lifted from its gums, baring ferocious pointed fangs. The German got out of the driver's seat and unlocked the padlock, swinging the gate open and kicking the dog as he did so. It slunk away, snarling at him over its shoulder.

"What sort of dog is that?" Monica asked nervously when he got back into the car. She didn't like dogs, even small ones; at that time Fifi had not yet acquired Sabre.

"A German shepherd – some people call them Alsatians," he told her.

"Has it a name?" she asked.

"No, just 'hund-dog'."

"Will it bite me?"

"Not if you leave it alone. It's a guard dog. I feed it and let it out of its kennel when I'm going away from home or when night falls. The rest of the time it's tied up."

She resolved to leave it strictly alone.

There was a servant in the house, a shuffling old man who came out of the kitchen at the back of the house when they arrived and stood with his head bent and his hands folded, waiting for orders.

"Bring me beer," said the German and when it appeared, in a glistening silver-coloured tankard, he downed it in one. He did not offer Monica a drink but, greatly daring, she asked the servant for a lime soda which was very good and very cold.

They ate dinner – roast chicken with mashed potatoes and green peas followed by strong black coffee. When they finished he got up without a word and told the servant, "Go now. Lock the kitchen door."

Then he strode on to the verandah and disappeared into the darkness. When he came back he told her, "The dog's loose so don't go outside or try to get away."

That night he subjected her to painful, abrupt and brutal sex and before she fell asleep she resolved to leave him as soon as she could.

"You should have gone straight away," said Stevie when she reached this point in her story.

"I couldn't. That dog was roaming about outside so I thought I'd wait to leave when he was away at his office," she said. "But when he did go, he locked me in and turned the dog loose again. He told me it would tear my throat out if I tried to get out of the house."

She shuddered as she remembered her ordeal. "It was awful. He didn't go into the city every day. Sometimes he stayed in the bungalow for days on end and drank. That was when he beat me ... with a stick and with a leather belt. He enjoyed doing it; he liked hearing me scream. I was bleeding and bruised but he wouldn't stop. We had no neighbours except the buffalo people and they wouldn't have cared if he killed me."

"Christ," said Stevie through clenched teeth.

Sobbing convulsively, she went on, "I thought he would kill me. I thought I'd never see my mother again. But one night, after he'd beaten me much worse than usual, and cut me badly with a knife, the old servant took pity on me. When Gelhorn fell asleep he fed the dog bits of meat with something in them that made it sleep too, and told me to run away. I could hardly walk but I managed to get down that lane to my aunt's house ... I crawled the last part of the way on my hands and knees. Oh God, the pain! It was awful. I spent the next two weeks in hospital..."

She remembered Fifi's horrified face when she opened her door to frantic knocking at three o'clock in the morning. "Have you had an accident?" she asked as she brought the half-conscious girl inside. Monica was almost unrecognisable – her face was bruised, her eyes blackened, her body slashed and contused and she was suffering agony from broken ribs, a dislocated shoulder and what proved to be serious internal injuries.

It was a miracle that she'd managed to cover the two miles between the German's bungalow and her aunt's house. Fifi sent Parvati for Dr Bali who arrived very quickly, strapped up her ribs, relocated her shoulder, dressed her cuts and had her admitted to a hospital run by kindly nuns.

Bali reported the incident to the police and a khaki-uniformed inspector went to hear Monica's complaint. Both the girl and her aunt were reluctant to speak to him because they distrusted the police – too often they were on the other side – but he coaxed Monica and nodded sympathetically as he listened.

"You shouldn't have gone up there with him. This isn't the first time he's beaten up girls. Will you go into court and accuse him?" he asked her.

Monica shuddered. "No, oh no. I'm scared of what he'd do to me. I never want to see him again. I just want to get better and out of this place."

"In that case, if you won't lay a charge against him there's not much I can do. I'll send a man up there and warn him, but he's very arrogant. He has powerful friends I think," said the policeman.

"So nothing happened to him? He got off?" said Stevie in a hard voice.

"Yes, nothing. I kept away from the Ambassador after that and then someone told me he'd gone to Delhi – but he must have come back. I was so scared when I saw him in that car of his that I nearly died ... I thought he'd see me."

"Stop worrying. He didn't see you, and you're safe here," said Stevie. He held her till she fell asleep in his arms.

He woke first in the morning and saw her snuggled up against him with her hair over her face and her lips slightly parted, breathing softly like a baby. Who would want to hurt a girl like that? he wondered, but he knew the answer. The man he was thinking about would enjoy it.

Eight

Ralph the doctor was worried about Dee Carmichael when she went to see him for a check-up. He took her blood pressure and was alarmed to see that it was hovering just below a high level. She admitted that recently she'd felt tired and breathless.

"It's maybe not a very good idea for you to be stuck out in Chembur on your own right now," he said carefully, not wanting to alarm her.

"I'm not on my own. Bernice is there," she told him.

"Bernice who?" he asked as he began writing up her notes.

"Budgeon. The Budgeons are our PGs. They've been living with us for three months."

He furrowed his brow. "Bernice Budgeon? But she can't be much help. She's very anxious about her own pregnancy right now. She was in here yesterday for another test."

Dee shook her head. "She's so keen to

121

have a baby. She's convinced she's pregnant every month. Poor Bernice," said Dee.

Ralph said without thinking, "Well, it looks as if she can stop worrying. I think she's pregnant this time but the test'll confirm it." He suddenly realised he shouldn't be talking about one patient to another – but Dee was a friend, and she didn't gossip.

She sat bolt upright. "Really? That's great. She hasn't mentioned it! They've been trying for nine years to have a baby. She must be very pleased."

"She did seem pleased but, as I said, I don't know the results yet. They should be back by the end of the week. I examined her and remembered her name. Don't say anything about it, will you?" he said.

"Of course not. But I suppose you're right. Two problem cases stranded out in the country is not a very good idea. The only telephone is across the lane in Raj's house and we don't like bothering him. And Bernice can't drive."

"It certainly isn't a good idea. Maybe you should think of moving – and I want you to go to see a woman gynaecologist I know. She's very good and I don't like overseeing the confinements of my friends. You should be tested now for things like rhesus negative blood and she'll do all that. She's very up to date," he told her.

"Rhesus negative blood?" asked Dee.

"What's that?"

"Some new thing," said Ralph, "but nothing to worry about. I'm sure you don't have it."

Dee and Ben conferred and decided again to put off the question of moving but that they would have to scrape together enough money for her to consult another doctor whose expertise wouldn't be cheap. They reckoned they'd be able to pay the bill by selling their cherished Studebaker – but they didn't have to worry about that either for a bit because the doctor's bill wouldn't come in till the baby was born. Sufficient unto the day, they thought blithely.

Mindful of Ralph's caution, Dee did not say anything to Ben about the possibility of Bernice being pregnant though it worried her that if it was true, the first thing Nigel would do when it was confirmed was move his wife into the city. That meant the Carmichaels would lose the PGs' rent, which would make it impossible for them to keep their house. *Don't think about it*, she told herself, because she still did not want to leave the Gulmohurs in spite of Ralph's caution.

A week later Dee had her first appointment with her new doctor, a woman recently qualified in America and not long in practice. She had rooms in the ground floor of a block of flats off Warden Road.

Hanging in her waiting room was a brightly coloured print of an Anna Zinkeisen painting of a woman driving a dog cart with a Dalmatian running behind it. As she sat in the waiting room staring at this picture Dee felt the first real pang of homesickness sweep over her though it was not the sort of art she normally admired. She mentally shook herself and thought, *I know what's wrong with me. It's the horse that's made me sad.* The spirited-looking Arab between the shafts of the cart had made her think longingly of the horses that she had spent her youth looking after and riding.

She'd been in Bombay for almost three years and they were would not be due for leave till three months after her baby was born. She'd begun counting the weeks till delivery day, and after that till the day they went home which was romanticised in her mind as a place where it was never cold and wet but always green and beautiful. One night she had been horrified at herself because she and Ben had gone to see Marilyn Monro in *Bus Stop* at the cinema and when a winter scene was shown, Dee began to cry with longing to see snow again.

The new gynaecologist, Dr Bannerjee, was not much older than Dee herself. She was very smartly dressed in European clothes, and was dark haired, dark skinned, brisk and business like. She prodded Dee's stomach as she lay on the table, performed a swift internal examination and then pronounced that her patient was indeed pregnant – which was no surprise because the bulge was apparent, and the baby had already begun heaving about like a little dolphin. As far as Dee was concerned it had a distinct personality and this amazed and delighted her.

At the end of the examination, the doctor said, "There's just one more thing. I need a blood sample from you. There's a new test we do for rhesus negative blood. You don't need to worry about it because only one woman in a thousand has it and I've never had a patient with the problem … but just in case, hold out your arm and I'll take a sample for testing."

They parted like friends but a week later a letter marked "Urgent" was delivered to the Gulmohurs by the Chembur postman who had a BA degree but couldn't find any better job than delivering letters.

Dr Banerjee's stiff little note informed Dee that she was one of the minority who had rhesus negative blood and her husband should immediately go to Breach Candy hospital to have his blood tested. If his too was negative, there would be no cause for concern – if it wasn't, there could be problems.

At the hospital a cheerful Indian doctor

tested Ben's blood and came forth with the unwelcome diagnosis.

"Mrs Carmichael," he shouted cheerfully into a packed waiting room, "you've married the wrong man!"

"What exactly does all this mean?" Dee asked Dr Banerjee the next afternoon. "I've never heard of rhesus negative blood before. I thought the word rhesus was only applied to monkeys." She was not at all pleased at being the problematic one woman in a thousand.

There was a furrow of concern between the doctor's eyebrows. She agonised over all of her patients even when there was nothing to worry about and now there was this – her first rhesus negative case!

"I'll have to be honest with you," she said. "If the child's blood is not negative like yours, there could be a danger of miscarriage at certain stages, especially in the seventh month – and even if you go full term there's a danger that the baby could be born severely jaundiced. There's a method of changing the child's blood but it's a fairly new procedure – let's hope it doesn't come to that."

Miscarriage! The word rang in Dee's ears like a terrible threat and she clutched her swelling stomach protectively. Till then she'd taken her pregnancy fairly lightly, confident that everything would go smoothly, but now the most important thing in the world was to hold on to the child which she felt growing within her. If she went into labour when she was alone in the Gulmohurs or with only Bernice for company, what would happen? Her baby could die for want of medical intervention.

In a panic she left the doctor's consulting rooms and headed for Ben's office where, weeping, she stormed in to interrupt him at work, the first time she'd ever done such a thing.

"I've just been to the doctor and she's told me something awful," she sobbed, bursting into the little corner room where he worked.

"But you're fine, you look fine, you feel all right, don't you?" he said in confusion.

She leaned over his desk, ignoring the blatantly interested face of Balraj, the plump Indian who shared the office with her husband, and shouted, "I'm all right now but in my seventh month it can be dangerous because of my funny blood! I'm scared!"

He saw she was serious and got up to take her arm. "Come on, kid," he consoled her. "It's nearly finishing time so I'll drive you home. You're going to be all right and so's the baby." He was always good in a crisis and she began to believe that nothing bad would happen to her if he was around. With relief she gave herself up to him and climbed into the car.

She'd stopped crying by the time they reached Kemp's Corner where Ben and Guy, with Dee at the wheel of the car, had once gone on a midnight spree hanging road workers' lamps on various statues and stealing paving slabs to make a path in the Gulmohurs' garden. Ben must have been remembering that escapade too because he suddenly said, "Old Guy phoned me at the office today."

"Did he? Is he all right?" she asked. She hadn't seen Guy since he'd gone to live in the city.

"He's being transferred to Singapore next week." Ben's voice was solemn and she turned her head to stare at him.

"Does that mean that we'll have to give back the furniture?" she whispered.

"Yes, that's why he phoned. It's his company's furniture and they'll want it back when he goes."

"Oh God! What'll we do?"

"He thinks he can stall them for a while but they'll take it away eventually."

"What'll we do about Nigel and Bernice?" There was a note of panic in her voice when she asked the question.

"Christ alone knows," said Ben.

Theoretically the Gulmohurs was let furnished but all that actually belonged to the house was a couple of ramshackle beds and some chairs. Fortunately Guy worked for generous company who provided their employees with furniture and kitchen equipment, especially that great treasure in India, a fridge. They couldn't be hired and were very expensive to buy.

After he went to live in the city he'd left it all behind in the house for Ben and Dee to use, for they had nothing of their own. If his pieces were taken away, they'd be forced to rent more from one of the big furniture warehouses down by the docks where Bill had got Anne's piano – and that would be a big drain on their finances. The worst deprivation would be the loss of the fridge.

When troubles come they don't come singly. It was not yet dark when the Carmichaels drew into their parking space in front of the garage and saw that Nigel's car was already there with the back doors standing wide open. At the house front door stood a worried-looking Ali, the bearer, with his shoulders hunched up around his ears and a frown on his face.

He came running down the steps towards Ben and said hurriedly, "Sahib, Birbal the mali says he is going away."

"Why?" asked Ben and Dee together.

"Because there is an animal in our garden," said Ali.

Ben groaned and asked, "What sort of an animal?" The indoor servants usually panicked when snakes appeared but Birbal was skilled at capturing and killing them. He took such pride in snake hunting that often, when they returned from late-night cinema shows, Ben and Dee had to step over the neatly coiled corpse of a cobra, a python, or a boa constrictor – and once a knitting-needle thin krite, the most venomous snake of all – laid out on the front door mat.

This time it obviously wasn't a snake because Ali sketched a huge shape in the air with his hands. "Very big!" he said.

"An elephant?" Ben laughed, half disbelieving.

"No. The servants are afraid." Ali wasn't laughing. This was serious.

"How did it get here?"

"Nigel sahib brought it."

Ben and Dee groaned in unison. "Aw no!" cried Ben and rushed into the sitting room where Nigel and Bernice were sipping coffee.

"What's this about an animal in the garden?" he asked without preamble. "I told you that the animal lark had to stop. I don't want dogs or baby monkeys – or anything else – here. Have you got that, Nigel?"

Nigel looked up with a conciliatory look on his face. "It's all right, Ben, don't panic. It's perfectly safe, and I don't intend to keep it very long."

"What the hell *is* it?" snapped Ben.

"It's quite safe because it's wearing a muzzle."

"What the hell *is* it?" yelled Ben again.

"It's a bear – just here for a short visit," said Nigel softly.

Ben gave a strangled yell and began hopping about like a man dancing on a hot plate. "I don't believe this. A bloody bear! No wonder the servants are scared. Where did you get it?"

Nigel looked shamefaced. "I saw it on the road with its keeper and it was so pathetic that I had to stop. It looked at me as if it was asking for help so I just put it in the car and brought it home. All it needs is a rest and a square meal."

"Like what? The gardener? He's threatening to bolt, you know," snapped Ben furiously.

"I think bears are vegetarian," said Nigel solemnly.

"I don't care if it's a bloody gourmet, it's not staying here. Where is it anyway?"

Nigel gestured over his shoulder with his coffee-cup. "Out there, in the little shed at the foot of the garden. Its keeper is with it."

The little hut was Birbal's home. *No wonder he's leaving*, thought Dee.

By now the night had gathered in and Ben strode to the verandah rail to stare into the darkening garden. His knuckles whitened as

131

he gripped the wooden rail in an effort to control his temper. Then, with an effort, he turned and said, "This is too much, Nigel. You know what I feel about those stray animals you adopt. And that shed is Birbal's house. No wonder he's not happy about sharing it with a bear!"

Knight errant Nigel had one last try. "But if you saw it! The poor thing's starving. It looked at me with such pain in its eyes and I knew it was asking for help. All I want to do is give it some food and a few days of peace," he pleaded. There was a pitiful expression on his battered face.

"It's one of those mangy dancing bears, isn't it? The kind that're led through the streets? The men who keep them are cruel rogues – and I bet you're feeding its keeper too," said Ben.

"I had to bring the keeper so's I could get the bear," agreed Nigel.

"It has to go," said Ben firmly. "Go out and tell the man now."

Nigel looked stubborn. "Let it stay the night at least. There's such misery in its eyes. I can't turn it away now."

"Christ, you haven't made any promises to the bloody thing!" exclaimed Ben.

"Yes, I have," said Nigel.

For a moment it seemed that the two men were going to fight. They were both standing stiffly, glaring at each other. The only contribution from Bernice had been a "tut-tut" when Ben swore.

Dee put a conciliatory hand on Ben's arm. "Let it stay the night, Ben, so long as it goes in the morning," she said.

He swung towards her. "These things are dangerous. That's why they wear muzzles. And they're flea-ridden. And what about Birbal?"

"It's old and it's ill and it's hungry. Birbal'll be all right if it goes away tomorrow," said Nigel.

"For God's sake, you're not St Francis of Assisi," snapped Ben. "I've had about enough of this. But OK, it can stay the night. Make sure it goes in the morning, though."

"Do you want to see it?" asked Nigel, hoping that the sight of the bear would soften Ben's heart, but there was no chance of that. He strode off into the bedroom and shouted back. "No I bloody don't."

"Do you want to see it?" Nigel asked Dee. She was surprised to realise that she did. Armed with flashlights, she and Nigel walked down the garden path to the gardener's hut. There was no sign of Birbal but a hunched man with a white shawl drawn over his shoulders was hunkering down by a little bonfire of twigs. Lying beside him was what looked like a pile of scabby fur.

When he saw Nigel, the keeper leapt to his feet and began babbling away. Nigel, who understood little Hindustani, waved his hand at the bear, gesturing to be shown it. The keeper prodded the heap with a long stick and it shuddered, quivered and finally lumbered to its feet.

In the darkness, illuminated only by the beam of the torches and the dancing flames of the fire, it looked enormous and terrifying. Standing on its hind legs, it was over six feet tall, with a long snout confined in a leather muzzle through which shone puzzled yellow eyes. Round its neck was a thick leather collar studded with metal bosses, and a heavy chain tethered it to a stake driven deep in the ground. Its scrappy fur was black and worn down to its greyish skin in many places which made it look like a huge man wapped in a threadbare overcoat.

"Has it eaten?" Nigel asked, staring in pity at the shambolical figure.

The keeper looked back uncomprehendingly. "Khana?" asked Dee in her kitchen Hindi, pointing at the bear. The keeper nodded enthusiastically and rubbed his stomach. Dee, unsure as to whether he was saying he or the bear had eaten, decided to pacify Nigel. "Yes, he says it's eaten," she said.

"Good. I asked your bearer to give it bread

and fruit. I don't know what those bears eat really."

"Probably people," thought Dee but she understood why the bear had excited Nigel's pity. It loomed above them, its talon-less paws – the claws of dancing bears were pulled out by their keepers – hanging limply by its sides, its puzzled eyes glittering. It looked hopeless, as if it were waiting for some new act of cruelty to be inflicted on it.

"Poor thing," she said.

"Ask Ben if it can stay for a few days till it gets fattened up a bit," said Nigel hopefully, sensing her pity for the pathetic animal.

She shook her head. "No, sorry, I can't. He's really furious. It'll have to go tomorrow but at least you've given it one good night."

When she went back into the house Ben was lying in bed with his arms crossed behind his head fulminating about Nigel. "I've had it up to here – dogs and monkeys and now bears. What'll it be next? That man's crazy."

He turned on his side and looked up at Dee. "We have to leave here, you know. Your pregnancy can be better managed in the city, we're losing the furniture and nothing I say stops Nigel from bringing in more animals. We've got to face facts. We can't afford to live here on our own and the PG idea is a disaster. It's over."

She nodded sadly and sat down on the

bed. "I know. You're right. It's October now and the baby's due in January. It'll be safer for me to be in the city near the hospital when it comes. Your tour finishes at the end of March and we can go home for good then if we like."

"So we give up this house?" asked Ben as if he wanted her to be the one to take the decision. They both felt as if they were moving into a new, more serious phase of their lives.

"Yes," she said. "We'll go."

She lay down beside him and they reached out for each other and sighed. Later they'd work out what would happen next, where they would go. Probably they'd have to be PGs in their turn or caretake a flat for people home on leave till Ben's tour ended. What would happen to them after that they had no idea, but they were young and full of optimism. Something would turn up.

The thing they did know, however, was that their youthful, carefree idyll at the Gulmohurs was over.

Nine

Stevie and Monica had become well known at the Ritz where they usually installed themselves in a prominent booth near the door guarded by a prohibition enforcement soldier in shabby khaki, who always looked half asleep as he slumped against the wall with his rifle propped up beside him.

Another customer, an even more regular attender than they were, was a white man called Reuben, a quiet old fellow with a simian-looking, high-cheekboned face. He always sat alone and made no trouble until he'd had too much to drink when he was inclined to buttonhole anyone passing by and try to engage them in conversation. The rugby club regulars, who made up the staple of the bar's custom, tended to give him a wide berth because his English was fragmentary and his tendency to burst into dramatic Slavic tears at closing time embarrassed stoic Britishers.

The night after their visit to the Gulmohurs, Stevie and Monica were in the Ritz and Reuben was settled into his usual booth next to them with a bottle of beer and a plate of peanuts. Stevie, who was unusually tense that evening, suddenly jumped up and slipped into the seat opposite the old man. Curious, Monica picked up her glass and went over to join them.

The all shook hands across the table and Stevie encouraged Reuben to have a gin, an offer that was eagerly accepted. Pleasantries were extended: Monica was congratulated on her beauty, and Stevie on his possession of her.

"The most beautiful women in the world are to be found in India," said Reuben in his strange, guttural accent. "My wife was a local girl, from Poona, and she outshone the sun."

Outshone the sun: how lovely, how romantic, thought Monica and warmed to the old man. Stevie too smiled. "You were married to her for a long time?" he asked.

"Nearly twelve years. Not long enough, but she died young."

"You have children?"

"No, unfortunately."

"You have other family?"

"Not now; my home is far away."

Without preamble Stevie leaned across the table and abruptly asked, "Where was your home exactly?"

"In Poland."

"How did you come here?"

138

Reuben stared into the liquid in his glass, put it to his lips and swallowed before he said, "I came in the forties. One day I found myself in Bombay and stayed. It happened to many people like me. There is an old doctor down near the Taj who came for the same reason but earlier. He's from Vienna. I don't see him now, though. I've stopped going anywhere but here."

He lifted his head, stared into the younger man's face and suddenly began speaking in another language. Monica saw the instant change in Stevie who reacted as if he'd been stabbed. He shuddered and leaned back in his seat with his arms crossed over his chest as if defending himself, but his eyes never left the old man's face. Words she could not understand hung in the air between them and each one seemed to strike Stevie like a blow. After a bit, when Reuben stopped speaking, he nodded slowly. "Yes, yes," he said in English. "Oh yes."

Reuben was weeping now, his head bowed over the table. Monica, who was not used to displays of open emotion in men, stared round the bar in embarrassment, but Stevie stood up and put his hand on the old man's arm.

"I'll take you home," he said, and to Monica, "Go back to the flat in a taxi, Mon. I'll come home later."

It was two o'clock in the morning and she

was asleep before he returned. Next morning, she asked what had happened when he took Reuben home, but he stonewalled her questions. It was obvious that he did not want to tell her why Reuben was so upset.

Eventually, in frustration, she said sharply, "I didn't know you could speak Polish."

"I can't," he said.

"Then what was that language Reuben used when he spoke to you last night?"

"Yiddish." He looked defiantly at her as he answered.

"But..." She was nonplussed.

His face was hard as he said, "Don't ask any more questions, Mon." His tone was so different to the one he normally used that she didn't.

After that night, Stevie acquired an even greater taste for society and started to invite all and sundry to the flat. His lavish hospitality become famous among the expatriate British set. Beer and gin flowed and he handed out free tickets for movie previews as well as food and drink to his guests, so that he gathered more and more friends, amongst whom he became established as a well-meaning, eager-to-please fool.

In return for his hospitality he was invited everywhere the smart set gathered – to a party in the most exclusive block of flats; to a formal dinner in an old-style bungalow at Pali Hill; to Kandala in the cool foothills of the ghats for a weekend, and then to a Sunday barbecue at Marvi where the more prestigious companies owned palm-shaded beach huts by the side of an immense white stretch of sand with the white-tipped breakers of the Indian Ocean pounding in like galloping horses.

Wherever he went he built on his reputation for being an accident-prone but a pleasant and generous idiot. People who accepted his largesse laughed as they recounted his escapades. "Guess what that fool Stevie has done now," they said.

Monica watched his antics with growing puzzlement because she could not equate the man he was in society with the much more cautious, reserved and melancholy person he reverted to when alone at home. She began to wonder if he was putting on a show for the rest of the world or for her. Which of his personalities was the real Stevie?

Dee and Ben Carmichael were at Marvi for the Sunday barbecue as well. Monica and Dee went for a walk along the long hard strip of wet sand that edged the sea and, screwing their eyes up against the brilliant glare of sun on turquoise water, they watched Stevie powering through the surf with a surprisingly impressive crawl.

"At least he swims well so he's not likely to drown," Dee reflected, thinking of the other mishaps Stevie had recently suffered. Then she noticed that he was swimming with his opulent watch still on his wrist.

"Gosh, Stevie's forgotten to take his watch off," she said to Monica. "He'll ruin it – and it must be very expensive!"

"Oh no," was the reply. "It's all right. He even wears it in the shower. I've never seen it off his wrist."

"Goodness!" said Dee, thinking, in repetition of the universal theme, *It's just Stevie*, not realising that one day, far off in the future, another glimpse of his watch would trigger off a cascade of memories. She dismissed the matter from her mind then, however, because she was preoccupied by thoughts of departure from the Gulmohurs.

She and Ben left the party at Marvi before darkness fell and drove slowly home through the aromatic evening air that is peculiar to Indian village life – a mixture of jasmine, urine, incense, woodsmoke and curry.

She sat leaning her head on her husband's shoulder, grateful that their relationship was settling down to a deep and satisfying companionship. Their initial insecurity and caution towards each other was disappearing and she no longer thought about taking up her father's offer of a one-way ticket home.

The baby turned languidly inside her and

a rush of happiness flowed into her heart with its movement. Surely they were blessed by good fortune; nothing bad could possibly ever happen to them, she thought. Their present troubles, caused by perennial lack of money, were only transitory and trivial and would pass because Ben's career was now going well. Everything was sure to work out wonderfully because luck was on their side. She believed in luck as fervently as any of the worshippers who flocked into Hindu temples to worship the goddess Lakshmi.

"We'll have to tell them tonight," said Ben, suddenly breaking into the companionable silence as they drove along.

It was as if their minds ran on one track because she'd been thinking exactly the same thing and knew without any explanation what he was talking about.

"Yes, we've been putting it off, but we'll have to do it now," she agreed.

Though it was cowardly, she'd half hoped that Bernice and Nigel would be the ones to make the first move and opt for the safety of the city, so removing the unattractive job of giving them their notice. There had been no mention of them going, however, although more than two weeks had passed since Dee heard from Ralph about Bernice's possible pregnancy. Perhaps, she thought, the result had been negative and their PGs had no intention of leaving.

"We'll do it as soon as we get home," said Ben firmly, reading her mind again.

When they were back at the Gulmohurs they found the Budgeons, with the ever-present Jean-Paul, sitting under the stars in chairs set out on the lawn. There had been a distinct *froideur* between Nigel and Ben since the bear incident but, squaring his shoulders, Ben walked across the grass and sat down beside them.

"Nigel," he said without preamble, "I'm sorry about this, but Dee and I have decided that we can't afford to go on living here any longer. We're giving notice to the landlord next week and that means we'll have to be out by mid-November."

He sounded very matter of fact and made it obvious that there was no possibility that he might change his mind. Dee's heart was thudding as she stood on the verandah and watched the group under the trees but, amazingly Nigel didn't seem surprised. In fact he actually looked pleased.

Smiling, he stood up and said to Ben. "That's a relief. Bernice and I have been worrying about how to tell you we're leaving you. You see, my wife's pregnant and I don't think it's safe to leave her out here all day, with only Dee for company, so far from the hospital. She'll have to be looked after very carefully."

Dee managed to look surprised and Ben

144

didn't have to act for she'd said nothing about Ralph's indiscreet slip to him. She ran down the steps and went across to Bernice whose eyes were shining, and said, "That's wonderful! You must be very pleased. Congratulations to both of you! I'm so glad. I know how much you want a baby."

Nigel, beaming like a child at Christmas, leaned over to his wife and hugged her. Her face bore the expression of a Madonna receiving homage as he put both hands on her shoulders and kissed the top of her glossy dark head.

"We're delighted, absolutely delighted. It's what Bernice wants more than anything and I want it for her too, though as far as I'm concerned, she is and always has been the most important thing in the world," he said. His voice broke with such strength of emotion and Dee was so filled with respect for his intrinsic goodness that tears came into her eyes as she watched him.

The only member of the group who seemed unaffected by the prevailing goodwill was Jean-Paul. Tonight he looked even more essentially masculine and predatory than usual, and was quite unmoved by the highly charged emotional atmosphere around him. He was wearing khaki shorts, and his muscular bare legs were thrust out and crossed at the ankle in a negligent attitude. His tanned column of a throat sloped down into the white V of his open-necked sports shirt and he looked self satisfied, secretive and sly. In fact he almost seemed to be amused.

Jean-Paul and everything else was forgotten next morning, however, driven out by more immediate concerns. While Ben was in the shower, Dee lay in bed, and made herself a mental list of things to organise for a farewell party.

"There's such a lot to organise," she groaned later, looking over the breakfast table at him as he calmly ate a boiled egg and read *The Times of India*. They were on their own because, as usual Nigel had left at seven o'clock and Bernice was still in bed.

"Don't worry. I'll tell you exactly what to do. Guy and I put on lots of parties here and they were always the best in Bombay," said Ben. "This one'll be a wow because the best weekend to have it is at the end of the month and that's Divali. We'll fire rockets and put lighted candles along all the window ledges. It'll look great."

Divali, the festival of light, was Dee's favourite among the many Indian holy days. It was a joyous time when people honoured the goddess Lakshmi by putting lines of twinkling oil lamps along their terraces or windows at night and setting off brilliantly coloured rockets or firecrackers.

"I love Divali," she said. "But the

mechanics of this party are really bothering me. I know that the Gulmohurs parties are famous and I don't want to let your reputation down. If it's not a success people'll say it's because Guy's not here any more and that I messed it up."

Ben had no time for her lack of confidence. As far as he was concerned, they'd decided to have a farewell party so the next thing to do was get it properly organised.

"Don't be silly. It'll be a great party. Nothing'll go wrong. Stop worrying. What's going to be on the menu? That's the first thing for you to work out," he said in an effort to rally her.

She'd been thinking about the menu and it struck her that she'd never been at a Bombay party where really interesting food was served. It was always the same old stuff – curry and cold meat with bowls of brightly garnished trifle to follow.

"I thought I might try something different this time ... perhaps a few special salads with avocados and mixed peppers, sliced oranges in French dressing, fish in aspic, baked potatoes with tasty fillings, cheese tarts, things like that," she suggested.

Ben looked at her in horror. "Avocados? Fish in aspic?"

"Yes, the sort of thing they serve at high-class weddings in the summer at home. I've got a cookery book that tells you how to make them," she explained.

"Forget it. We'd better stick to the usual party menu – chicken curry, poppadums, Waldorf salad and cold meat. That's what people expect and our cook can cope with those dishes. I don't think you'd get him to make cheese tarts or fish in aspic."

She had to agree. Pasco their cook, never a cheerful man, had been extra churlish recently. Perhaps it was better not to ask him to extend himself. Sadly she accepted Ben's logic.

"OK. I'll type the invitations today," she said. "How many people do you think will actually come?"

Ben wrinkled his brow. "There should be about a hundred or a hundred and twenty on our list and the word'll get around so we'll have to expect gatecrashers. Maybe a hundred and fifty altogether – or even two hundred."

The prospect of such a crowd descending on them worried him not a bit but Dee was horrified and groaned aloud, "Two hundred people! Oh God, we can't afford it. What have we let ourselves in for? What about plates and glasses, knives and forks for all that crowd? What about chairs?"

He swept these trivial worries aside. "We don't need chairs! People bring blankets and sit on the grass. All we have to buy is food and ice because everybody brings their own booze, the Gym lends us glasses and Raj Kapoor'll send over some crockery, he's got any amount of it. We just have to go across and ask him. That reminds me; we should warn him well in advance about the party, because there'll be a bit of noise and he usually sends his family away whenever we have a big do here."

"Sends his family away! Why?"

"Because of the din, the music and the cars in the lane, that sort of thing. Besides, people wander about a bit when they get drunk – you know what our gang are like."

"They'd better not wander too much here or they'll end up in the jungle."

"Raj's doorman looks out for them and the locals are pretty decent. They take stragglers down to the main road where they can get taxis."

"Oh my God," thought Dee again for she had never actually experienced one of the really mammoth Gulmohurs parties which had become legendary. Since she arrived the entertainment had been more restricted due to lack of cash. "What have I let myself in for?" she asked herself again.

When Ben left she sat on at the breakfast table with her chin in her hands thinking and making notes.

If Raj had to be warned about the noise, what about the other neighbours? Who else should be told? High on the top of the hill behind the house lived a holy man in a little stone-built hut with a long narrow pennant fluttering from its roof. He rarely came down and she had never seen him. With any luck the din of the party wouldn't reach him away up there so she decided to forget about him.

In the middle of the lines of the fruit farm's pomelo trees on the other side of the rapidly drying river bed, which formed one boundary of the Gulmohurs' garden, was the house where her friend Shadiv used to live, but he'd gone now and his flat was empty. The fruit farm manager had an office on the ground floor of the house but was only there during the day so the party would not disturb him.

Then she remembered the fast-driving German who lived higher up the hill, in a bungalow like their own embowered in jungle undergrowth and scrub. In spite of the offhand way he behaved it would only be polite to warn him about the party – perhaps they should even invite him to attend.

I'll go up and see him one afternoon soon, she decided. *In the meantime there's so much to do...*

As soon as Ben left for the office, she sat down to type out the invitations on her old portable Underwood in its rigid black box, which reminded her so forcibly of her time as a newspaper reporter that she was gripped by a sudden agony of regret for the job she had left behind when she married. But she drove those unproductive thoughts away and started to pound on the rickety keys. Her working table was set up beneath the trees and as she sat in the dappled shade, ticking off names on her guest list, she did not let herself think of the actual meaning of the words that appeared on the sheets of paper in the typewriter carriage. It was best to concentrate on the matter in hand.

COME AND HELP US SAY GOODBYE TO
THE GULMOHURS
ANY TIME AFTER 9 P.M. ON
SATURDAY OCTOBER 29th
BEN AND DEE CARMICHAEL
BYOB

BYOB meant Bring Your Own Bottle. That was essential because there was no way she and Ben could afford even a single bottle of beer for each of the hundred people on her list. Laboriously typing with two fingers, as many newspaper reporters of her acquaintance did, she produced a pile of invitations, economising by getting three on each sheet of paper. They were stacked on the table beside her, then cut up and folded so as not to need any envelopes. Peons from

Ben's office would start taking them round to his friends' places of work tomorrow, thus saving the cost of postage.

The Carmichaels were having a party and the Gulmohurs was famous for its parties. It was essential that this last splash was the best that had ever been held there.

Ten

To Monica's surprise, the pursuit of pleasure had become the chief object of Stevie's life. No longer did he spend even part of an evening with her on their Malabar Hill terrace but went out partying till dawn whenever he could.

As far as work was concerned he seemed to have lost interest in it altogether and rarely showed his face in the Paraworld office any more, leaving the running of it to Ajay and his staff. Ajay did not openly complain about this, in fact he actively encouraged Stevie's truancy, though he took the opportunity of sending a memo to another US-based vice-president – not Stevie's uncle – complaining about having to carry Stevie as dead wood. In fact it had to be admitted that the company's business went on unaffected whether he was there or not.

Staying up till the early hours of the morning meant that Stevie rarely rose before noon. Monica was usually up first and tried to visit her mother before he was out of bed but if they did not get to bed until dawn that was not always possible.

Once up, however, he was fired with a new enthusiasm for touring Bombay, as if his visit to Chembur had sharpened his taste for seeing the sights. Behind the wheel of his enormous car, he drove through suburb after suburb of the city, and then started venturing into the undeveloped countryside. With Monica sitting beside him, he covered the twelve miles of potholed road to Thana where a causeway connected Bombay island with the mainland, and the day after that he went even further out, up the coast to the old Portuguese fort at Bassein.

He always wanted Monica's company on those trips, quizzing her about the places they drove through, and though she did not complain, she silently fretted as she sat beside him because when he had gone to work, she had been in the habit of spending the day with her mother who was steadily weakening.

Eventually, when she had not been to the chawl for four anxious days, she refused to accompany him on another one of his jaunts.

"What's wrong?" he asked.

"Nothing's wrong. It's just that I haven't been to see my mother for almost a week and she's ill."

154

He looked distressed, saying with genuine concern, "I didn't know you had a mother. You never said anything about her."

"She's not very well but the cool weather should make her better soon," said Monica, hanging on to that slim hope as usual.

"Let's go and visit her now," said Stevie, jumping up.

She shook her head because she did not want him to see the obvious poverty of her home. "No. I'll go alone. She'd be shy if you called on her without warning," she claimed.

He gave her one of his unexpectedly shrewd looks. "She shouldn't be; I won't criticise," he said. "I'll take you to see her now but if you don't want me to go in, I'll wait outside for you. Come on. I can tell you're worried about her."

She yielded. "That's true. I am worried. She's been very pulled down though she pretends to me that she's better. For the last few days though I've had a funny feeling that she's not well ... I've been dreaming about her."

"Get dressed and we'll go," he said.

On the way to Colaba he bought a big bunch of flowers and two paper bags full of fruit – mangoes, oranges, grapes and a juicy pineapple. They parked in the chawl, causing a great deal of interest, and Stevie paid a small boy a rupee to guard their car from thieves who would strip it of its windscreen wipers and hub caps if it was left unattended. Then they climbed the stairs to Bernadette's room.

She was looking even worse than her daughter had feared. Lying on her string bed beneath the window with her eyes closed, she could already be a corpse. Her once springy dark hair looked lank and lifeless, her colour was a drained pale ochre and a sheen of sweat pearled her forehead. The sound of their footsteps on the bare floor did not wake her.

When Monica laid a gentle hand on her mother's thin forearm, the closed eyes opened and she stared up uncomprehendingly. It was obvious she did not at first recognise the person leaning over her. "Mama," she whispered in a dreamlike daze, "Where's Fifi?"

"I'm not your mother. It's me, your daughter," said Monica, feeling panicked.

"Of course," said Bernadette in a stronger voice, collecting herself. "I was dreaming, dear; of course it's you. Don't you look well."

"So do you," lied Monica whose heart had sunk at the pitiful sight of her mother.

Bernadette struggled to sit up and looked around dazedly. Monica gestured across the room to where Stevie was standing in the open doorway.

"I brought my friend to see you, Mama," she said.

Bernadette's delighted smile animated her face. "Come in, come in, have some tea. My ayah will bring it now. She'll have heard you arrive. She's very good to me, Monica."

The gentle ayah slipped into the room and stood smiling, waiting for orders.

"Make us tea," said Bernadette in a lordly tone. In order to impress the guest, she was acting her memsahib role.

As they drank the tea, Monica was grateful to Stevie for the natural way he behaved. There was not a trace of condescension in his manner and he was kindness itself to Bernadette who was obviously charmed by him but could not resist bombarding him with the sort of questions that her daughter had never dared to ask.

"Is your mother alive?" was the first.

He shook his head. "She died when I was young."

"Your father, then?"

"He's dead too, I'm afraid."

"Sisters or brothers?"

"I had a sister but she died when she was sixteen." His voice cracked a little as he said this and Monica looked at him anxiously because she'd never heard this before.

Bernadette sighed. "I had a sister who died aged seventeen. It's so sad and hard to bear. So you're the only one of your family still alive?"

"I've an uncle in New York. He took me into his family after my parents died."

"So you're American! Were you born in New York?"

"No, I was born in Berlin."

"Then you're German." Bernadette's voice was anxious because she remembered Monica's unfortunate experience with the man calling himself Hans Gelhorn.

His jaw clenched and his tone was cold. "No, I'm not German. I'm American now."

Monica felt the conversation was verging on sensitive ground so she diverted Bernadette by asking about her health. "Oh, I'm much better," was the reply. "I'm always better in the cool weather and there's a lovely breeze at night now. Sometimes I wish I was able to walk to Cuffe Parade and watch the sea."

Stevie looked at Monica and said, "We'll drive you to the sea. Would you like that?"

A look of longing crossed Bernadette's face. "I'd love it. But I might not be able to get down the stairs to your car."

Stevie would brook no objections. "Of course you can. We'll carry you and then I'll take you for a drive." He looked across at Monica whose eyes were glittering with unshed tears. "Get your mother ready and I'll bring the car to the foot of your stairs. It'll be easy to get your mother into it. Then we'll go for a tour of the city," he told her.

Bernadette weighed next to nothing now and, as Stevie said, it was easy to get her down the stairs. She placed her sticklike legs carefully on each step and tottered in their arms but she was brilliant with excitement. "I've not been out of that room for nearly three months," she kept whispering. "This is wonderful."

They propped her up in the corner of the long back seat and put cushions behind her head and back. Then they were off.

First they drove through Colaba, past the Afghan Church to the Point and back by Cuffe Parade. When they were opposite a lane leading back to the chawl they stopped.

"More?" asked Stevie looking at Monica who glanced back at her mother but Bernadette seemed to be infused with new life as she exclaimed at the things she saw out of the open window.

"A little more," she pleaded, so they went along Marine Drive, up Malabar Hill and down to Kemp's Corner. Still Bernadette was enthusing, "I've not been in this part of the city for ten years. Look at those new blocks of flats. Aren't they lovely!"

"Home now?" asked Monica. Her mother's face fell, however, so she said to Stevie, "Go out to the racecourse. It's not far."

When they reached it, Bernadette spoke

up again. "I don't suppose you'd take me to Chembur to see my sister? We've not spoken to each other for years and I'd like to make it up with her before I die."

It was the quiet time of the afternoon and the road was not busy so they made Chembur from the racecourse in less than half an hour. The door of Fifi's house was standing ajar and Leela's face appeared at the kitchen window when their car drove up. Monica got out of the front seat and ran inside. Fifi was lying asleep on the sofa with *Eve's Weekly* over her face to keep off the flies.

"Auntie, Auntie, wake up. You've got a visitor. Come and see who it is!" Monica cried.

Fifi sat up. "Is it Carole?" she asked.

"No, but it's a big surprise. Come and see."

Grumbling and brushing her hair out of her eyes, Fifi followed her niece to the front door and stopped in amazement when she saw the imposing car. Stevie got out and opened the back door to reveal Bernadette enthroned among her cushions and with both hands outspread. "Felicia, dear sister," she cried and burst into tears.

Fifi fell into the car, crying too, and the sisters hugged each other for a long time while the others walked away to give them a little privacy. Eventually they separated and Fifi stuck her head out of the car to scold

Monica and say, "What are you waiting for? Bring your mother in. She must have something to eat. She must have tea."

Bernadette was helped into the house and installed on the sofa, plied with tea and sticky jellabies that attracted even more flies, and gushed over by her sister.

"You don't look a day older than the last time I saw you," lied Fifi.

"Neither do you. I'm sorry it's been so long. I can't even remember what we fought about," said Bernadette.

"Neither do I, but that's all in the past. It mustn't happen again. You've been ill. Who is looking after you?"

"I have an ayah," said Bernadette proudly. "A very good woman. Monica is paying her."

All three women looked at Stevie who they knew to be the actual paymaster of the ayah, but he only smiled.

"You must come and stay here," pronounced Fifi. "I'll look after you. There's plenty of room and it's cool under the trees." She would brook no protests. Her sister was to be put to bed in the upstairs bedroom and Monica should go back to Colaba to collect some clothes and her mother's medicines.

"You'll stay with me till you're better," said Fifi, and the offer was accepted though they all knew that recovery was impossible.

It was only a matter of time before Bernadette died.

As Stevie and Monica eventually drove
away from the house on the golf course, she
sat silently weeping beside him. He put his
hand on hers.

"Your aunt will look after your mother
well," he said. "It's the best place for her
now."

She nodded. "I know that. I've accepted it.
It's just so sad that it's taken such a long
time for them to make up their quarrel –
and now she's dying. I can't pretend she
isn't any more. She knows it too."

He sighed. "At least she'll die in comfort,
Mon; not every one does. Give your aunt
whatever money she needs for doctors and
medicines and that sort of thing. I'll pay."

"You're very kind to me," she told him in
a faltering voice. "You don't have to be..."

"I like you," he said. Like, not love, she
thought, and she was glad that their
relationship was on that much easier level.

As they were waiting to join the traffic on
the main road, the white Mercedes swept
past with the blond-haired man driving.
Stevie's hands tightened on the steering
wheel. "He's going towards the city," he said
as if to himself.

Then he turned to Monica and told her in
a definite tone, "I want to see where he
lives."

She stared at him, her eyes huge and scared. "Now? Why?"

"I just want to see it. You can stay hidden in the car if you like."

"All right; it's up the same lane as the Carmichaels' place. Do you remember where that is?"

He gestured with his thumb toward the left. "Along there, about half a mile." And he turned the steering wheel in the opposite direction to the one he'd originally intended.

There were no cars parked outside the Gulmohurs' garage door and although the doorman at Raj Kapoor's was leaning over the gate watching the world go by as usual, he did not appear to register any interest in them.

Stevie drove slowly up the lane until Monica said, "It's just here. There's the gate. He keeps it padlocked, and if he's away the dog'll be roaming the compound. I hate that dog."

The words were barely out of her mouth when a huge Alsatian came bounding up the drive and put its front paws on the top spar of the gate before throwing back its head and letting out an enormous baying sound.

Ignoring it, Stevie got out of the car and walked up to the gate. "Is this the only entrance?" he asked.

She shook her head. "You can get in by

walking up the river bed when the river's dry. But there are snakes there and you have to be careful. Besides, the dog roams the creek at night and it would tear your throat out if it got the chance."

He stared ahead. "Where does this lane go?"

"It runs out in the jungle. After this it's only a path and then it's nothing."

"What's on the other side of that hill?" He pointed at the wooded slope rising above them.

"Trombay where the American refinery is and where they're building a new harbour. That's where Nigel Budgeon works – you remember, the man we met at the Carmichael's."

Stevie nodded. "Sure, he said he was building there, didn't he? That French guy worked there too, didn't he? But we can't get to it through here, can we?"

"Not unless we walk through the jungle and that would take hours. There's a road that cuts off just past Chembur and heads for Sewri. You can reach it that way but it's a long way round."

He stood staring round with his hands on his hips, ignoring the snarling dog. When he returned to the car he said to Monica, "That's it, then. This is where he's been living."

"Yes, this is where he brought me. You've

no idea how isolated it feels when you go down to that house. And it's bleak inside, too – like a fortified barracks. He has lots of guns."

"Has he? That's interesting," he said and bent down to have another look at the padlock before he started the car again. Their sightseeing trip was over but Stevie was silent and abstracted all during their drive back to the city. He seemed to be working something out.

Eleven

"The trouble with knowing someone as nice as Nigel," Dee said to her husband, "is that in an argument he always leaves you feeling like a rat, no matter how angry you are with him when you start out."

"I wonder if he had the same effect on the chaps he fought in the boxing ring," replied Ben.

"If he did, he'd have ended up world champion," said she with a grin.

They were standing at their open gate feeling guilty as they waved farewell to the disappearing Ambassador car which was carrying Nigel and Bernice to a suite of rooms in the Ritz Hotel.

Before she left, Bernice had told Dee that she and Nigel had originally hoped to save most of his salary during their two years in Bombay and that was why being PGs had suited them. However, now that she was pregnant, he was determined to go overboard as far as expense was concerned and had booked them into the hotel.

"He says I deserve to be waited on hand

and foot and live in air-conditioned comfort till the baby's born," said Bernice complacently. "He says what's money, after all?"

According to her, he'd also insisted that she become a patient of Bombay's most distinguished obstetrician – an internationally famous professor who had devised a special technique for preventing miscarriages.

"You should go to see him too," said Bernice, "especially since you have that funny blood group ... But he's expensive of course. Five hundred rupees a consultation and seven thousand for the delivery."

Dee shivered. Her lady doctor charged a hundred rupees for a consultation and two thousand for the delivery. Even that was a problem she and Ben were trying to ignore and she nurtured a secret hope that her father would be moved to a fit of generosity by the delivery of his first grandchild.

"What does he do that's so special for all that money?" she asked.

Bernice leaned forward and said in a confidential tone, "If there's any possibility of miscarriage he stitches you up ... He's done it for several famous Hollywood stars and he's going to do it to me the moment I develop any bad symptoms. Anything's better than miscarrying."

"What! How awful! You mean ... really stitch you up?" It sounded hideously utilitarian, even misogynistic, to Dee.

Bernice did not share these misgivings. "It's such a good idea!" she enthused.

"I think it's awful. What about making love?"

The corners of Bernice's mouth went down. "Really, Dee, that's not important when there's a baby to consider, is it?"

"Wouldn't Nigel mind?" asked Dee who could not imagine life without the consolation of love-making, even at her stage of pregnancy, and had every intention of going on doing it until the last minute. Bernice was only just over two and a half months pregnant which meant she and Nigel could be sexless for about nine more months, because she would certainly not start love-making again for quite a while after the delivery. Poor Nigel, Dee thought.

"Nigel doesn't worry about things like that any more than I do," said Bernice primly. "All he wants is for me and the baby to be safe."

Dee remembered this conversation as she watched the Budgeons' black car disappear from view, then, as they walked back to the house, she took her husband's hand and said, "That's it, then. Let's go to bed!"

After they'd made love her thoughts reverted to the loss of their PGs. "You don't think we were unreasonable about Nigel and all his animals, do you?" she asked.

Ben shook his head. "No, I don't. He'd have started bringing in beggar families next. The man's a walking bleeding heart."

"But he's so likeable. I think being in India must hurt him a lot; he'll see so many things that affect him badly," said Dee.

"Yeah, his withers are easily wrung. But he *is* a nice guy. The Pathans who work on that site of his worship him. They'd follow him to hell and back. They'd kill for him! And you know what Pathans are like – not easy to impress," replied Ben.

Dee did know what Pathans were like because Ben employed several of them as guards on his various sites and they were all touchy, proud and intensely quarrelsome. Fortunately Ben got on well with them too, though perhaps not as well as Nigel.

"Maybe this baby they're having'll take up his attention and divert him from good works. He'll have his hands full with Bernice and the Ritz must be costing him a packet," Ben went on. "But you know, in spite of that, he insisted on paying me a month's rent in lieu of notice. I wasn't going to take it but he made me. He said it was his contribution to the going-away party."

Dee groaned. "That makes me feel even worse. We were rotten to them ... I know what I'll do to make it up to them. I'll go into the Ritz once a week and play Scrabble with Bernice as a penance! Did he say they'd come to the party?"

"He said they wouldn't. He's terrified of Bernice losing the baby by being jolted about on rough roads. He seems to think she's made of eggshell china."

There was no danger of Ben thinking that about his wife, however, because he then said, "Come on, get up, you can help me put up the loudspeakers."

She gaped at him. "What loudspeakers?"

"In the trees, for the music at the party. Guy and I always did it. He climbed the ladder and I handed up the stuff. Do you want to go up the ladder or will I?"

"Ben, I'm pregnant!"

"But you're all right," he said. Then he saw the expression on her face. "OK, I'll get Birbal to carry the equipment. All you'll have to do is pass up the wires."

It took the rest of the day to erect the loudspeaker system to Ben's satisfaction. Three speakers were dotted around the garden, high in the trees, and Dee watched them going up with disquiet. "They'll make an awful lot of noise," she said, staring up at her husband who was halfway up a tree. "I bet there's more amplification for music here than at the Trooping of the Colour."

Ben took that as a compliment. "Do you think so?" he asked, jumping down and standing with his hands on his hips surveying his handiwork.

"But what about the neighbours?"

"As soon as I've done this I'm going over to tell Raj."

"Won't the German hear it?"

"Yes. We'll let him know too ... but right now I'm going to put on Satcho to hear how he sounds."

He sounded so loud that flocks of birds rose screaming into the air and flew around in panic the moment the *Muskrat Ramble* began. The two sinister vultures that always brooded on top of the tall palm trees by the well were disturbed out of their vigilance over the district and flew off too, naked necks sticking out and flapping their wings in a threatening fashion as if they were planning revenge.

Encouraged by the success of his electrical work, Ben then went across the lane to confer with Raj about the racket which he could not have avoided hearing. It was midnight before he came back, well lubricated by Raj's whisky, and by that time Dee was deeply asleep.

Next day, after he left for his office, she set about planning the menu and by noon had prepared it as well as she could, bearing in mind the advice to keep it simple. With a list of ingredients in her hand she made her way to the kitchen quarters by walking through the garden and past the garage to the back door.

Pasco, the cook, was taken by surprise as he was taking his ease in the shade on a string bed, lying back and smoking a bidi. His knobbly bare feet were the only bit of him that was in the sun. When he saw her, he threw the bidi away and rose reluctantly, making clear his view that she was abusing her position by penetrating the servants' quarters without being properly announced.

"I've made a list of the food we need for the party on Saturday," she said holding out the sheet of paper.

He did not take it and she realised that once again she'd given offence. He could neither read nor write. Her face reddened.

"We're expecting about a hundred people," she said, deliberately underestimating the number because she knew Pasco would over-cater.

He did not bat an eyelid. "Yes, memsahib."

"I wanted to know how much money you'll need to buy the food and so I made this list ... perhaps you can tell me if I've allowed enough. I thought we'd need twenty-five chickens; two hams; ten legs of roasting lamb; forty lettuces; fifty apples and fifty oranges; ten pineapples; a hundred bananas; ten cabbages for coleslaw salad; at least a hundred tomatoes; seven dozen eggs..."

She was reading off her own list and the length of it appalled her. The cost would be awful. If she was to go into the market to buy all that stuff, she'd expect to spend about four hundred and fifty rupees but Pasco would get it all for much less. The market traders always inflated their prices for white women who did their own shopping and Dee had learned to leave it to the staff.

"How much cookbook money will you need?" she asked.

"Seven hundred rupees," said Pasco promptly.

She reeled. "Seven hundred! But I thought—"

He flashed his eyes at her. "A hundred people will eat much food and this house has been well known for putting on a good table. It will cost seven hundred rupees – perhaps a few less but I will bring home what is not needed." *Some chance,* she thought.

Though the average cost of food for a month – even when Nigel and Bernice had been there – was only about three hundred rupees, she was intimidated by his dumb insolence. His implication was that this party she was putting on would not be as good as anything given in the past.

Feeling like a dog with its tail between its legs, she went back through the house to the bedroom where she took from its hiding place in her underwear drawer the seven hundred rupees which was Nigel's generously given rent – all their worldly wealth till Ben's next salary went into the bank on the last day of the month. A little warning voice in her head told her not to hand the cookbook money over to Pasco till the day before the party and so she stuck the precious notes back in the hiding place again, thinking, *Let's hope we can live on leftovers till we finally move out.*

The encounter with Pasco had so dispirited her that she felt incredibly weary and lay down on the sitting-room divan to read a battered library copy of *The Pickwick Papers,* which usually cheered her up. However, but she only managed a few pages before falling asleep.

When she woke again the world seemed dreamlike, still and silent, for it was three o'clock in the afternoon, a time when all life in India seems to come to a temporary halt. A soft breeze was ruffling the branches of the trees outside the open window and the sweet smell of freshly cut grass wafted in from the garden.

Oh God, I'm going to miss this place so much, she thought with a terrible pang. But there was no use brooding. The decision was made. She sat up and slipped her feet into sandals, remembering her doctor's advice to walk at least two miles a day. That would be a good cure for the blues.

She took her time, wandering slowly up the lane towards the tree-covered hill, pausing to admire yellow-trumpeted flowering creepers that clambered over the cactus hedge and then to look across at the military-style ranks of glossy-leaved citrus trees that filled the acreage of the fruit farm. These ramrod-straight trees gleamed like emeralds in the sunshine because their leaves had not yet been covered by the fine dust which would have turned every growing green thing to a uniform shade of beige by the time the rains came round again next year.

Shadiv used to live over there, she thought as she always did when she looked across the nullah at the farm. She hadn't seen him since she discovered she was pregnant and knew that she could not leave Ben in spite of how desperately she loved Shadiv. Though three months had passed she was still ravaged by the realisation that she was capable of loving two men at the same time and wondered if she was in some way aberrant.

Shadiv's name was not on the party guest list because seeing him again would be too painful for her, but she had continually wondered how he was since he had moved into the fashionable flat on Malabar Hill.

Had prosperity changed him? What books was he reading? He'd be able to buy them from Thackers now because, from the gossipy articles about film stars in *Eve's Weekly* which she read in the doctor's consulting room, she knew that his career had taken off in a big way and he was being talked about as India's answer to Hollywood's Tony Curtis. She was not sure whether he would consider that a compliment.

A line of pale green feathery bamboos marked the course of the nullah that divided the Gulmohurs from the farm, and she followed it with her eyes. You could get to the German's bungalow by following the river bed, she realised.

The German! That's where she'd go. She'd call on him and invite him to the party. Ben had written him off as unsociable, but inviting him to the party would be a way of warning him about the noise from those loudspeakers. She'd also take the oportunity to ask if they could borrow his bearer for the party night because there would be too much work for Ali and his little assistant, a boy called Jacob, to manage on their own and they needed all the help they could get. Anne had already offered the services of Gopal but Dee doubted if he'd be much help. He never extended himself at home so he was unlikely to do so when he was in someone else's house.

She wandered up the lane at a snail's pace, swinging a length of twig she'd broken off a tree as she went. There was not a soul about and not a sound except for the crunch of her feet on the dried-up mud of the lane, though, as always in India, she was prickingly conscious of hidden eyes watching her. They might be human eyes, they might be animal eyes, but though she was alone and unprotected, she was quite unafraid.

People were waking from their afternoon rest by the time she reached the fence that barricaded the buffalo camp off from the lane. Fascinated, she stopped and stared through the open gap in the stockade at a cluster of palm-thatched houses built round a sun-baked square of earth where nothing grew.

I wish I could go in there, she thought but knew she must not. The camp people were very hostile to strangers because, as well as selling buffalo milk into the city, they had a lucrative illegal sideline in brewing illicit liquor – a palm toddy that cost a few annas a bottle and tasted so vile it could barely be stomached unless mixed with Coca-Cola. Even undiscriminating drinkers like Ben and Guy only bought it when in dire straits. Ben said that the smell from it was so rank that he was nauseated when a bottle was opened in a closed room so he always uncorked it on the verandah. You had to be really desperate for a drink to taste it, he said.

A few lanky, sinewy-looking women were emerging from the huts, adjusting their cotton saris, yawning, stretching in preparation for another round of tasks. Beautiful children, naked except for little scraps of dirty vests but with thick lines of kohl lovingly painted round their enormous eyes, scuffled in the dust or trailed after their mothers. The pungent smell of woodsmoke hung over everything like an invisible veil.

Suddenly the peace was shattered by a big tan-coloured pye-dog with a curling plume of a tail, who spotted Dee and rushed towards her baying ferociously. A gaggle of other dogs joined in and the women paused in their gossiping to look towards her.

She tried smiling. None of them smiled back and their eyes were hard as they stared at her. Some of them called to their children as if they were afraid she was going to touch them. They must have known who she was because they passed her in the garden on their way to and from the well every day of the week, but none of them gave any indication of recognition.

If only I could talk to them. How I wish they'd tell me about their lives, about the things that concern them. I wish I could tell them that I'm pregnant and scared by the prospect of child bearing. They'd be able to tell me what it's like, how to bear it, she thought as she backed awkwardly away. It was only in books that someone like her could strike up a friendship with women like them.

The guard dogs stopped their pursuit of her when she crossed to the other side of the lane but they stood in the camp entrance baying ferociously as if daring her to come back. She went on walking up the lane for a few more yards till she reached the closed gate of the German's house.

A huge padlock and chain secured the hasp and the white paint on the wood was blistered and peeling away in long strips. Hanging from a tree branch by the gate was a rusting metal bell with string dangling down from its clapper. She pulled the string and the bell gave out a loud, harsh clatter that started the buffalo camp dogs off barking again.

The only reaction from the German's side of the gate was the appearance of a huge Alsatian that came bounding up the overgrown driveway, which looked as if few cars ever drove over it because clumps of flowers and grass were sprouting between the tyre ruts. The Alsatian kept on running till it reached the gate when it leapt in the air as if intending to clear it. The attempt failed and instead the dog put its front paws on the top rail and drew back its lips at Dee, showing black gums and ferocious teeth.

God, I hope it can't get over that gate, she thought. The baying dog weighed more than she did and was wearing a thick leather collar adorned with brass studs that made it look exceptionally threatening. It was behaving as if the dearest wish of its heart would be to tear out her throat.

"Good dog," she said in what she hoped was a conciliatory tone. She liked dogs and they usually liked her but this one was a real challenge. Knowing that it was essential to stand her ground and look the dog in the eye, she steeled her nerve. "Good dog," she said again in as firm a voice as she could manage.

The dog shook its ruffed head and gave a low throaty growl that seemed to say, *I'll kill you and enjoy doing it.*

Dee put her hand in the pocket of her skirt where she knew there were a couple of mint sweets that she'd brought along for refreshment on her walk. She took one out, unwrapped it, and, making an effort to stay calm, tossed the sweet over the gate towards the slavering animal.

It stopped barking and sniffed at the sweet, sniffed again and then gave it a tentative lick before gobbling it up. Bribery did not mellow its temper, however, and it was throwing itself at the gate again when Dee saw a man in a white shirt and khaki shorts coming up the drive towards her.

"*Hund, hund!*" he yelled at the dog, which went silent, turned and slunk away as if it was afraid of being beaten.

Though they had been neighbours for all her time in India, she'd never seen the German on his feet and out of a car. He was tall and well built, in his early fifties, probably a contemporary of Nigel. His hair was pale blond and very straight with a lock falling across one side of his forehead. He was undeniably still handsome, and today, fortunately, prepared to be courtly.

She smiled at him. "Hello," she said. "I'm your neighbour from down the lane. Sorry to drop in on you like this but we're having a party next weekend and—"

"Hello," he said, smiling too and without a trace of a foreign accent except a slightly guttural undertone to his voice. "I recognise you. Sorry about my dog but it's trained to see off intruders. Come in and have a beer. I'll unlock the gate."

He produced a key from the top pocket of his shirt and opened the padlock. The gate swung back easily on well-oiled hinges. There was no sign of the dog when Dee stepped through and the padlock was quickly secured again behind her.

"Those people in the camp are all thieves," said the German as he turned the key. "They'd steal the dirt from beneath your fingernails."

She laughed. "They don't bother us but I don't suppose we've got anything worth stealing really. Hello again, I'm Dee Carmichael."

He bowed. "Gelhorn, Hans Gelhorn," he said, and gestured with his hand to indicate that she walk down the drive in front of him.

For an odd moment she thought, *What am I doing? I'm usually pretty cautious but here I am, on my own, in the middle of the jungle with this man. What if he's some sort of maniac?* But she looked back over her shoulder at him and saw him smiling benignly, which reassured her slightly.

His bungalow was built on much the same plan and of the same materials as the Gulmohurs – exterior walls of roughly cut blocks of stone, a ridged asbestos roof, a long wooden verandah along its front. But whereas the Gulmohurs was distinguished by the enormous red flowering tree at its gate that gave it its name, and by the bougainvillaea that branched over its walls as well as its lovely garden and expanse of emerald green lawn, this house seemed to huddle miserably in an unkempt wilderness. The end gables of Dee's home were covered with flowering jasmine and a huge creeping liana that could have sheltered Jane and Tarzan, but the German's walls were stark and bare. The whole place looked unloved.

His front door was open showing a dim interior and as they approached it, Gelhorn said, "Please go in and sit down. I'll fetch some beer."

She looked over her shoulder and said, "I'd rather have a soda, if you don't mind."

"That will be no trouble," he replied in a courtly way.

The main room opened on to the verandah. Like the house, it was forbiddingly spartan and contained only two big leather armchairs and a massive sofa with the stuffing hanging out of its back, grouped round in a huddle as if they were looking at a central point in the middle of the floor. Dee paused as she walked into the room because of a throat-catching, pungent smell that permeated the room: drifts of what seemed to be smoke were coiling round in the corners. She didn't take time to speculate about that, however, because what struck her most forcibly was the line-up of guns that adorned the back wall. The place looked like an arsenal. She quickly counted two double-barrelled shot guns, a sporting rifle and three smaller handguns displayed one above the other, all oiled and gleaming like precious jewels.

"Go out and sit on the verandah," said her host. "The smoke might irritate your throat."

Gratefully, she did as she was told. The

verandah, like so many in Bombay, contained the usual cane sofa and two armchairs with cushions covered in a faded green fabric. A broken-open sporting gun lay on the top of a table with a tin of oil and a cleaning cloth beside it.

When he came back with the drinks, her host insisted, "I must apologise for the smell. You see, I have had to light a fire in the room next door to drive away the cobras."

She was taken aback. "Cobras? Inside the house?"

"They've been nesting in the roof beams of my bedroom and some Indians I know told me that the best way to drive them out is to light a fire in a buffalo's skull. They hate the smell so they go away," he told her in a tone that he might have used when making an observation about the weather.

She drew in a breath and gave a tentative laugh. "It does smell rather strong. No wonder they go away."

Gelhorn sat forward in his chair and asked eagerly, "Would you like to see it?" His eyes were striking, a very pale shade of blue. She'd once read that very blue eyes were the sign of a criminal personality.

Must I? she thought, but for some reason, perhaps because she felt he was testing her, she nodded and said, "All right."

Her host seemed pleased that she'd

accepted what was clearly a challenge. He walked across to a door at the back of the main room and threw it open. "Just look in there. The snakes are up beside the fan," he said.

The furniture of the room had all been pushed back against the far wall but a hideous heap smouldered in the middle of the bare marble floor. What was recognisably a buffalo's horned head was burning away with its eyeballs literally popping out and a stream of acrid smoke rising from the top of its skull. Its teeth glittered horribly as if it was laughing. Dee didn't dare to lift her eyes to the roof to see the snakes. All this was bad enough.

"Ugh!" she said and felt herself gag.

He laughed and drew the door closed. "Horrible, isn't it?" he said with satisfaction.

I've got to get out of here, she thought. It was obvious he was relishing her discomfort and she began to wonder if he was as sober as he appeared.

Keep calm, she told herself, determined not to let him see how disconcerted she felt, *take him on at his own game.* So she went back to the verandah and sat down in her chair. She even managed to smile as she sipped her drink. "I hope your anti-cobra cure works," she said. "It would be awful if you suffered that smell for nothing."

"If it doesn't get rid of the cobras I'll shoot them," he said, gesturing at the gun on the table.

"I've heard that if you kill a cobra, it takes revenge on you," she told him.

He laughed. "I've faced worse enemies than cobras."

What did you do during the war? she suddenly wondered. He would certainly look right in a black and silver uniform and jackboots.

She smiled again and changed the subject. "You must be wondering why I've come to see you. It's because of our party next weekend. There'll be a lot of loud music till pretty late, I'm afraid. My husband and I would be very pleased if you'll come down and join us because it's our farewell to our house, you see."

His eyes showed interest. "You're leaving India? Where is your home?"

"We're Scots ... but we're not going home yet. We've still got some months to go before we go on leave but we're moving into the city because I'm having a baby and this place is too isolated."

He ignored the bit about the baby and said, "You're Scots. The ones whose men wear kilts. The Ladies from hell! Like the Germans you are a warlike people."

He raised his glass in a toast to her and she smiled frostily. Her father had been a Lady

186

from Hell fighting in the First World War and the memory of the trenches still haunted him.

"Will you come to our party?" she persisted, deciding it was time she went home.

"I might," he said. "It depends what work I have to do, but in any case I don't mind your music. I've heard it before."

"Do try to come," she said politely. She shifted forward in her chair in preparation for standing up but remembered the second reason for her errand. "Oh, I was also wondering if your bearer would like to earn some extra money by helping our boys on the night of the party," she told him.

He shook his head and said, "I've no bearer at the moment. My man left me last month and I look after myself now. Living alone means there's not much work and I find that those Indian servants are all just thieves."

That's what he said about the buffalo camp people, she thought. *He seems to be suspicious of the entire world.*

She stood up and said, "I'll have to go now, I'm afraid. My husband will be back soon and I don't want to walk down the lane when it's getting dark."

He didn't attempt to detain her. She felt she'd fulfilled her function by being visibly shocked by the burning buffalo head.

"I'll walk to the gate with you," he said.

"My dog'll attack you if I'm not there to see you out. That's what it's trained to do."

At the big gate they parted cordially enough. "Do try to come to the party," she repeated though she didn't really want him there.

"I will," he said and she could tell that he too was lying.

Twelve

The precise writing on the face of the blue airmail form told Anne that the letter was from her father.

She tore it open anxiously and ran her eye down the meticulously spaced lines. The writing only covered half of the page: he had nothing detailed to suggest or anything momentous to report.

Twice she read what he had to say and then slowly tore the letter into tiny pieces and set fire to it in a tin ashtray. She didn't want Bill finding any bits and start trying to stick it together.

Because it was so short it had not been difficult to memorise.

My dear daughter, reading between the lines of your letter it seems to me that you are suggesting we might provide you with a home if you decide to leave your husband.

As your mother and I warned you at the time you took your hasty step, you

189

have made your choice and must bear the consequences. You are not specific in your complaints about your domestic circumstances but it does not seem that you are short of money or that your husband is betraying you with other women.

If we took you in and he tried to come after you, your mother's nerves would be very agitated and she cannot bear scenes or upheavals, especially since her health is much more frail these days and such things cause talk among the neighbours.

Another reason we cannot help is because there is an extra demand on us at present. Your sister Diana is getting married just before Christmas. Her prospective husband is a banker, slightly older than she is, but eminently suitable and in receipt of an excellent salary. Your mother and I send you and your daughter our very best wishes.

He seems to think I was asking for money, but I wasn't, she thought bitterly. *Of course, I shouldn't have written to him.*
She had sent an appeal for emotional support rather than material assistance for she desperately needed reassurance. It was impossible to talk about her worries to Bill, partly because he was the cause of most of

them but mainly because he simply refused to take anything she said seriously. Perhaps he was afraid to.

"Have a drink and forget about it," he always said when she told him that the attacks of lightheadedness that had plagued her occasionally since childhood seemed to be getting more frequent. There were times now when she had no recollection of what had happened only a few moments ago.

Normally those attacks passed quickly but recently they had been accompanied by a feeling of nausea and she had begun to be afraid that she might die suddenly and leave Liza to the erratic care of her husband. If only her parents would take in the child – but she had not spelled out her concerns clearly enough for them to know that was what she was asking.

Sometimes depression claimed her so badly that she was unable to think clearly or to talk about it even to her closest confidante and only real friend, Dee. She knew Dee had noticed something was wrong but whenever she broached the subject Anne cut her short. In truth she was terrified to tell anyone about the attacks which so worried her. *I ought to go to see a doctor but I'm afraid*, she thought. Then she recalled her father's letter again and wept a little. If only he had written something like, "We love you. We want to see you." That would have helped her through this bleak period of her life.

She imagined the pleasure her mother was getting out of Diana's marriage. There would be a cake to order, cards to have printed, invitations to be sent out – all the sort of thing that would have been done for Anne herself if they'd approved of her choice of husband.

She'd never got on very well with Diana, a boring, whining, mousy-looking girl who had always been in Anne's shadow. Diana would undoubtedly be glad that her sister was not going to be present at the wedding.

Anne got up and stared through the open window at the aquamarine stretch of Back Bay in front of her house. How awful, she thought, to be miserably unhappy and scared of dying in this place. Although it was beautiful, it was very far from home.

If only, if only ... If only she hadn't married Bill in such a hurry, before she'd really got to know him. His jealousy had not become obvious until after the honeymoon but it had been growing more intense and more violent ever since. Now she could not even look at a man without him threatening her with violence.

The letter home had been dashed off after he threw one of his terrible rages and accused her of contemplating an affair with a well-known Bombay roué, a man who openly boasted that he'd had every woman in their set who was worth having. A lot of women, their vanity activated, fell for his line – but not Anne who was sufficiently secure in herself and too intrinsically moral to be swayed by his implication. She had never even contemplated sleeping with him, or anyone else, but could not convince her husband of that.

Her mind went back to the night before she had written to her father. She wished she could have told him the truth about her situation because she knew he was not so unfeeling as to ignore a genuine plea for help.

"If I ever get you cheating on me," Bill had threatened, backing her against the wall of their bedroom with his hands around her throat, "I'll kill the guy and then I'll kill you. I really will."

She'd placated him at last and, as usual, it ended by them making violent love, but the erotic thrill of that, which once excited her, had long ago worn off.

She walked away from the window and sat down at her piano to tinkle out a tune. What came out was one she actively disliked – "April Love". She strummed it with a wry look on her face. Bill said it was their tune. How long ago was it since they'd met? Over eight years. It seemed an eternity.

As usual she ended up making excuses for

him, telling herself, *I'm being unreasonable. He's not a bad man. He loves me – he even got this piano for me. He's jealous, that's all. He behaves like he does because he loves me too much. I suppose I'm lucky compared to a lot of the wives here whose husbands are off chasing other women all the time.* Even Dee's Ben still had a roving eye and Dee watched him warily all the time though he was devoted to her.

But it wasn't just Bill's jealousy that was the trouble. She was worried by growing signs of serious instability in her husband and was afraid that one day he'd snap completely. His frustration at work, which fuelled his rages at home, grew worse every day and his employers were rapidly losing patience with him. He was rude, he was insubordinate, he was deliberately obstructive and she knew too that he was dabbling in things which could turn badly sour on him.

In the beginning of their life together she'd been tolerantly amused by his fixation with criminals and crime, but little by little she began to realise with dread that he was serious when he talked about becoming a gangster. From time to time he'd discuss with her illicit plans he dreamed up, but fortunately none of them had ever come to anything – until recently.

Through his working-hour outings to illicit drinking dens near the factory where he had his office, he'd met a group of renegade Muslims who were not above drinking and breaking other kinds of laws, secular or religious, as well.

In his cups a few months ago, he'd confided to her that he was contemplating getting involved with a gun-running syndicate that sold firearms to Pathans for smuggling to the North-West Frontier where a series of mini-wars seemed to be waged all the time. What he did for this syndicate was unclear but it mainly involved hiding crates of firearms in the mill where he had his office and sometimes delivering them to pick-up points in company vans. It was dangerous, she knew, it couldn't go on, and every morning when she woke she was afraid that this would be the day when Bill's criminality would be discovered. What would happen to them then?

She wouldn't be able to plead ignorance of what he was doing because for months she'd been benefiting from the fruits of his enterprise. From time to time he gave her bundles of high-denomination rupee notes and said, "Go out and spend these. Use them in little shops or cafés. We want to change them into smaller notes as soon as possible."

She held the money with shaking hands. "What if I someone wonders where I get so much cash?" she asked.

"They won't. They never suspect white women of doing anything wrong and they'd think it normal for you to be spending big money like that anyway."

She still had most of the money lying hidden in the flat because she was afraid to spend it. Every day since he'd given the notes to her, Bill asked if she'd spent much and she'd say, "Yes, I spent some in Crawford Market and I ordered three new dresses," or something of the kind. He was pleased and didn't ask for any of the change back because he was generous and liked her to be well turned out.

In fact the sums she spent were only paltry but she led him to believe she was getting through a good deal more than she actually was because when she'd built up a lot of ten and twenty-rupee notes, she started putting money in her bank account. It was what she thought of as her "just in case" money. In case she had to bolt suddenly.

Before very long she had over three thousand rupees safely deposited in a private account at Lloyds Bank in Hornby Road. She only ever paid in, never withdrew, and took care to conceal all evidence of this account from her husband, hiding her pass book at the bottom of Liza's toy box. Bill was not above secretly searching her handbag and reading her letters for evidence of infidelity but never went into the toy box because he was very much a hands-off father.

Thinking about the toy box, made Anne wonder when her daughter would be returning from her morning walk with the ayah. She went back to the window and stood looking out for a few moments till the two of them came in sight walking up the pavement on the same side of the road as the houses. Liza was clutching the ayah's hand and looking up at her as she talked – in which language, her mother wondered? Anne's heart filled with a deep and painful love for the child. No matter what happened, she had to safeguard Liza.

As they came clattering up the stairs, she played a nursery rhyme on the piano to welcome her daughter who cried, "Mummy!" and came running across the floor with her arms out. Then she said, "Auntie Dee's just parking her car in the garden. She's coming up to see you."

"Good," laughed Anne, sweeping her daughter into her arms and holding her up towards the ceiling. "Will I put you up on the beams so's you can look down on her like a bird?"

"Oh Mummy," said Liza tolerantly. "You know that'd be dangerous!"

Anne laughed and set her on the floor again as Dee came in. She looked excited and her baby bulge was hardly showing today beneath the loose pink shirt and cotton trousers she was wearing. "I've come to ask if you'd like to come to Breach Candy pool with me, but first I want to call in at Stevie and Monica's because we need more bearers for the party. Your Gopal's not enough and they've got a nice old boy working for them that I want to borrow," she explained.

"Yes, Breach Candy!" cried Liza and Anne nodded but as she did so she felt one of the strange sensations come over her and she was forced to sit down suddenly.

Dee noticed at once that her friend's face had gone pale and her eyes seemed unfocused. "Are you all right?" she asked. "Have you any brandy? Let me get some for you."

In an instant, Anne recovered herself. Standing up quickly, she said, "What do you mean? I'm perfectly all right." But she was still pale and seemed to tremble slightly. Seeing how intently Dee was staring at her, she said sharply, "Well, are we going to visit Monica then?"

"All right, but I'll drive. Come on, my car's outside," said Dee firmly. To her relief Anne did not argue or want to take her own car as she usually did.

It was cooler up on Malabar Hill than down by the sea and they drove slowly with the car windows open, the breeze ruffling their hair. Stevie's penthouse was spectacularly beautiful because Monica had called in a garden specialist who filled the terrace with big pots of flowers and shrubs. With her ivory skin covered with diaphanous scarves to keep off the sun, she was taking her ease among the flowers beneath a shady parasol. The last thing she wanted was any more of a tan than she already had.

The arrival of visitors delighted her and she plied them with coffee. As Anne sipped hers she watched the Anglo-Indian girl bustling about in her prettily swishing skirt. She'd seen Monica around at parties with various men for several years and thought her brittle and predatory, but now she seemed surprisingly vulnerable and much more likeable. Stevie was obviously having a good effect on her.

Dee made her request for the loan of a bearer as the old man, whose name was Vijay, lingered behind them listening. Monica looked at him for confirmation before she said, "Of course, we'd be delighted to lend you Vijay. Stevie and I will bring him with us in the car. Will we come early so's you can be ready before the crowd arrives?"

"That would be tremendous," Dee responded gratefully. She was about to say something else when there was a confusion at the open doorway and Stevie appeared smiling broadly.

"I thought I'd drop in for a drink and it's nice to find so many lovely ladies on my verandah," he complimented them with unusual gallantry.

They laughed back and Anne said, "We're just leaving. We're going to Breach Candy."

"At least have a proper drink here first," said Stevie. "We've got cold beer and you can't get that at Breach Candy. I hate the tepid cola they serve in that place."

They sat drinking beer around a glass-topped table in the elegant sitting room with an air-conditioner purring away in one corner as Dee told them about her plans for the party. She talked excitedly. "We're buying all our permit points in beer and putting them on ice in the bath. Ben's rigged loudspeakers up in the trees and he's spending hours sorting out which records he's going to play – all the usual ones of course: Chubby Checker, Louis Armstrong, Benny Goodman and Nat King Cole. He's also going to string coloured lights all round the garden because it's Divali. I only hope he doesn't electrocute himself."

Monica asked, "Do you need any help with the food?" She knew Ben and Dee were always hard up and, having had bitter experience of that, knew what it meant.

"The cook's going to buy everything at the market on the morning of the party and I'm sure he's out to cheat me but I can't do anything about it," Dee said, sobering as she remembered the glum Pasco.

"Don't let him get away with it," said practical Monica. "Buy a lot yourself. There's a very good baker in Chembur who makes splendid double rotis. You can order as much as you need from him and he'll deliver them to you on Saturday afternoon. I'll do it for you if you like because I'm going to see my mother out there tomorrow. It'll be my contribution to the party!"

"And I'll give you a couple of huge Edam cheeses that Bill brought home the other night. Heaven knows where he got them but they're the sort that are coated with red wax and look like footballs. The problem is he doesn't like cheese and neither do I so I'll be glad to find them a good home," said Anne who was also very aware of what a drain on the financial resources of Dee and Ben the catering for this party was going to be.

As Anne talked she was aware of Stevie watching her and felt a flush creep up her neck and her heart starting to beat very fast. *Why is he staring at me like that?* she wondered. She was intensely aware of him but unsure whether he was admiring or adversely criticising her. Lifting her head she looked directly into his face. The intensity of his stare scared her and she shifted awkwardly in her chair, not sure of what she felt herself. Though she wasn't tired, she couldn't suppress a big yawn.

Dee, seeing her friend's sudden discomfort, thought she was having another of her peculiar turns but Anne smiled to show that she was all right so Dee relaxed again, feeling happy and reassured by the generosity of her friends, and launched into the tale of her visit to the German's bungalow.

"The oddest thing happened yesterday," she said. "It still makes me shudder. I went up the lane to invite that German chap – Gelhorn – to our party..."

From the corner of her eye, Anne saw Stevie's face tighten when Dee mentioned the German's name. Monica too looked uncomfortable for some reason, but Dee failed to notice and swept on, "When I got there he told me he had a nest of cobras in his bedroom roof and was burning a buffalo's head in the middle of the floor to drive them away. It was the most horrible, macabre-looking thing I've ever seen! And the smell was nauseating. I think he only invited me in to see what my reaction would be. Ben says that burning a buffalo's head is what the priests are called in to do when he finishes factory buildings. It brings good luck and drives away evil or something ... but Gelhorn doesn't strike me as being particularly superstitious. Perhaps the buffalo-camp people were pulling his leg about the cobras. He doesn't seem to have much time for them or them for him as far as I can see."

"I hope you didn't stay long in his house," said Monica, leaning forward on to the table.

"No, I didn't. That buffalo head looked so horrible I practically took to my heels and ran all the way home. He keeps the place locked up like Fort Knox. His dog roams the garden slavering for a bit of human flesh and you can't get out of the gate unless he comes with you and unlocks it. He even carries the key in his pocket in case you try to make a getaway. He seems in dread of being robbed by practically everybody."

"Why on earth did you go up there in the first place?" asked Stevie in a tight voice.

Dee looked surprised. "I went to invite him to the party – and to ask if his bearer would work for us on the party night, like I've asked for your Vijay. But he hasn't any servants now, apparently. His bearer has left so that was a non-starter ... and I'm sure he won't come to the party either."

"He won't be any loss," said Stevie and his voice was even colder than before.

When they left the flat Anne was pale again and suddenly asked Dee if she would mind driving her and Liza home instead of to Breach Candy. "I think the sun's too much for me today," she said. Though Liza was disappointed she was a good child and didn't make a fuss.

Dee dropped them at their door for Anne pointedly said, "I want to sleep now. Don't worry about the party. It'll be all right, and we'll come early to help you with the last-minute arrangements."

Worried, Dee drove away wondering how to pass the rest of the afternoon. The library was always a good refuge; she'd go there, she decided.

The old building was surprisingly cool, because it was so cleverly situated that it caught the breezes off the sea even in the hottest weather. She climbed the steps, which were getting more difficult to negotiate as her pregnancy advanced, and found her favourite clerk behind the desk.

On an impulse she asked him, "Do you have any medical books?"

He beamed and darted out from behind the desk, pointing to a distant stack. "In there. Many medical books. Which disease?"

"I don't know. A general textbook would be best."

Eventually they decided that she might find what she wanted in Beaumont's *Medicine* – a fourth edition published in 1942. It was a big book, bound in red, and she carted it across to one of the desks and started to browse.

Anne's manner when she became ill

reminded Dee of a man who used to work for her father. He'd been epileptic and though Anne didn't collapse into fits as he had done, she displayed the same fixity of stare and abstractedness that he had shown. Dee looked up "epilepsy" in the index and as soon as she read the entry for *"Petit Mal"* she knew she'd struck gold.

> The patient might be quite unaware of the occurrence of the attacks ... They suddenly stop speaking or remain motionless for a second or two ... The eyes deviate and there may be yawning.

That was exactly how Anne behaved today, thought Dee.

> During the attack there is a brief loss of consciousness or the patient may fall to the ground.

That had happened once but Anne had insisted she'd only fallen over because she tripped.

The worrying part came at the end of the section.

> Another type of minor attack is characterised by what is known as a "psychic equivalent" in which the patient may, for example, become a

homicidal maniac or perform automatic actions of which he is unconscious.

Dee closed the book with a slam, thinking, *What nonsense. That could never happen to my friend!* Then, when she had calmed down, she opened the book again and turned back to the relevant pages to see if there was any cure.

"Potassium or sodium bromide," it said. "Luminal..." Whatever that was.

"Belladonna" ... Mental worry and over-fatigue are injurious; a regular mode of living, with open-air exercise and avoidance of alcohol should be enforced.

How Victorian it all was. She gave the book back to the man behind the desk and left the library in a mood of deep depression.

Thirteen

Because it was such a long drive from the Ritz Hotel to Trombay, Nigel had to be out of bed by five o'clock in the morning but he didn't mind. After dressing himself in the bathroom so as not to disturb his sleeping wife, he tiptoed back into the bedroom and gently kissed her cheek. She always gave a soft little whimper and snuggled further down beneath the blanket which she needed now because it was so beautifully cool in the air-conditioned room.

Nigel straightened up and gazed down at her with adoration. He loved her with every fibre of his being and, even after nearly ten years of marriage, could scarcely believe his luck at being her husband – and the father of her soon-to-be-born baby.

"I'll see you tonight, darling," he whispered as he left the room with his heart singing.

Bernice lay with her eyes closed pretending to be asleep. Nigel's ponderous attempts at making as little noise as possible annoyed her intensely. He was so anxious to please her all the time that she wanted to crack a whip over his head and make him perform like that dancing bear.

They'd met when she was working as a typist in the London offices of an international construction company that employed him as a site manager. He came in one afternoon, tanned like an Arab, fresh from a big project in the Gulf.

God help me, she remembered, sitting up in bed and reaching for her hidden cigarettes – which Nigel did not know she still smoked – *I thought he was glamorous!*

The cigarette, a Benson and Hedges out of a filtered tin which was meant to keep them fresh but didn't, lightened her mood and a smile crossed her lips as she remembered that she had something special to look forward to. Jean-Paul was coming this afternoon.

When the cigarette was stubbed out, she lay back, pulled up the cover and slept again, dreaming of Jean-Paul.

Nigel sang as he drove through semi-deserted streets. He stared around as he went because there was always something going on in Bombay so the streets were never entirely deserted. When he got to the thickly populated district near the cotton mills, his gaiety left him and he sobered up because he had to overtake a sad little procession. A body was being borne to the burning ghat by a quartet of running men. Lying in her best sari on the rough stretcher which they carried on their shoulders was a woman with a single garland of marigolds and silver tinsel piled on her chest. He could see her sharp nose pointing up towards the lightening sky and her hair was still dark and lustrous in the shine of his headlights. She wasn't old ... perhaps she'd died in child-birth and one of the men carrying her was her husband.

The thought grabbed his tender heart like a cruel fist and almost made him cry out loud, "Dear God, don't let Bernice die." If she died he'd want to die as well. He was far more concerned about her than about any baby. In fact if they never had a child it wouldn't matter a jot to him, but she wanted one so much...

Dawn was breaking when he reached the construction site and his Pathan labourers were wandering aimlessly about as all Indians seemed to do early in the morning. He tooted his horn and heads turned towards him. Then arms were raised in salute and voices rang out in greeting. They liked him and he liked them. He didn't think he'd ever worked with a gang of men he'd liked and respected more.

They were as agile as monkeys and now that the scaffolding had gone up on the towering jetty, he marvelled daily at their fearless dexterity and head for height. Bare-footed they climbed along swaying bamboo struts barely thicker than a suburban garden's clothes pole, many feet off the ground or over the sea, without safety harnesses or helmets. They were utterly fearless, and so far, thank God, there had been no serious accidents.

He'd heard that the skyscrapers of New York were built by Red Indian steel constructors and he was sure that his Pathans could equal these legendary men any day of the week. He knew too that they took their sexual pleasure with boys and a number of nubile youths ran flirtatiously to and fro around their camp, but that didn't bother Nigel. Live and let live, was his motto.

Grinning, he climbed out of the car, eager to start another day, as the malik – the head-man of the gang – came striding towards him. This man, Mehmet Ali Khan, was well over six feet tall, and had eyes as green as emeralds. Adding drama to his magnificent appearance was his full beard, dyed a brilliant shade of henna red to show that he'd completed the pilgrimage to Mecca.

"What today, sahib?" he asked. His English was fragmentary but good enough for them to communicate. In fact he was more fluent in French than in English because at one time in his life he'd worked on dhows sailing to and from the French

210

outpost in Djibouti where dejected legionnaires filled the cafes and tired whores in black patrolled the streets.

Nigel squinted his eyes at the growing structure of the harbour wall towering above them. "Keep on building," he said. "Some men are coming to investigate another area of sea bed for the last bit of the jetty. The diver's going down this morning."

"The Frenchman?" asked Mehmet Ali.

"Yes, I expect it'll be Jean-Paul who goes down. The other chap's in hospital with dysentry," said Nigel.

Mehmet Ali shrugged. He didn't like Jean-Paul and made no secret of how he felt. Because of a sense of loyalty to his friend, Nigel would never discuss the divers with the Pathans so he did not know the exact reason for Mehmet Ali's dislike. Perhaps, he thought, it was the way Jean-Paul swaggered around, arrogantly flaunting his masculinity in his brief bathing trunks; or perhaps it was the scornful way he looked at the workmen. From the Frenchman's conversation, Nigel knew he disdained homosexuals and had branded all the Pathans as disgusting deviants.

If he was to be honest, Jean-Paul was not exactly Nigel's cup of tea either, for he obviously thought of himself as a lady-killer, and sized up each woman he met as if assessing her potential in bed. Also, he and

Nigel could barely talk to each other because Jean-Paul seemed to know less English when talking to him than with anyone else. But Bernice liked him and that was enough for her husband to be friendly to her protégé.

"It's so wonderful to have someone to speak French with," she had enthused to Nigel when they first met the diver. "My French has been getting so rusty and I'm going to take this opportunity to sharpen it up. Besides, the poor boy's so lonely and homesick. He misses his mother and he knows no one out here. That terrible crowd of Ben's at the rugby club are not his sort at all ... he's too sophisticated and intelligent for them."

So, on behalf of Bernice's linguistic skills, Nigel sat for night after night and weekend after weekend listening to his wife prattling incomprehensibly to the young man. He did not doubt that her grasp of the language was excellent because Jean-Paul seemed to know exactly what she was saying and answered with great enthusiasm.

One of the first things Nigel did when he arrived on site every morning was to visit his miniature zoo. He'd organised a little stockade with rough kennels where he kept his pye-dog and her puppy as well as several other motherless pups, baby monkeys and some terrified feral cats that he picked up on his journeys to and from work. He'd have kept the bear there too but the Pathans persuaded him against that.

Yusuf, a simple-minded boy from the workmen's camp, who had been delegated to feed and clean out the animals, was sitting by the gate with the fluffy white puppy clutched lovingly to his chest when Nigel appeared.

"You good man, sahib," he said and beamed delightedly. Nigel's heart was touched. He put his hand in his pocket and fished out a five-anna piece which he handed to Yusuf. It was received with rapture and the boy began to bend down over and over again like an automaton, touching his forehead to the ground in front of Nigel's feet and murmuring blessings.

"You are my mother and my father," he chanted over and over again. Nigel was embarrassed and backed away.

Work went on till about ten o'clock in the morning when a distant whirring sound was heard from beyond the headland. Soon a red rubber dinghy, its bow riding high out of the water because of the thrust of its powerful engine, came roaring into the stretch of water alongside the site.

Three men climbed out at a floating platform on which an air-pumping unit was set up and Jean-Paul got out of the dinghy, turning to wave at Nigel who stood with his hands on his hips staring across the water. He watched a while longer and saw the Frenchman being prepared for the dive. Dressed up in his heavy diver's suit with the metal helmet on his head, he looked like an alien from another planet. With a huge splash he was let down into the water and Nigel turned away.

The diving went on for about an hour and a half with Jean-Paul bobbing up from time to time to report his findings and receive more instructions. When the men were satisfied, the dinghy headed for the shore. The engine was switched off at the end of a line of planks that made a walkway on to the land and Jean-Paul, in shorts and a shirt, strolled up to Nigel.

"Bonjour, mon ami," he said with a flashing grin, almost as if he was being mocking.

"Hello," replied Nigel. "Good day's work?"

"Yes, we 'ave finished. Now I go back to the city ... it is easier on water, much queeker."

Nigel nodded. "It must be. It takes me over an hour to get back to the hotel at night, more if I hit the busy time."

Jean-Paul shrugged as if to say, *That's your hard luck.*

Nigel went on trying to be matey. "So it's off to Breach Candy now, is it, for you?" he said, gesturing towards the sun that was beating down from an aquamarine sky. The other man's deep tan testified to hours of sun worshipping.

"The 'ospital?" Jean-Paul furrowed his brow.

"No, no, the swimming pool." Nigel made swimming motions with his arms.

Jean-Paul laughed, "Perhaps, but I have a lady to see first." Then, after nudging Nigel meaningfully in the ribs, he left, reboarded the dinghy where his colleagues were waiting and they roared off leaving a wake of furiously surging water behind them.

About half-past three, fresh from the library and feeling dejected about her findings in the medical textbook, Dee parked her car outside the Ritz. She had been on her way to the Gym to wait for Ben to meet her at half-past five but then she remembered her resolution to play Scrabble with Bernice as a recompense for being horrid to the PGs.

Three thirty-three, she thought, looking at her watch, that's just about the time Bernice used to wake up and come out on to the verandah rattling that bag of tiles. She'll be ready for a game.

Dodging the sinister-looking old fortune teller who always lurked at the hotel's main door and who filled her with terror, she ran inside and asked the desk clerk which was Mrs Budgeon's room.

He recognised her and smiled. "Number eighty-five," he said. "Tea is going up with room service now. Go up in the lift with him."

She and a silent boy waiter in a white uniform, carrying a napkin-covered silver tray, shared the lift and when it stopped, the door of room number eighty-five was facing them. Dee stood behind the waiter as he rapped on it. "Tea," he shouted and there were sounds of someone shooting back the bolts.

The door was swung open and they were confronted by Jean-Paul looking like a bronzed Greek god with only a white towel knotted round his slim hips.

For what seemed an eternity Dee and he stared at each other over the waiter's shoulder till from the room behind came Bernice's voice. "If it's room service with *the, mon cher*, tell him to bring it in."

Jean-Paul stepped back without saying anything but Dee stood still in the corridor as if frozen to the spot. Over his magnificently muscled shoulder she saw Bernice appear, in her familiar cotton housecoat and with her hair flowing down to her shoulders. Through the open inner door she caught a glimpse of a dishevelled bed and her heart seemed to solidify like stone.

"I'm so sorry," she gabbled. "I just dropped in to have a game of Scrabble with

Bernice ... I didn't know she was busy."

She backed away towards the lift door, still talking stupidly. The words "sorry" and "Scrabble" seemed to fall out of her mouth like olive stones.

Jean-Paul disappeared and Bernice filled the door frame. *Will that bloody lift never come?* thought Dee, pressing her finger frantically on the button. Amazingly Bernice was smiling.

"How kind of you," she enthused. "Do come in. Jean-Paul dropped in to have a chat with me and asked if he could have a shower before he left ... it's so hot out today, isn't it, and he's been working. He's just leaving."

The lift door creaked open at Dee's back. She stepped inside, still gabbling, "Sorry to have called without an appointment. I'll come again ... goodbye."

She descended to the ground floor in total confusion.

She was sitting in the Gym, with several unopened copies of *Country Life* on the table in front of her, when Ben arrived. He was surprised at how flustered and out of sorts she looked.

"Are you OK?" he asked.

"Yes, oh yes," she hurried to say. She couldn't tell him about Bernice and Jean-Paul. She couldn't bring herself to say, "Nigel's being cuckolded" *After all, I might be jumping to conclusions. I might be wrong*, she told herself – but she knew perfectly well that she wasn't.

While Dee and Ben were driving home, Anne was sitting on her bed watching her husband storm up and down the floor, frantically punching one fist into the palm of his other hand and cursing. From the bathroom at the far end of the room came the sounds of splashing as the ayah washed Liza and prepared her for bed.

"The bastards, the bastards," cursed Bill. "I told them what they could do with their job. I said, all right, I'll take the tickets and go. I'm not working out any notice. You can run your bloody plant on your own. See how they like that. They don't know a spanner from a claw hammer. Bloody useless, all of them ... We can get our stuff packed up over the weekend and fly on Tuesday."

Her eyes followed him as he stamped to and fro. "Where are we going?" she asked in a small voice.

He stopped in the middle of the floor and stared at her. "Well, there's no point going home, is there? There's nothing for us there. I thought Australia. I asked for tickets to Sydney."

"Without asking me?" Her face was white and set.

"I couldn't ask you, could I? They called me in and fired me, just like that. You didn't expect me to take that, did you? I said that I'd leave at once and go to Australia."

"I don't know anyone in Australia," she said.

"Neither do I. But you didn't know anybody here when you first arrived either."

She said nothing, just kept on looking at him in an unblinking way that he found very unsettling. "Christ, what's wrong with you? You knew we were going soon. All we've got to do is put a few things into suitcases and push off. We'll close the door behind us and go. My money's being sent on to Sydney, the furniture is the company's and so's the car."

She looked around the spartan room. There was nothing in the whole flat she wanted to take with her. *Four years with nothing to show for them*, she thought.

"I don't think I want to go to Australia," she said.

He leaned towards her, his face reddening, and shouted, "You've no bloody choice. When I go there'll be no money and no place for you to live. You'd better get packing."

She leaned back against the pillows and closed her eyes. "You do the packing. You've done everything else," she said. One of her headaches was starting and she felt as if a metal band round her temples was being steadily tightened.

Making contact with the outside world was frustratingly difficult in India. When Ajay's phone rang in the Paraworld office as the last of the staff were leaving in the evening, he grabbed it, thinking it was his wife who frequently telephoned to remind him of errands he must do before coming home.

"Hah!" he snorted into it and then his entire manner changed because through a blast of static he heard an American voice. It was the vice-president to whom he had written his complaints about Stevie.

The man at the other end was brief. They were summoning Stevie home. Ajay was not to be bothered with him any longer. "Buy him an air ticket," he was told. Was Stevie there to give some idea of when he might be leaving?

Ajay looked around the empty office. There was no sign of Stevie of course. "The office is closed," he said.

"Closed? You mean it's not open yet?"

"No, it's closed. It's after six p.m. here."

"Oh sure, I forgot. Tell him to ring his uncle, then." The caller hung up.

Even though he was one of the few people in Bombay lucky enough to have a tele-phone in his flat, after a visit from Ajay,

Stevie spent most of the evening in frustration trying to call New York.

Eventually he managed to book a slot for seven o'clock the next morning and when it came through he asked Monica to go and have a bath while he shut himself in the bedroom in order to shout at his uncle over an indistinct and hollow-sounding line.

When she judged the call was over she came out again fully dressed and made up to find him looking very cheerful.

"Well, that's it, Mon. If everything goes to plan, I'll be back in the States by the end of the week," he told her.

She sat down on a chair beside a little table on which lay an open copy of the latest *Eve's Weekly* and tried to hide the deep disquiet this announcement caused her.

"So soon?" she asked, sounding very calm and offhand as she flipped over the pages.

"Yeah, probably. Maybe at the weekend. It all depends."

Of course, she thought, *he's made no commitment of any kind to me, and he's never told me any lies like Bob did.* She had no reason to reproach him.

"Is there trouble at home?" she asked. Though they'd been together for nearly two months she knew little about his family or background apart from the fact that his only living relative seemed to be his uncle.

"Not really. Not any more than usual. It's

221

just that my job here's almost over – with any luck," he said.

There was no reply she could make to that but she privately thought that if his work was finished he hadn't exerted himself in any way that she'd ever seen. She could almost count on two hands the number of whole days he'd spent in his office. That Ajay man seemed to run the whole show.

He walked across the room and hugged her. "Don't worry, Mon. I haven't forgotten about you. I'll make arrangements for you. If you want entry into America, I'll fix it. My uncle's got friends in high places."

She shook her head and kept on looking down at the magazine. It was open at the horoscope page, she noticed wryly. "I can't leave my mother. She's not going to get any better but it might drag on for some time yet. I'll only leave if – I mean when – she dies."

He understood completely. "If it was my mother I'd do the same," he said in a tight voice. "I wish I'd had the chance."

"When you leave I'll go to Chembur, to Fifi's. The last time I saw Dr Bali he told me he thought Mama won't last till Christmas. He said that she's going to need drugs to kill the pain too." There was a crack in her voice that showed her sorrow and terror of what lay ahead.

He reached out and took her hand. His

grasp was the grasp of sympathy and friendship, not of passion. "Don't worry about the
drugs. I'll buy as much as you think you'll
need before I go and I'll put money in the
bank for you in case it's not enough, and for
everything else."

"You don't need to. We'll manage. Fifi's
glad to be in contact with my mother again
and she'll help me."

"Take my money. I've got plenty – and
anyway, I owe you a lot," said Stevie
earnestly. "It was lucky for me that we met
because you've backed me up to the hilt,
and you know what I mean. I'm sorry it
couldn't be anything else, Mon, but I'm not
looking for that ... I can't feel enough."

She stared up at him now with her eyes
swimming. "I understand, but this has been
a good time for me. I'll never forget it – or
you."

"Will you help me finish things up before
I go?" he asked, leaning forward.

"Of course," she said, wondering what
sort of things he was referring to. She did
not have long to speculate.

"Listen," he said and started to talk.

He spoke for over an hour and when he
finished she was looking at him with
mingled fear and admiration on her face.

"You don't have to help if you don't want
to or if you're afraid," he said.

She shook her head. "I want to help,"

she told him.

It was noon before they were ready to leave the flat and start making their arrangements, bustling about purposefully, not speaking much because their heads were full of the things that had to be done. It was best for them to go out separately, they decided, because they'd get more done that way.

"After I've fixed things up at the office, I'll arrange to get the medicine for your mother," Stevie said.

"And I'll go to Chembur," she told him.

On her way to the golf course, she remembered her promise to Dee and stopped the taxi at the bakery in Chembur village. When she strutted in, magnificent on her high heels, to order forty double rotis – the word for the large-pored, stodgy loaves that passed for English-style bread in India – the baker, a large, fat, very black and very sweaty man goggled at her. "Forty? When for?"

"Tomorrow evening. They've to be delivered to the English people in the Gulmohurs, next door to Raj Kapoor."

He nodded, impressed. "I know where it is," he said. Everyone knew where the famous Raj lived.

She paid for the bread and got back into the taxi, feeling the eyes of half the village street boring into her back.

The house on the golf course looked like a

safe haven as she drove up. Its door and windows stood open to the breeze and the dog's nose could be seen jutting out of its kennel but it stayed silent as if out of consideration for the sick woman upstairs.

Fifi was looking magnificent. Having something to fill her mind and someone to care for brought out the best in her. She spoke to Monica in a whisper, holding on to her arm at the foot of the stairs. "You'll find her a bit vague maybe but she's quieter today. I gave her something and there's not so much pain. The priest came yesterday but she's not ready for him yet so I sent him away."

Monica nodded. "I'm getting some very strong medicine for her. With luck we'll bring it tomorrow. Do you think you'd be able to inject her? It's morphia and it acts quicker that way."

"Of course. I won't hurt her," said Fifi proudly.

Bernadette was lying beneath a vast white cotton crocheted coverlet that had been made by Carole, who was surprisingly skilled with her hands. So much had the sick woman shrunk and dwindled through the ravages of her illness that the hump she made in the bed was hardly visible, but her eyes were still vividly alive and she was staring expectantly at the door when Monica tiptoed in.

"Star of my heart," she whispered. "I've been thinking about you. I've been praying that kind man will marry you and take you to America."

Monica lied. "Yes, he's leaving soon and he's going to take me with him. We're flying out just after Christmas so you'd better be well by then or I won't be able to go."

Bernadette smiled faintly. "I think everything will be all right by that time. Where in America will you be living?"

"In New York."

Bernadette had always been an ardent fan of the movies and remembered every one she'd ever seen. She sighed. "Oh, New York. Central Park and all those big tall buildings – the Empire State Building, Wall Street! And wonderful department stores. I can see you in a long fur coat like the one Elizabeth Taylor wore in *Butterfield 8*. We went together to see it, do you remember? I wonder if it will be snowing like in *Holiday Inn* when you get there. I've never seen snow."

"I remember *Holiday Inn*," said Monica, biting back tears. *I'll get a long fur coat – a mink coat – one day, just for my mother's sake,* she silently swore.

"How do you feel today?" she asked, kneeling by the bed.

"Tired. But Fifi is very good. She comes and helps me in the night if I feel pain. She rubs my back and last night she gave me a little bit of opium ... Then I had the most wonderful dream about swimming in the ocean. She bought it from a woman in the village."

Monica looked over her shoulder at her aunt who was standing in the doorway listening. "That's kind," she said. "It must have cost a lot, though. Don't either of you worry. I'm getting you some stronger medicine that will take your pain away completely."

Bernadette closed her eyes. "You are a blessing to me," she whispered. "You've been a blessing every hour of every day since you were born."

Monica laid her head down on the bed and sobbed. "I love you, I don't want you to leave me. You must get better."

Now it was Bernadette's turn to solace her. Seeing their dark heads huddling together, Fifi turned slowly away and walked down the stairs. They needed and wanted no one else at that moment.

Stevie didn't turn up to fetch her so it was midnight before she returned to the penthouse on Malabar Hill where she found him in the sitting room, with his feet up on the cream-coloured couch and a glass of whisky on a side table. What stopped her in her tracks was the fact that his left arm was tied up in a sling.

She pointed to it. "What happened?"

"I went to Breach Candy hospital and that young Indian doctor with the lisp bandaged it for me."

"Is it cut?"

"No, I said I'd tripped and dislocated it or something."

"Does it hurt very much?"

He laughed. "Not really. It's OK. Sit down, Mon, and have a whisky. You look exhausted. This bad arm of mine isn't going to hold me up in any way."

Fourteen

Friday began at dawn for Dee who opened her eyes as the sun was rising and felt a mixture of panic and anxiety sweep over her.

For a moment she wondered what else could be worrying her other than the ever-present anxiety of the party. Then she remembered Bernice and Jean-Paul ... What still stuck in her mind was Bernice's incredible coolness, the way she'd smiled as if she and Dee were in some way complicit. She'd said nothing to Ben about calling on Bernice in the Ritz, preferring to mull it over in her mind for a while before she spoke about it as she did with most problems.

They were probably quite innocent; I must have jumped to the wrong conclusion. I've a suspicious mind, she told herself. She didn't want to believe anything else because she couldn't bear the thought of the innocent and trusting Nigel being so deceived.

She rubbed her fists into her eyes as if to

eradicate the memory of what she'd seen and gave herself up to her main worry. *Oh God, tomorrow's party day.*

She was terrified of letting Ben – and the house – down. This had to be the party to end all parties in the Gulmohurs.

He lay deeply asleep by her side. *If I'm worrying, why shouldn't he be doing the same?* she thought but managed to resist the temptation to nudge him awake.

Mentally she ticked off her action list. The cutlery, crockery and glasses were all borrowed and stacked up in the kitchen; extra help had been called in for the servants; the music was under control and loops of coloured light bulbs had been strung through the branches of the trees. Ice for cooling the beer bottles still had to be collected but that could not be done till tomorrow. Monica had promised to order the bread.

Both of the bathrooms had to be thoroughly cleaned with fresh towels and soap put out ... vases of flowers must be arranged in the sitting room and candles put on the trestle table that held the buffet and the little oil lamps along the window ledges ... On and on her mind ran, deliberately avoiding the major concern – food.

Disquiet seized her when she thought about that, but she reassured herself. *Don't worry, you're not trying anything spectacular, it's just ordinary party grub.* Yet the anxiety niggled on.

It had to be Pasco that was causing it. He'd been acting so peculiarly recently, ever since he heard they were leaving. Ben had found Birbal and the boy Jacob permanent jobs on his construction gang and Ali was to go with Ben and Dee, but they knew they would not be able to afford Pasco as well, so they'd asked all their friends if anyone needed a first-class cook. Eventually they had found him a job with an Australian couple in Pali Hill for more money a month than he was earning at the moment. They thought they'd played fair with him – but now she wondered if he shared that opinion. What else did he expect, she wondered?

As the light grew stronger she noticed there was a gap between the curtains through which she could see a section of the garden – the twisting path that led to the well, overhung by the leafy branches of neem trees, an archway heavy with mauve bougainvillaea, and a brilliant corner of the canna bed. As she gazed out, Birbal appeared, crossing the grass and dragging his green hose behind him. He was by far the blackest person she'd ever seen for his skin shone like an overripe blackberry with a lovely purplish sheen that reminded her of shot silk. His head was completely shaved except for a long, thin pigtail of black hair that straggled down to his shoulders from the crown of his head.

The pigtail was to be used by the gods to haul him up into a higher caste when he died because he was from a very low caste who had no expectation of salvation otherwise, she'd been told by a disdainful Mohammed before he departed from the household. The gradations of society in India never ceased to amaze Dee and she was horrified to realise that as far as all the people around him were concerned, sweet-natured, innocent Birbal was the lowest of the low.

He came from a very remote area of Bihar and the language he spoke was not understood by any of the other servants. He could only talk to them in fragmentary Hindi, about as much as Dee herself could speak. When she had first arrived and asked him questions about the flowers in the garden, they had to be relayed through Mohammed who had been in charge of the household. She had seen the gardener's puzzlement by the way his brow sank down over his worried eyes and he grunted out a few monosyllables in reply. Yet she liked him best of all the servants because he was her most constant companion. With him, however, she was in the same frustrating position that she was in with the buffalo camp women – longing to communicate but unable to breach the barrier that divided them. They were isolated from each other by lack of language but she wished she could ask where he came from, what his childhood had been like, what he believed in. Did he have a family back in his village?

When she lay reading in her homemade hammock or sunbathed beneath the trees, Birbal would be busying himself around her, watering, hoeing, nipping dead heads off the flowers. Every now and again he'd wordlessly present her with a perfect flower, and once a dead, very green, tree snake, as a sort of trophy. She felt a transference of unspoken friendship between them.

I'll miss you, Birbal. I'll never forget you, she thought as she lay in bed and watched the squat little mali in his white dhoti watering the lawn in the early dawn. Tears pricked her eyes as she contemplated leaving this paradise. Not only would she never forget Birbal, she'd forever remember the Gulmohurs as the perfect house, a place of ideal happiness. It was their Shangri-La and in a way she was frightened to leave it for who knew what waited outside in the other world?

She turned and lay on her other side, tearfully pressing her face into the pillow. Above her head the ceiling fan slowly turned, ruffling the sheet that covered her. In the hot weather she would be wet with sweat even so early in the day, but now it was cool and pleasant, so cool that goose-pimples rose on her back because of the slight chill.

When she padded through to the bathroom, the bath was already full of bottles of beer, waiting for the ice, so she stepped into the shower and stood beneath its big rose, letting water run down over her head, drip off her breasts and make runnels over her swelling belly. She wondered if the baby shared her delight in the warm, flowing deluge and pressed her hands against her abdomen, trying to make contact with the hidden person within her.

Her time beneath the shower calmed and cheered her and she was happily humming when she went back to the bedroom to dress. As she squeezed past the end of the bed, Ben sat up and grabbed the end of the big towel she'd wrapped round her body and pulled it off. "Come and lie down here beside me," he said, patting the mattress and throwing off the sheet to reveal his erection.

She laughed and hopped in beside him. "You are a randy old so-and-so," she told him, putting her face against his shoulder and smelling the wonderful dry, musky smell that always turned her on.

When they'd made love, she felt able to tell him about her visit to the hotel and her suspicions about Bernice and Jean-Paul.

He lay silently listening and thinking, but after a bit he said, "Shit! What a bitch."

"It's maybe not as bad as I think," she said. "It could have been quite innocent. Bernice slopped around all day in her housecoat too when she lived here..."

"Aw, come on," said Ben, who had no doubts. "They're at it. That Jean-Paul would screw a hole in a wall and Bernice's been making cow's eyes at him for weeks."

"I hope Nigel never finds out," said Dee.

"Well we're not going to tell him and I bet she isn't either," said Ben. "What I hope is that the kid she's carrying isn't half French."

Dee sat up and agreed, "God, I hope not too. I do hope it's really Nigel's."

"Well, let's also hope for his sake then that it's born with a broken nose and cauliflower ears," laughed Ben. Their day had begun.

It turned out to be a good one and some of Dee's anxieties about provisioning the party were solved because immediately after breakfast Divali presents started coming in from Ben's contractors.

In the India of the Raj, when a European man was in a position of influence and able to give out contracts, preferments or assignments, it had been generally expected that his goodwill could be won by gifts or, more accurately, bribes. This system dated back to the days of Warren Hastings and Robert Clive when nabobs lined their pockets

and made vast fortunes by the fruits of privilege and bribery.

Some of the senior Europeans still in Bombay in the 1950s made no bones about looking forward to seasonal bounties – at Christmas and Divali in particular. A few were blatantly greedy and would accept nothing less than wads of money or jewellery, but Ben refused to be bribed and scorned those who were.

For the first couple of years of their marriage, no one had bothered to bribe him anyway because he was too junior and had no influence to wield, but since his career had begun to take off and he had been given his own construction sites to run, he was attracting more attention. When approaches were made to him, he let it be known that he was not for buying. He'd accept small seasonal gifts because to send them back would be an insult – but no money, nothing big or valuable.

Last Christmas they'd received a bottle of whisky, some flowers and a bundle of yellow dusters which, for some reason, were received with rapture by the servants. Since then Ben's influence had obviously grown even greater because while Dee was sitting at breakfast, an enormous cornucopia of fruit – oranges, apples, guavas, grapes, pineapples and limes – arrived, and was swiftly followed by a huge basket of nuts, a hamper

of mangoes, and several bouquets of flowers.

During the course of the morning more gifts came rolling in – three bottles of whisky, even more fruit and mangoes, three dozen eggs, and a huge pink and silver cardboard box that turned out to be full of sickly milk and sugar based Indian sweetmeats. At about eleven o'clock a man came up the lane on a bicycle with a large basket full of fireworks, rockets and jumping jacks with which to celebrate the auspicious night to come.

What was more disturbing, however, was the delivery of three dejected-looking hens which Birbal tied to a tree at the kitchen door with strings round their legs.

"What on earth can we do with those?" asked Dee when she saw them.

"Eat them, memsahib," said a delighted Ali.

When the full array of Divali bribes was assembled, Dee realised that they provided part of the solution for her catering problems. Now she needn't commission Pasco to buy any more fruit, eggs or nuts because they had enough to see them through the party and for several days after as well.

When she went into the kitchen with the cookbook money she saw at once that Pasco had also realised the significance of the gifts. He was visibly sneering as she said, "We won't be needing so many provisions now, so I've kept back two hundred rupees. Here's five hundred. That should be more than enough to buy everything else we need for the party."

He took the money with bad grace. It was obvious that she'd done him out of a good profit from his shopping expedition.

Monica heard Stevie groaning in his sleep early in the morning. Anxious, she nudged him and said, "Are you all right? Are you ill?"

He opened his eye and stared at her as if he had no idea who she was. "Oh, Mon, yeah, sorry. Was I shouting?"

"You were moaning. I thought you were ill."

"I'm not ill. I'm a bit anxious, that's all."

She put a cool hand on his cheek. "About tomorrow, you mean? Don't worry. Everything's going to be all right. Go back to sleep, it's not six o'clock yet."

He turned on to his side and drifted off to sleep again. She lay awake for a little while and then very quietly got up, dressed and went off to church. Outside the flat she hailed a taxi and told the driver to take her to Colaba. She was feeling very positive, probably more positive and sure of herself than she'd ever been, and wanted to make her confession to the priest in the church where she'd worshipped all her life.

Sunlight was slanting over the paved floor when she pushed open the church door. The confession box smelled of cigarettes – Charminar, a cheap Indian brand. The priest had obviously been smoking them because when he slid back the grille, the smell became stronger. Today the voice from behind the screen was that of a lean-faced Spanish Jesuit who'd known her for years, and she was glad it was him.

Encouraged, she began to tell how worried she was about her mother's approaching death and whether she would be able to cope afterwards. He listened in silence so she went on talking and heard herself saying, "I'm much happier now, father; I'm not pretending any longer. I know I'm neither English nor Indian – I'm half caste and proud of it. I've stopped being angry because some people look down on me ... I know there's a lot more important things in life than the colour of your skin."

When she finished, he sighed deeply and said, "I'm glad you are more secure in yourself. I'm glad you've accepted that in God's eyes all people are equal, and as far as the future goes, you must be guided by your faith and your conscience. In your heart you know what is right and what is wrong. I will pray for you and for your mother ... I will pray that she has a peaceful death and is welcomed by the saints in heaven."

Then he handed out a conventional penance – so many Hail Marys – and told her to go in peace.

She felt more resigned to what lay before her when she stepped out of the church. The traffic was now much heavier and she walked slowly in the direction of the chawl where she still retained her mother's room. On the way she passed the tea-shop and saw old Maya sitting on the step, gazing blankly at the passing world.

"Maya," said Monica, "have you eaten yet today?"

The old woman looked up. Her black eyes, once sharp and lively, glittered with a bluish sheen that showed she was almost blind. In spite of that, however, she recognised Monica by her voice.

"I've had some tea. How is your mother, little one?" she asked.

"She's very ill. In fact she's dying. She's living with her sister in Chembur now," was the reply.

Maya shrugged. "We all die eventually. But when life is good we should enjoy it. You'll be sad when she goes but there's still a lot to enjoy ahead for you."

It sounded as if she was making a prophesy and, though the impassive old woman had always slightly scared Monica, she was even more encouraged and cheered by her now than she had been by the priest. As if to keep the gods of India on her side as well, she fished into her handbag and produced a twenty-rupee note which she handed to Maya. It was received with evident surprise but no extravagant gratitude.

"So much?" Maya asked, holding it close to her face. Five rupees would keep her in food for the best part of a week but twenty would last for a month.

"It's Divali," was Monica's reply as she turned to leave.

When she turned into the chawl, neighbouring women came running up to enquire after Bernadette who'd always been a general favourite. She told them the same as she had told Maya, that her mother was dying. There was no point glossing over the truth any longer because she'd stopped trying to convince herself that her mother's illness was not fatal. Her problem now was to come to terms with reality.

The room smelt stale after having been shut up unaired for so many days. She threw open the window and fetched a jug of water from the communal tap for the plants which were dying in their dry pots. Then she fluffed out the pillows and mattress and hung them over the verandah rail before she went back inside and found a battered old suitcase beneath the bed.

In it her mother kept official papers and

mementoes, a few fading, tattered black and white photographs, a baptismal certificate for Monica, yellowing birth certificates and the death certificate of her mother, Monica's grandmother.

Folded into Monica's birth certificate was a stiffly posed photograph of a proud-looking Indian soldier in a regimental uniform. There was not a doubt in her mind that this man was her father and she studied him with keen interest. He was tall, erect, proud and savage looking with pale-looking, glittering eyes and a stiffly waxed moustache. Even she could see the resemblance between herself and this nameless man who'd fathered her. The knowledge that he'd been a pure-bred Indian of ancient lineage and traditions, knowledge which once would have mortified her, now filled her with pride. It gave her roots.

Leafing through the other scraps of paper that summed up her mother's life, Monica wanted to weep at the sadness of it all. There was a baptismal certificate and a few school reports testifying to how clever her mother had been when attending Deolali cantonment school.

"A child of singular intelligence and sweetness," said one, written in a precise European hand and signed, "Stella Sinclair, Head Teacher".

Checking her mother's birth certificate,

Monica saw that she'd given birth to her only child when she was seventeen years old. Now she was dying at forty-two. So all Bernadette's hopes, her beauty, her sweet and cheerful nature had gained her nothing. Her life had been a struggle to survive, to keep herself out of the trough of misery and poverty that had swallowed up old Maya.

Monica closed the suitcase and said aloud, "That won't happen to me. I'm going to leave more than this behind me."

But she knew that her mother would be comforted if she took the suitcase to her now, so she closed it up and was carrying it tucked under her arm when she went out of the room and locked the door behind her.

The woman Miriam was waiting for her on the landing. "How is your mother?" she asked in a gentle voice.

"Very ill. She won't be back. I'll pay you what I owe you now but I won't be needing you any more. Thank you for what you did."

She passed over some more money which Miriam took with a gesture of gratitude and said, "I'm sorry. She is a good woman. I hope she is not in bad pain."

"That's under control. We have good medicine and my aunt is looking after her well."

"Will you be living in this room again? I

have a friend who would rent it if you aren't."

Monica frowned as if she was working things out, but then said, "I'll keep it for now; I might need it again soon. Keep an eye on it for me, will you?"

Miriam said, "My son lives down below and he'll watch it for you. Please give my best wishes to your mother. I hope she has an easy death."

With tears filling her eyes Monica walked down a little alley between two big houses and emerged on to Cuffe Parade.

Unknown to her, one of the houses she passed was Nirvana where the Connors lived and where Anne was taking breakfast with her daughter, sitting with her chin propped on her hand as she listened to the chattering child.

Who will you marry, I wonder, she thought. *If I don't like him, what will I do? Will I cut you out of my life completely? No, I couldn't do that, no matter who you chose.*

Liza was talking about a friend she'd made in the play group she attended. "Louisa says she's going home soon. Where's home? Isn't this home?" she said.

"She's probably going back to England," said Anne.

"Maybe I'll see her there," said Liza.

"You might, because we too will be going back soon."

She was spreading butter on Liza's toast when she heard Bill stumbling into the room behind her. Turning in her chair she saw that his eyes were bloodshot and swollen and there was a heavy stubble on his chin. He looked like a tramp.

"Daddy!" cried Liza. "When are we going home like Louisa?"

Bill stared at Anne. "You've been talking to her?"

"No, I didn't. She asked me the same question. Her friend's going home, you see."

He said to his daughter. "Maybe you'd like to go to Australia. Where the kangaroos live."

She had a well-loved fluffy toy kangaroo and clasped her little hands in delight. "Kangaroos! Real ones. I want one of them."

Bill sat down beside Anne and said in a reasonable voice, "It would be best if we went to Australia. A new start and all that. We'll have enough money to set ourselves up comfortably. I've got a stack of cash hidden away by now..."

Her heart sank.

Australia was the other side of the world, and stranded out there she'd never see her family again. Another thought struck her – if she went to Australia with Bill, she'd never get away from him.

But it was necessary to dissemble so she smiled and said, "They say it's a lovely country and perfect for children ... all that sunshine and swimming."

Inside, however, she was not smiling for she felt as if the gates of a cage were closing round her. She was quite unaware that for a few moments her consciousness shut down and she sat staring out of the window at the sea like a woman in a trance.

When she came to, she felt as if she'd been on a distant voyage and Bill was saying, "You never listen to a thing I say, do you?"

"What did you say?" she asked.

"I said we'll clear out after the Carmichaels' party. There's nothing to keep us here, is there?"

"Can I tell Dee we're going?" she asked.

"No, keep it to yourself. I don't want people coming round here with bills – the petrol station and the grocer, that sort of stuff. If the servants get to hear we're clearing out they'll spread the word."

Like a lot of other Europeans in Bombay, Bill preferred to live on credit, running accounts on for months at a time. Anne frowned. "But they'll see us packing the suitcases."

"No they won't, because we'll do it all at the last moment and only take one case each. They'll think we're going away for a few days – that's what we'll tell them anyway. There's nothing here that's so special that you can't live without it, is there?"

She looked around. The only thing in the house that meant anything to her was her child.

Fifteen

The day of the party

When they were first married it had amused Ben Carmichael that his new wife would look out of the bedroom window every morning and exclaim, "Look at that sky! It's going to be a lovely day."

Eventually, slightly exasperated, he said to her, "It's always a lovely day here except during the monsoon and then it rains all the time." So she stopped saying it but never stopped thinking it. Early mornings at the Gulmohurs, when the sky was a brain-piercing shade of blue and there wasn't a cloud in sight, never ceased to fill her with a feeling of wondering disbelief. She was half afraid that the expanse of blue above her would suddenly cloud over.

That summed up the basic difference between her and Ben, she thought. He totally accepted that, except during the monsoon, it was always going to be glorious weather; he believed that things would always be

248

wonderful. She was more doubting and had to keep on mentally pinching herself.

Looking out of the window on the morning of the party she bit back her naïve old comment because she knew he thought it stupid, but that did not stop her gazing out at a sparkling world with delighted amazement. It *was* going to be a beautiful day.

Ben had got up before her and was already running about in a black and yellow rugby shirt and the baggy, fraying old khaki shorts that he wouldn't allow her to give away because he loved them so much.

"I'm off to fetch the ice," he called, grabbing a hundred-rupee note from Dee's drawer and dangling the car keys from one finger before running into the garden. He liked having definite things to do and was always bursting with energy. She was sure he'd go on racing around like that till he was ninety and would outlive her by years and years for already she was beginning to slow down and fancied a more sedentary life. *Perhaps that's only because I'm pregnant, though*, she told herself.

When Ben disappeared she decided to conserve her energy so she climbed back into bed, took up *The Pickwick Papers* again and decided to stay out of the way till the ice arrived. When that happened he'd be sure to think of something for her to do. She often told him that he couldn't carry out the simplest job – not even hanging a picture – without a coolie and the coolie was usually her. With a happy sigh, she turned over a page of her book and began to read about the downfall of Mr Jingle.

In other flats and houses scattered throughout the city of Bombay, under the same clear sky, other guests at the party were preparing for their day and looking forward to the evening.

On Apollo Bunder, in a "chummery", a large flat shared by four bachelors who worked for Lloyds Bank, an argument was going on over the breakfast table about how much drink should be taken to the party. The four men, Colin, Alexander, Roy and David, couldn't decide whether three or four bottles of gin would see them through the night because they expected that the festivities would last till dawn – and maybe even into the next day. In the end they decided to take a bottle each.

Colin, the most senior of the four, began marking the labels of gin bottles with their names because that was the sensible thing to do when going to a BYOB party. There were always some unscrupulous people who only took half-bottles which they drank up quickly and then started on other people's. Cautious guests marked their bottles and made sure that the servant in charge of the drink knew which were theirs.

"Just in case a bottle each isn't enough, you'd better fill hip flasks as well," said Colin, writing away with red ink in enormous capital letters.

In a luxury flat in a 1930s building on Marine Drive, Malcolm, a senior employee of a shipping company, was filling up an almost empty gin bottle with water from the bathroom tap before marking it with his name. This was partly parsimony and partly an attempt to prevent his alcoholic wife, Nora, from getting so drunk that she would make an exhibition of herself again. Nora's favourite party trick was to strip naked and try to perform a belly dance.

"I'm a senior man now, darling," Malcolm always reminded her before they went out. "Belly dancing is all right for chokras' wives but not for a burrah sahib's."

Sober, she agreed with him, of course, but forgot after a she'd had a bit to drink. He didn't think she'd tumble to his watering trick because she always drank her gin in Coca-Cola and was likely to be more than half drunk by the time they got to the party and unable to taste anything properly.

He had his own party drink – whisky – in a hip flask and didn't care that the tap water which his wife would be swilling down in her innocuous gin was teeming with amoebae and germs. Maybe she'd get something awful – with any luck.

In a less grand, dark and gloomy ground floor flat on Warden Road, Philip, a junior employee of an insurance company, was chatting pleasantly to his wife, dark-haired Pammie, about the party and discussing who would be likely to be there.

"It's a pity the Carmichaels are leaving that lovely house," she said. "We've been at some super parties there, haven't we?"

"We have indeed," he agreed, smiling at her and wondering who she would seduce tonight. They had a peculiar marriage. Both of them were rampantly unfaithful and predatory, but they stayed married because on the morning after any debauch, like conspirators, they titillated each other with graphic details about their conquests.

In his doting parents' ramshackle house at the end of Grant Road, Dadi, the twenty-one-year-old son of a Parsee diamond merchant whose safes contained jewels worth several maharajah's fortunes, was hoping that tonight would be the night he lost his virginity. He'd heard wonderful stories from Ben and Guy about the bacchanalian goings-on at their parties, and was trying to talk himself into a state of sufficient confidence to make a pass at one of the rapacious married ladies, who, he'd also heard, were as eager for an adventure as he was himself.

After a rugby match a few months ago, he'd mentioned his eagerness to lose his virginity to Guy and said, "I don't know what to say to a woman. I don't know how to bring the subject up."

Guy laughed and replied, "All you have to say is 'fancy a fuck'? You'll get a few slaps on the face but more acceptances, especially out here."

Dadi stood looking at himself in his bedroom mirror and rehearsing this chat-up line. Did you shrug your shoulders casually when you said it, he wondered? Or did you look intense? He tried both ways, acting them out in the mirror, and decided that the casual way was best.

By this time it was nearly eleven o'clock and in the Gulmohurs Ben was unloading the ice from the boot of his car. Two huge blocks, wrapped in sacking, were man-handled into the bathroom by him and the servants. Eventually he appeared on the verandah where his wife was sitting and, wiping his hands on his shorts, said, "That's OK; the ice is in. It'll not all melt away till tomorrow night at the earliest. I got enough to sink the Titanic."

Dee, dressed in a long towelling robe, looked at him with a harrowed expression on her face. Then she rose and started wandering up and down, wringing her hands like Lady Macbeth.

"What's the matter with you?" he asked.

"I've just remembered I've not bought any Cokes," she groaned.

He laughed. "That's no trouble. Give me the rest of our money and I'll go down to the village and buy some." But she didn't sit down and went on groaning.

"Now what?" he asked.

"I'm so worried. There's no sign of Pasco. He should be back with the food by now."

Ben looked at his watch. It was ten past eleven. "He'll have a lot of stuff to bring. It might take a bit longer than usual," he assured her. *She's such a worrier*, he thought.

She ran both hands through her hair. "I'm worried sick. What if he doesn't come back?"

"Aw, he won't do that. He'd not be able to take up that job with the Australians if he did," said Ben.

"I don't trust him, I just don't trust him. I've felt bad about him from the moment we started planning this party," moaned Dee. She was filled with a terrible dread.

When Pasco had not appeared by noon they went round to the kitchen quarters where they found Ali in a state of agitation almost as bad as Dee's.

"Where's Pasco? Where's the food?" asked

Ben bluntly.

Ali shrugged to signify he had no idea. "He has gone," he said.

"Did he say anything to you about running away?"

"No, sahib, and he's left his box. He's maybe had an accident."

"An accident!" Dee seized on the idea with relief. "We could try the hospitals," she said to her husband.

"If he's in the hospital he won't be coming back to make our chicken curry," he told her and she relapsed into despair.

"Let's see his box," he said to Ali.

Pasco's box was stored in the garage where he slept on a string bed. It was unlocked and when opened they found it contained nothing except some folded-up newspapers.

"Well, you're right. He's done a runner with our money," said Ben, standing up. "How much did you give him, Dee?"

"Five hundred chips," she replied and burst into tears.

Sixteen

Taking the morphine to her mother was Monica's first priority on Saturday morning.

Stevie had got the drug from a disreputable chemist friend of Ajay's and he assured Monica that even after he went back to America, she would be able to get more if she needed it by ringing a certain phone number. For the meantime, however, he'd procured a considerable amount – enough for at least ten days – and they carried it to Chembur partly as pills and partly as a liquid in little glass phials nestling on lumps of ice in an insulated box, the kind people took on picnics or to the beach to transport their beer.

Stevie drove with one hand because his left arm was still in its sling though it did not seem to inconvenience him very much. When it was necessary to make a gear change, he sometimes asked Monica to do it but most times he managed on his own.

Fifi was looking agitated when they

arrived at the house and grabbed Monica as soon as she got out of the car. "Your mother's had a bad night, with a lot of pain," she whispered.

They hurried upstairs and found Bernadette grey faced and sweating, though she knew her daughter and grasped her hand tightly, saying, "I wish this was over. I want to die."

"No, no," said Monica but inside she was saying, *Yes, yes*, because the agony which she saw her mother suffering horrified her. Beseechingly she looked at Stevie who nodded and went downstairs and soon was back with a loaded hypodermic.

"Where will I inject her?" Monica asked, taking the needle from his hand.

"In the arm or in the thigh. It doesn't matter." He turned away as he spoke because the sight of hypodermics upset him.

The dose was strong and within a few minutes Bernadette's groaning and tossing had stopped. Eventually she fell into a deep sleep.

The three of them went downstairs again and sat in cane chairs at the door staring in sorrowful silence at clumps of thick-trunked mango trees growing on the green sward of the golf course.

"I think we should all have a beer," said Stevie eventually and got up to take three bottles of local Lion brew out of the ice-box in the boot of his car.

When their glasses were filled he silently toasted the women and they drank gratefully. Monica's eyes were swimming with tears.

"It won't be long now," said Fifi, reaching over towards her niece.

"Just give her a shot as soon as she feels any pain," Stevie told her. "Use a full phial every time. It's a big dose. She won't suffer."

Monica gave a convulsive sob and the faces of the other two showed deep sympathy. "That's true. She won't suffer. She'll sleep away," whispered Fifi.

"I know. It's just that I can't bear to lose her. I love her so much." Monica gulped and wiped her eyes with the back of her hand, not caring if she looked swollen faced and ugly. She wanted to tear her clothes and keen like a mad woman but she had to keep control in case she disturbed the sick woman upstairs.

Stevie stood up and put an arm around her shoulders. "I'll bring in the bag with your dress and shoes for the party out of the car now and go back into town to take Vijay to the Carmichaels'."

"Do I have to go to that party?" she asked him.

He stared down at her, pity in his expression. "Yes, you have to go. I'm sorry, but I need you. I can't go without you."

Fifi, never one to go against anything a man wanted, nodded in agreement and looked at his bandaged arm. "If you're going back to the city, how can you drive like that?" she asked.

"I'm all right. The gears are on the steering column and I can change them without moving too much," he told her. "Look after Mon, will you? I'll come back for her about half-past eight."

He drove back to his flat again, and pottered about for a while before he changed into evening clothes, carefully transferring another pack of morphine pills from his shirt into the pocket of his white sharkskin jacket. It looked as if he was carrying a pack of cigarettes there. Then he hurriedly packed some ordinary clothes and his passport in a suitcase before he summoned Vijay.

The old man was smartly dressed up in a long, stiffly starched white coat, white trousers and a scarlet turban with a little golden plume made of cheap metal stuck in the front of it. On his feet he wore immaculate white pipe-clayed tennis shoes.

"Gee, aren't you a swell," said Stevie, impressed.

Vijay smiled faintly. "When I was young I worked for a big officer, a general, who had seventeen servants working in the house and all the men were dressed like this."

259

"Things have changed, huh?" said Stevie, impressed by how dignified and proud the old man looked.

"They have changed," agreed Vijay.

"How old are you?" asked Stevie.

"I think I'm seventy-five."

"You shouldn't be working any more."

"You are my last sahib. When you leave Bombay, I'll go back to my village. I've got land there and a wife and two sons; all I need now is enough money to buy a buffalo."

Stevie looked solemn. "A buffalo, huh? Listen. I'm sorry but I'm going away. I want to give you some money to make up for leaving so soon. Then you can go back to your village."

He fished into his trouser pocket and brought out a wad of notes. "Here's six hundred chips. Is that enough for a buffalo?"

Vijay looked at him in frank amazement. "It's enough for two buffaloes," he said.

"Then take it. When I'm back in New York I'd like to think of my money buying buffaloes that'll swim in one of your water tanks every day and pull your cart over the fields."

Vijay carefully folded the money and made a sign of respect. "May all your enterprises be blessed with good fortune," he said.

"Thank you; they'll need it," said Stevie fervently.

He and the old man loaded his bag into the car and rode out of town companionably together. When he reached the Gulmohurs' lane, he parked well past the gate, and they walked down towards the house which they found in chaos. Ben, looking stricken, met them at the door and said, "Christ, Stevie, I don't think there's going to be a party tonight. Dee's having hysterics."

"Why? What's happened?"

"Our bloody cook's done a runner with the cookbook money and there's nothing to eat except fruit and the bread Monica bought for us."

Stevie laughed. "Is that all? Some people could make a party on bread and fruit. Anyway, I don't suppose food's a great attraction to the people who come to parties in Bombay. Any I've ever been at always serve the same thing – curry and cold meat that's guaranteed to give you gut rot."

"OK, you think it's funny, but we've no curry or cold meat, good or bad. And no money to buy any. The cook's cleaned us out."

"You've got to have a party. I'll give you some money," said Stevie, suddenly serious.

"No, you bloody won't," snapped Ben. "We're not charity cases. I think we should call the whole thing off."

"You can't," said Stevie equally vehemently.

"Why not?"

"Because – because it's too late, because people'll be on their way here already. You should have done it long before now if you were going to cancel."

Ben was reluctantly forced to agree to that. "You're right, we can't stop them coming now. We've no phone and neither have most of the people we've asked. There's no way of contacting them. We'll have to let them come."

"Yeah – and when they arrive tell them what's happened and give them the option of going home or staying. I bet they stay," said Stevie.

While they were talking, Anne and Bill appeared, with their sullen servant Gopal bringing up the rear carrying rugs and bottles. At the sight of them Ben threw out his hands and cried, "Go in and speak to Dee, Anne, she's in hysterics."

"Why?" Anne looked startled.

"She'll tell you."

Anne turned and ran to the bedroom where she found Dee lying on her back in bed with her arms crossed over her eyes. She was still dressed in her towelling bathrobe and her face was bloated with crying. She looked up when her friend went in and gave a heart-rending groan.

Anne sat down on the bed and said, "Pull yourself together, Dee. What on earth's happened?"

Dee sat up and thumped both fists on to the mattress. "That bastard Pasco's run off with all our cookbook money. There's no food. And I so much wanted this to be the best party that had ever been held in this house! I'm a failure. I knew something awful would happen. I knew I couldn't do it."

"What nonsense. It's not as bad as you think. You must have some food in the house."

Dee looked angry. "I'll tell you exactly what we've got – dozens of oranges, apples, guavas, some pineapples, about four kilos of grapes, two baskets of mangoes, about fifty bananas, thirty-six eggs, three live hens, two cheeses – your cheeses – and piles of bread. Oh yes, and a box of those sticky Indian sweetmeats that make you feel sick if you eat more than one of them."

Anne laughed. "Well, that's pretty impressive. We'll put it all out and let people help themselves. And we'll boil the eggs and make a salad with them. I like egg salad. You said you've got three hens too, didn't you? We could roast them and mix the flesh in the salad with the eggs. It'll be interesting if nothing else."

"Those hens are alive, Anne! Who's going

to kill them?"

Anne got up. "Somebody will. I'll put Bill on to it. Go and have a shower and get yourself dressed. Leave it to me to organise things in the kitchen. The garden's looking lovely with all the fairy lights in the trees and the Divali lamps are lit ... it's like paradise out there. Music and loads of booze are all that people come to parties for anyway."

"Do you think we can do it?" asked Dee with a flicker of hope lightening her swollen eyes.

"Of course we can. People'll think it's funny. This is going to be a memorable party, you mark my words."

While Dee was showering and dressing, Anne went back into the sitting room to chivvy the men and stop them drinking. Tying a folded sheet round her waist to protect her scoop-necked black dress – black was her colour because it accentuated her satiny white skin – she grabbed Stevie in passing. "You needn't think that bandage of yours will let you off. You're going to help me with the food," she said.

She set about ordering the other men around too. "I need somebody to kill three chickens and one of the servants can pluck them. We've got plenty of time if we get moving now. Nobody ever turns up for a party like this till about half-past nine or ten o'clock."

They got moving. Bill killed the chickens and Stevie, apparently unhampered by his bandaged arm, helped Anne with preparing the food and organising the setting of the table. As they worked together, they talked and laughed, but luckily Bill was too busy to notice.

By the time Dee emerged, looking fresh and pretty in a long smock, the chickens were roasting in the oven, eggs were boiling in a huge pot and the kitchen, normally a forbidden area to sahibs and memsahibs, seemed to be full of people, all laughing and talking as they chopped and peeled.

Dee cried out, "Anne, you're wonderful! It's going to be all right, isn't it?" A surge of energy and optimism filled her as she looked at the festive buffet table that was beginning to emerge under Stevie's and Anne's care. They bent over it together in companionable co-operation and then Anne turned around, face glowing, obviously enjoying herself.

"Go and sit down, Dee, take it easy. We're in control and we don't want to share the glory," she said.

Stevie, who was piling mangoes up in a pyramid using his good hand, grinned too. For the first time he looked really unself-conscious and animated as if he was genuinely enjoying himself.

By nine fifteen everything was ready. Ben

put Frank Sinatra's *Songs for Swinging Lovers* on the record player, and Dee's favourite track, "You Make Me Feel So Young!", came booming out from the loudspeakers among the trees. While Ben went off to shower and change into black trousers, white shirt, red cummerbund and black bow tie like the other men, Stevie drove to Fifi's house to fetch Monica who soon appeared, dressed in a skilfully draped dark blue silk gown and looking magnificent. Grief and pent-up emotion about her mother had her in its grip and lent her a new gravity that enhanced her loveliness.

Because she did not want to cast a gloom on the party, she said nothing about her worries but smiled at everyone and joined them as they stood in a group on the verandah to toast each other with whisky from one of the bottles Ben had got as a Divali gift.

"Here's to the best party ever," they cried and linked arms as they clinked their glasses. The last Gulmohurs party – a party they would all remember for the rest of their lives – began.

Seventeen

At half-past nine, headlights blazing, horns tooting, a stream of cars came jolting up the lane, drawn to the brightly lit garden like moths to a flame.

Loops of coloured bulbs glowed among the trees and flickering flames from tiny earthenware lamps, like the sort the Romans used, twinkled along the tops of the walls. A dance floor, dusted with chalk, was marked out on the upstairs terrace and the pots of plants – crotons, mother-in-law's tongues and Christ thorns – that usually stood there had been removed in case some obstreperous guests chucked them down on to the grass below and brained other party-goers in the process.

"Won't You Come Home Bill Bailey?" alternating with Dave Brubeck's "Take Five" blared out over the treetops and made wild animals in the jungle hunker down in their hiding places and stare around with glittering eyes, wondering where the danger was coming from. Birds roosting in the trees fluttered up from their perches in sleepy alarm. The holy man in his little stone house on the summit of of the hill stirred out of his peaceful trance and shifted his arms and legs from the lotus position. It was difficult for him to focus his mind on eternity, as he liked to do at night, while that din was going on.

The labourers in the fruit farm and the people in the buffalo camp, who had finished their evening meals and were about to go to bed, sat gossiping round the fading embers of their cooking fires, tutting their tongues in annoyance. The party was not a surprise to them for they'd watched the preparations with keen interest but it irked them that the racket would last all night. They knew that from past experience.

The oldest buffalo farmer, a tetchy fellow of eighty-two who'd seen off many annoyances in his time, told his sons that he was going to load his bandook – a blunderbuss dating from Mutiny days – and go down to blast the revellers if the noise went on after midnight but he was restrained, given a drink of palm toddy and persuaded to go to bed.

The Pathan doorman in Raj's house, vastly intrigued by the goings-on, leaned on his gate and watched every person who went into the Gulmohurs. He didn't mind if they partied till dawn because he slept all day and worked all night anyway and besides, he would welcome a diversion tonight because he had his own plans.

Taking advantage of the absence of his employers, he'd invited some of his compatriots from the construction site at Trombay to pay him a visit so that they could have their own party. Already a goat kid was roasting on a spit at the back of the house. They would sing, eat and talk all night without interruption because Raj was away from home, taking the opportunity to visit his actress mistress at Juhu while his wife and family were in Darjeeling, where they'd decided to go when the forthcoming party had been announced.

In the third bungalow on the hillside, the German who called himself Hans Gelhorn sat on his verandah and watched the lights of arriving cars and people thronging into the Gulmohurs through field glasses. He hated the music they played because his taste ran to Schubert or Wagner, and anything else sounded like a cacophony to his ears.

On the parapet in front of him stood a fresh bottle of whisky and a glass. He planned to drink it all tonight because it would be impossible to sleep unless anaesthetised by alcohol. Something rustled in the undergrowth below and he gave a little whistle which was answered by the dog slinking out of the bushes on its belly. Satisfied that it was the source of the noise, he tossed a peanut down to it and told it, *"Gut."*

The dog caught the nut and turned round to go back to its job patrolling the compound. The uncultivated state of the garden was deliberate because tangled undergrowth provided another line of defence for the house. It would take a machete to cut a way through the thorn bushes and cacti. The only easy access was by the main driveway, though the dog had made a little path down the steep bank into the nullah, which it used to get at the sweet-tasting water which flowed through when the river was running. It would be very difficult for a man to make his way up there without being heard.

Suddenly Dave Brubeck stopped and "Let's Twist Again" took over. Hans Gelhorn flinched and poured himself another drink, a double. Soon he'd be drunk enough to flop into bed and sleep till morning, confident that his dog was on guard.

Down in the Gulmohurs, as each group of guests arrived, Dee or Ben warned them about the food problem. "There's bread and cheese, chicken and egg salad and lots of fruit, but nothing else. The cook did a runner with the market money today," they explained.

Everyone who heard this tale laughed.

"Who cares?" said the bank chummery boys, summing up the general attitude. "So long as there's plenty to drink it doesn't matter." In fact, the lack of food seemed to be a party bonus point. It was something to talk about, something to break the ice.

On the narrow stretch of grass that led from the main gate to the lawn, a long trestle table covered with a white cloth had been set up and manned by Vijay and Gopal, both of whom could read English and were able to decipher the owners' scrawls on bottle labels. Thirsty guests were served in thick tumblers, borrowed from the Gym, from the ranks of bottles of beer, gin, rum and whisky. The boy Jacob was detailed to run back and forward with dirty glasses to a huge tub of soapy water at the kitchen door, where Birbal gave them a cursory dip and wipe before Jacob took them back again.

Ali, backed up by two servants from across the road, who had been ordered by the Pathan doorman to go and help because he did not want them muscling in on his own party, comprised the food serving staff. They were all excited and beaming, smart in fresh white uniforms and little black pork-pie hats, and it didn't matter to them that they would still be working when dawn broke. They were earning extra money and none of their employers would want much work out of them tomorrow.

Anne and Bill spread a rug out beneath a tall tree beside Stevie and Monica who'd picked a pleasant place beside the flowering gardenia bush to spread their carpet. Bill was agitated and voluble, trying as usual to impress Stevie with his menace and hardness. He didn't seem to be making much of an impression, however, since Stevie lay on his side as if half asleep with his head propped up on his good arm and only nodded solemnly as Bill expounded his theory of life.

"You've got to watch out for yourself in this world. Everybody will do you down if they can – even the people you think are your friends. You've got to get in first, that's all. I'm leaving my job here because it's a dead end. I'll never make any money at it and I'm at an age when I've got to start making cash."

He had already excised from his mind the uncomfortable fact that he'd been fired.

"What are you going to do instead?" asked Stevie suddenly.

Bill, who was rapidly getting into the voluble stage of drunkenness, put a finger alongside his nose and grinned. "Lots of things. I've got my finger in plenty of pies, and take it from me there's some good ones out here. The hard men think they're tough but they're just amateurs. Guys like Jack Spot could run rings round them. I might try my luck in Australia or I might stay here ... I've got a few Indian friends who know how to work the rackets."

"I'd have thought that getting involved with Indian crooks could be dangerous," said Stevie.

Bill laughed. "That's what they want you to think. But there's Europeans keeping their heads down out here that have been running good rackets for years and nobody's taken them on, not even the police. Like that German who lives up there." He pointed towards the dark hillside.

Stevie felt Monica stiffen beside him but he sounded mild as he said, "Oh, I don't think he can be a crook. He's into importing and exporting I believe."

"Importing and exporting what? Gold and guns, that's what," sneered Bill. "I'm telling you, I've heard enough about him to put him in jail for ten years."

Stevie looked around and said in a low voice, "In that case you'd probably be safer to keep it to yourself. Have a whisky." From a hip flask he poured a generous slug into Bill's glass.

"I was drinking gin," said Bill, "but what the hell!"

He knocked it back but though Stevie held a glass to his own lips as well, he didn't swallow.

The party was hotting up. Ralph the doctor arrived, quarrelling as usual with his skinny, elegant wife Rosemary whose tongue was so sharp that it could cut glass. They were engaged in an endless war of attrition in which each tried to out-insult and betray the other – and because they still loved each other, the betrayals seared like sabre cuts.

As soon as he arrived Ralph swigged down his first whisky in Coca-Cola, and within a very short time was running around playing the fool and dropping the end of the stethoscope which he carried in his dinner-jacket pocket down the trouser fronts of other rugby players. His antics caused great hilarity and usually ended with fake scrums in the middle of the lawn.

Many of the people who had seen Ralph in this state of apparent intoxication before wondered why he felt compelled to act like that. The persona that he took such trouble to conceal was actually intensely serious. His favourite reading was Latin poetry.

Smelling sweetly of imported Roget and Gallet's carnation soap and wearing a beautifully tailored white sharkskin jacket very similar to Stevie's, Dadi, the Parsee boy, arrived in a taxi with a bottle of rum and a dozen bottles of Coca-Cola. Everything about him breathed money but his enormous, limpid brown eyes betrayed innocence as he surveyed the dancing, chattering, drinking guests.

Pammie, who was sitting on the verandah steps swinging her long brown legs in time to the music, stood up and walked towards him. In an instant she'd decided he was to be her quarry for the night.

She went up to him and caught hold of the lapels of his jacket, pulling him towards her.

"You must dance with me," she said, kissing him open mouthed on the lips.

He kissed her back and put his arms around her, hardly able to believe his luck. It's going to happen, he exulted, it's actually going to happen, and I didn't have to say a word!

Donald Brewer-Neal, the roué, had brought his wife and arranged for his mistress, a dyed-blonde Eurasian called Gloria, to turn up at the party as well. Gloria was a magnificent specimen of humanity, built like a brood mare and oozing sex, with swelling breasts, magnificent legs and spreading hips. Any day now she'd be out-of-control fat but it hadn't happened yet. Tonight she was as luscious as an overripe mango. She and Donald's wife Deirdre hated each other like poison and spent the first couple of hours of the party shooting looks of loathing across the dance floor at each other.

As usual it would be Deirdre who cracked first. After she'd drunk half a bottle of gin she always launched herself at Gloria, screaming insults, red-taloned nails clawing. Their cat-fights marked the end of the first phase of every party and when that happened, the more decorous members of the gathering made for home.

Alex, one of the chummery four, who, to his own horror, found that in drink he was more attracted to the men in the party than the women, adopted his usual avoidance technique and took over the record playing. Swiftly he sorted through Ben's collection and alternated trad jazz with swooning, dance-style music. Nat King Cole was followed by Benny Goodman; Chris Barber by Glen Miller. As the night wore on, sentimental music gradually predominated and couples swayed beneath the trees and on the terrace, knee to knee, pelvis to pelvis, breast to breast, while Harry Belafonte, Sinatra or Cole crooned over them.

Dee's careful obstetrician hadn't warned her against drinking while pregnant and she had three nips from Ben's Divali whisky before her nervous anxiety about the party began to subside. After that she began to enjoy herself and went from group to group, making conversation and looking for someone with whom she could really *talk*.

As always when in drink, she longed to

have the sort of conversation that explored subjects like "why are we here?" or "what is goodness?". Ben was a good talker in sobriety, but preferred to dance and shout and wave his arms around after drinking. As he got jollier, Dee became more solemn and philosophical. As a consequence they tended to drift apart at parties, meeting only now and again to dance smoochily to some evocative number like "The Story of My Wife".

By midnight, the crowd of guests, which had grown to almost two hundred as Ben had predicted, began to shrink a little. The party was going well, the buffet table in the sitting room had been systematically plundered of its colourful display and no one seemed to be complaining of hunger. Gradually Dee's thinking was becoming blurred. She'd entered a strangely woolly, benevolent state of mind which, for her, always preceded an overwhelming desire to go to sleep.

Like someone in a dream, she wandered over the dew-covered lawn in bare feet – a delicious experience – and found Monica sitting mournfully alone under the trees. In the dim light it looked as if there were tear marks on the girl's cheeks so Dee slid down beside her and said, "You're looking very sad. Are you all right? Where's Stevie?"

Monica looked up, rapidly wiping her

eyes, and said, "He's dancing with your friend Anne. I think he's sorry for her because her husband's such a horrible man."

Dee nodded. "Yes, he is pretty awful, I'm afraid. He talks a lot of nonsense, doesn't he? But does he know Stevie's dancing with his wife? He's horribly jealous and never lets her dance with anyone but him."

Monica shrugged. "He went off to fetch some drinks and hasn't come back yet."

"Then I hope Stevie and Anne get back before he does," said Dee. She tried to focus her eyes enough to see across to the drinks table in search of Bill but the world seemed to be swimming in a grey fog so she gave up.

When she looked back at Monica, however, her sight was good enough to see that the other girl was miserable and had indeed been crying. Her sympathy was awakened at once. "Don't worry about Stevie," she said. "Anne won't steal him."

"I know that. I don't mind him dancing with other people. I'm not myself tonight because my mother's very ill. In fact she's dying." All her sorrow, all her worry and grief about Bernadette came out in a rush like water when a sluice gate opens. It was easy to talk in the darkness with a sympathetic listener beside her and the scent of gardenias making her head swim.

Dee listened in silence and in sympathy

put a hand on Monica's which was lying clenching and unclenching at the grass. The change in the girl was startling, she reflected. She'd seen her at parties in the past but hadn't liked her much because she'd always seemed very brittle and artificial. Not only that but she'd put on terrible airs, telling people that she was English and was going "home" soon. Dee had thought it stupid to playing such a ridiculous part but, as she got to know Monica better, she realised she was not in a position to criticise because she had never been subjected to the insults and denigration Monica and her family had known all their lives. If the fantasy of "home" comforted her, why spoil her dream?

But the weeping Monica was so vulnerable, and the sorrow and sincerity of the way she talked about her mother so genuine that Dee's heart was touched and she felt a rush of real feeling. "I'm so very sorry. Where is your mother now?" she said.

"In the house on the golf course, just a couple of miles down there." Monica pointed down the lane. "Her sister, my aunt, who lives there, is the mother of Carole, the girl who used to live here with you."

Dee was genuinely surprised. "Gosh, really? What a coincidence. That means you're Carole's cousin. How is she? It was a pity about what happened."

"She's gone to Calcutta but she'll be back before very long if I know her. Her mother's nursing my mother tonight but I'm still worried. I want to be there when she wakes up. What if she dies before I get back?" Monica's voice cracked again and with her composure lost she looked like a frightened child.

"Why don't you go home now? I'll drive you down there if you like," said Dee.

Monica shook her head firmly. "I couldn't do that. I promised Stevie I'd stay, you see ... He wants me to wait till he's ready to go." She seemed confused, as if she regretted revealing so much of herself to someone else. She gathered back some of her reserve as she sat upright and said in a different tone of voice, "My mother'll be all right till dawn. We gave her some very strong medicine before we came out and Fifi's with her."

Dee stood up and asked, "Do you want me to find Stevie and ask him to take you back?"

Monica shook her head. "No, definitely not." Her voice was totally controlled. The old Monica was back.

If Stevie really was dancing with Anne, Dee thought, then they would be up on the terrace so she climbed the stairs and wandered about among the dancers looking for them till she was found by Chris, a friendly, freckle-faced bachelor, who held out his hand inviting her to dance with him. She laughed and patted her swelling stomach but Chris shrugged. "Dance with me anyway," he said, so she did. Stevie could go on dancing for a bit, she thought. Monica didn't really seem to want him summoned back for her.

Chris sighed into her hair as they circled the floor in the middle of other amorous couples, few of whom were married to each other. "What is it that happens to people in this country? What makes us all so randy?" he exclaimed, looking around.

"It's the smell, I think," she said solemnly.

He held her back from him and gazed into her face. "The smell! You must be joking."

"No, I'm not. The smell of India really gets me – incense and woodsmoke and white jasmine, the one they call Queen of the Night. I can almost get drunk smelling it."

He shook his head. "And pee and cow dung and filthy sewage! No, I don't think it's that. I think it's the feeling that you've left your old self behind in Europe and can do what you like, be who you like, when you get out here. You can recreate yourself ... I noticed it when I came out on the boat. The moment we were through the Suez Canal, all the women became raving nympho-maniacs."

Dee laughed again. "You must have loved it."

He shook his head as he twirled her round on the floor. "No, because the ones who made a set at me were never the ones I wanted."

She was prevented from replying by an outbreak of angry shouting and they stopped dancing to turn and stare at the far side of the dance area where they were no lights except the Divali lamps and the brilliant moon that hung above the house like an enormous silver lantern. What looked like a pair of Japanese Sumo wrestlers were struggling back and forward with their arms round each other and their heads down. Some of the onlookers were laughing, and a few men shouted encouragement. "Come on Stevie – knee him in the goolies!" cried Colin.

Then Dee saw with a feeling of dread that one of the fighters was indeed Stevie and the other was Bill. No one was shouting any encouragement to him.

"Stevie's fighting that roughneck who's married to the good-looking woman," said Colin scornfully. "Go on, Stevie!"

In fact Stevie, who nobody thought had any strength at all, was giving a good account of himself and seemed to be winning, till Bill suddenly jumped away from his opponent to grab a beer bottle that stood on the terrace parapet. Viciously, with his face contorted into a mask of evil, he smashed it against the wall and went back into the fray holding the jagged end in front of him. It was sickeningly obvious that he intended to push the broken glass into Stevie's face and no one was near enough to stop him.

At that point most of the jeering onlookers realised that the fight was serious, and some rushed over to try to put an end to it – but they were too late.

How it happened no one was ever very sure though there were several theories. Some people said Bill tripped, others were sure that Anne had jumped in and deliberately pushed her husband down, while there were some who swore they saw Stevie go into a low crouch and perform an adroit judo throw that took Bill off his feet. Whatever happened, one thing was sure. In a split second Bill went from menacing Stevie with the broken bottle to squirming on the ground with blood spurting from his own neck.

He rolled sideways and blood splashed over the white wall of the terrace while Stevie stood alone with one hand over his face. Slowly he took it away and stared into his palm while Colin ran across to him and turned his chin towards the light.

"It's OK," he said. "He missed you."

"I felt him hit me," said Stevie slowly.

"That must have been with his hand and not the bottle, because you're not cut," Colin told him. "You're lucky. There's not a scratch on your face, just a bit on your arm, nothing serious." Stevie shook himself like a dog coming out of water and turned to walk away. Though there was blood on his white shirt, it wasn't his blood.

Anne and a few men were leaning over Bill in the dark corner. Then one jumped up to run to the edge of the terrace, and shouted down into the garden, "Tell Ralph there's been an accident up here."

Anne, hair and eyes wild, was gazing down at her huddled husband like an avenging fury in black. Her face was chalk white and she seemed speechless. When Dee ran across to her, her arm felt icy cold and she seemed unaware that her friend was beside her.

The tension among the group staring helplessly down at the huddled, moaning Bill was broken when Ralph came running across the room behind the terrace. Once again he'd done his party trick – gone from being a rollicking drunk to stone-cold sober in a matter of seconds. He didn't need to be told what had happened because he went straight to the injured man, pushing his way through the shocked bystanders.

"Christ," he said through gritted teeth

when he lifted Bill's head. The flow from the wound increased and a puddle of blood that looked hideously black in the dim light began to form beside Bill.

Ralph looked round at Dee, his face grimly set. "Get me towels and a darning needle and white cotton. Tell Rosemary to bring our car to the gate. He must get to hospital straight away."

Bill struggled to sit up and was told abruptly, "Lie down. I'm going to put a couple of stitches in that gash."

Ralph carefully stitched the edges of a gaping wound together with needle and thread from Dee's sewing box before tying a thick muffler of towels round Bill's neck. Apart from a few groans when the needle went in, Bill stayed totally silent and the only sound was stifled sobs from Anne who still seemed to be unaware that people were around her. In fact she looked catatonic.

There was no sign of Monica or Stevie and, in the garden below, other revellers, unaware of the drama going on above their heads, set off another volley of rockets and firecrackers. A kaleidoscope of brilliant, shooting colours from the bursts in the night sky illuminated Ralph's face as he hauled the injured man to his feet.

"Somebody help me get him into my car," he said and three men, followed by a still silent Anne, carried Bill downstairs, through the front door and on to the back seat of the car that sat with its engine purring at the gate. Ralph got in beside his patient and said to his wife, who was at the wheel, "As fast as you can make it, Rosie. There's no time to waste."

Rosemary was throwing the car into gear when Anne suddenly came to life. She leapt away from her friends and hurtled herself down the steps to grab the front passenger seat door handle. "Take me with you, take me too," she said. Then, as she scrambled in, the car drove away with a screech of tyres.

This drama had all been enacted in only a few minutes so when Dee went to find Ben she discovered that he knew nothing about the bloody fight upstairs and neither did a lot of other people at the party.

"Old Ralph'll fix him up," Ben said unconcernedly when Dee told him Ralph had taken Bill to the hospital.

Little by little, however, word got round that Bill Connor had been in another fight and got himself injured. Like Chinese Whispers the story grew till it was being said that he'd wandered off into the jungle where he'd fallen foul of a jaguar. It was true that a few of those big cats had been seen on Chembur hill from time to time, but mostly they kept out of people's way.

The mundane truth was not so exciting so

it didn't get around so fast. There was nothing really unusual in the fact that he'd seen his wife dancing with another man, gone berserk and made a murderous attack on her partner. No one was quite sure how it came about that he was the one to be injured but it was generally agreed that he'd stumbled and fallen on the broken bottle that he'd meant to use on Stevie.

The general opinion was that the most interesting thing about the incident was that Stevie had been involved but for once escaped unscathed. "Trust old Stevie, always in trouble," people said. "Lucky he wasn't hurt though."

Bill didn't get much sympathy. "He's a nutcase. It serves him right. Pity a jaguar didn't get him," was the general opinion.

It was half-past one in the morning. Rockets still soared into the sky and firecrackers were going off like rifle shots all over the garden as if the place was under attack by a gang of Second World War commandoes. Nat King Cole had been replaced on the record player by Chubby Checker and, Bill forgotten, people were whirling and whooping again like mad things – they'd got their second wind.

By this time more than half of the revellers had gone home and only about fifty were left. The ones who survived to this stage would go on partying till dawn. Dadi and

Pammie were entwined in an amorous embrace in the hammock; Philip was with someone else's wife; Donald was kissing Gloria in a corner; Chris had found a pretty doe-eyed Anglo-Indian girl who someone else had brought to the party and was dancing again and Stevie and Monica had disappeared, back to the house on the golf course, Dee hoped.

Staggering, tension draining out of her, she found her husband in earnest drunken colloquy with a group of friends, arguing about rugby tactics and reaching no conclusion. "I'm exhausted. I'm going to bed," she told him and he nodded in agreement.

"Good idea," he said. "This'll go on for hours yet. It's been a great party."

A great party! she thought. It certainly had all the required ingredients – a bloody fight, a drama, lots of romances going on, plenty to talk about for the days to come.

"I haven't let you down after all," she said aloud to the house as she laid her head on the pillow. Within seconds she was sound asleep.

Eighteen

In the servants' compound behind Raj Kapoor's house ten partying Pathans sat round a red-hearted bonfire and stared up at the moon in the midnight purple sky above the roof of the main house, admiring the coloured tails of rockets that were being fired across in front of it from the next-door garden.

"They will all be drunk there now," said Mehmet Ali, the malik and their acknowledged leader. "You would have to be drunk to enjoy the awful noise they call music."

Someone laughed, bending forward to light his bidi from a twig taken out of the fire. "They are young, just chokras," he said.

"And stupid," said Mehmet Ali. "My man Budgeon sahib won't be there. He has too much sense."

Guttural grunts of agreement responded to that and the talk reverted to Nigel who was universally admired by everyone in the party. In his absence they complimented him on his manliness, his sense of fair play and his lack of prejudice.

"He doesn't think of himself as something special like a lot of the others," said Mehmet Ali, and Yusuf, who was sitting behind him cuddling the white puppy that he took with him everywhere nowadays, said, "Yes, he is a great man, a hero like Iskander."

"Has he got a woman – or a boy?" asked one of the men who had recently joined the work gang.

"He has a woman to whom he is in thrall," said Mehmet Ali. "He told me that she is having a child soon. I said my wish for him was to have a son."

"Yes, yes," agreed Yusuf softly under his breath. "Yes, the good man must have a son."

"His wife is a lazy, spoiled woman," said Raj's doorman who never missed anything that went on in the neighbouring properties.

His audience looked expectantly at him, waiting for more. "She lies in bed every day till noon and only gets up to play chequers. When he comes home she bullies him, shouts at him. He never raises a hand to her but what she needs is a good beating. The servants from over the road told me about her. She has left their house now but they say that she has been making up to some French man who works with her husband ... they think maybe the child is not his."

It was as if he'd lobbed a grenade into the

middle of the party. His visitors sat bolt upright and stared at him, horrified. "Tell us more," said Mehmet Ali angrily.

There were no secrets in India. Everywhere prying eyes watched the reactions and movements of employers who blithely led their lives as if they were free agents. Little did they know that every action, every nuance of expression was noticed and commented upon.

"The servants next door have seen her and the French man touching each other and he was always there hanging over her. His name is Jean-Paul..." The door man pronounced it like "jumble", as if it was one word.

"The diver with the yellow hair?" asked Mehmet Ali in a hard voice.

"Yes, that's the one."

Mehmet Ali slammed a clenched fist hard on the ground beside him. "She should be killed. They should both be killed. They have betrayed a good man."

"How do you know that?" asked the doorman.

"Because of what I've overheard that Frenchman who jumps into the sea saying to his friends. I speak his language, you see, and he doesn't know I do, so he's been boasting about some woman who's hungry for him, who can't get enough of him. I didn't know who it was he meant, though! I thought it was some silly girl. I'd have slit his throat from here to there if I'd guessed the truth." He drew one finger along his throat and his eyes glittered like a wild animal's.

Then he groaned, remembering something else he'd overheard. One of Jean-Paul's colleagues had laughingly said, "You'd better take care you don't get caught by her." But Jean-Paul had shrugged.

"There's no danger of that. She's married and her husband's a fool. I'm quite safe."

When Mehmet Ali told this to the gathering. Yusuf sank his face into the puppy's fur and cried out, "It's wicked. She must be a bad woman. I hate her, I hate her. The punishment for her sin is to be stoned to death."

"The woman is weak and not to be considered. The one to hate and who we must punish is that Frenchman," said Mehmet Ali. "I've never liked him and now I know why. He is making a fool of a good man. If he and she pass off his child as Budgeon sahib's, that is unforgivable."

"What is to be done?" said a voice from the back of the group round the fire.

"We could offer to remove the other man for him ... that would be easy, a stabbing in the middle of the night would be enough. The police would never find out who did it because the assassin could be well out of Bombay by the time the body was

292

discovered in the morning and there'd be no motive to link them together. But we can't tell him because he loves the woman and he wants the child. He doesn't know she's cheated him. I'll have to think about this," said Mehmet Ali, his translucent eyes glittering like the eyes of a devil.

He stood up, a wrathful avenger, drawing his shawl round his shoulders and casting a long, sinister shadow away from the glare of the fire. Yusuf stood up too, his none-too-clean face smeared with tears and with a fierce, fanatical gleam in his eyes.

While the Pathans were involved in their discussion of Nigel's marital confusions, they did not notice that the stream of rockets soaring into the sky had tailed off and that only one or two firecrackers were still being detonated in the nullah or in the shrubbery over the road. The party was running down; a few couples continued to dance, clutched tightly in each other's arms, but they were hanging on rather than standing up. The music too seemed to be dwindling, with the same record being played over and over again, sometimes stuttering on for several minutes when the needle stuck before someone noticed and lifted it up.

All the food in the Gulmohurs had been eaten and the few people who still wanted to drink were desultorily helping themselves at the drinks table, emptying any leftover bottles of their dregs. The exhausted servants were stretched out on string beds beneath the trees at the kitchen door and dozing off. Soon it would be another day.

Then, all of a sudden, in a chorus of birdsong, dawn broke in a burst of colour. It was Sunday morning.

Ribbons of light were streaking the sky when Monica bent over her mother's bed and whispered, "You've been moaning in your sleep, mama. Let me give you more medicine."

Very gently she turned her mother on to one side and slid the hypodermic needle into an almost fleshless buttock. Bernadette flinched a little, but managed a feeble smile and slipped back into sleep.

Fifi, standing behind Monica, put an arm around the sobbing girl's shoulders and said, "It won't be long now."

Monica sank her face into her aunt's breast and groaned, "But I want her to live forever. I don't want her to die. I want her to stay with me."

"Not like that, she wouldn't want to live like that," said Fifi, gesturing at the little body on the bed. "Let me send for the priest. It's time now."

"All right. I'll get the priest," said Monica, sliding out of the housecoat she was wearing and dressing in the day clothes she had been wearing the previous afternoon when she first arrived at her aunt's house.

Together she and Fifi went downstairs and found Stevie lying on a leatherette sofa, sound asleep but fully dressed in his black evening trousers and a bloodied white shirt. There was a long narrow scratch on his hand with a crust of dried blood along it.

Monica shook him. "Wake up, wake up. I want to go to Colaba to fetch a priest for my mother."

He groaned and turned over but didn't wake. Fifi said, "Let him be. Why's his shirt marked like that?"

"He was in a fight," said Monica shortly, bending over Stevie again and saying urgently, "Get up, you must take me to Colaba to fetch the priest."

"You needn't go to Colaba. We can send Leela for the local priest," Fifi told her.

Monica looked fierce. "I don't want him. He's a nasty old soak. I want the Spanish Jesuit from our own church, the one she knows." She bent over Stevie again and shook him more vigorously till he opened his eyes.

"Is it over, Mon?" he asked staring at her.

"Yes. I mean no. My mother's still alive. She needs a priest and you must take me to fetch him. It's too early to pick up a taxi."

He did not protest, only got shakily to his

feet and rubbed his hands through his hair as he said, "OK. Let's go."

Fifi, always more considerate of men than of women, still protested on his behalf. "At least let him have a cup of coffee first," she said to Monica. "Your mother will not die yet."

"It's all right, I'll go now," said Stevie but he drank the cup of coffee that Leela brought before he went. As she watched them leave, Fifi noticed that his arm was no longer in a sling. *So it must be better*, she thought. At least he'd be able to drive unhampered.

The Spanish Jesuit was finishing early Mass when Stevie's car drew up at the Colaba church door. Monica ran inside and grabbed his cassock arm as he was walking into the vestry. "You must come with me, Father," she said. "My mother is dying and she needs you."

"I'll walk over soon," he said for he'd recognised her and knew where she and her mother lived.

Monica hung on to his sleeve, however. "No, no, she's not in the chawl any more. She's with my aunt in Chembur. I have a car waiting outside. Please come with me now."

He looked into her distraught face. Tears filled her lovely eyes and her dress was crumpled and stained which, he thought, was a bad sign because, even when very poor, both she and her mother had always been immaculately clean.

"Let me change and fetch what's necessary then," he said and went into the vestry, returning almost at once with a small suitcase.

They did not talk much on the return journey. Stevie hunched over the wheel with his face screwed up in concentration as if he was fighting to stay awake. Monica, on the front seat beside him, wept quietly and knotted a soaking handkerchief in her hands. Though he noticed her pathetic state, the priest offered no consolation yet. The time for that would come.

Fifi, waiting in the doorway when the car arrived, was surprised to see that the priest was a tall, thin, handsome but austere-looking white man who stepped out of the car like an athlete. "She's upstairs," she said as he swept past, taking the stairs two at a time on his way to dispense absolution to her sister.

Shivering though the sun was warm on her skin, she turned back to the other two who were still sitting side by side in the car. The driver's and passenger doors were both open.

"Can I go up too?" Monica asked but her aunt shook her head. "No, what goes on between them is private, there must be no one else listening. Come in out of the sun and eat something."

"But what if she's too doped to speak?"

"She won't be. She'll know she's being granted absolution."

Monica put her hands over her face and swayed in her seat. Stevie put his arms round her. "Hold up, Mon," he said. "I've got to go now too. I told you that, didn't I?"

She gathered her wits and nodded. "Yes, yes, I know. You've been very kind. I don't know what I'd have done without you."

"Or me without you," he told her. "I'm sorry but I must go soon. The plane's at noon. You can stay in the flat till things are sorted out for you. I've told Ajay to give you whatever help you need. Everything's taken care of for you."

Fifi watched and listened, not bothering to hide her surprise at this exchange. "You're going away now?" she asked him in a tone of incredulity.

"I've got to go. My plane seat's booked. Monica knew about it," he said.

"My God, but her mother's not dead yet. What's going to happen to her?" Fifi's outflung hand indicated her niece.

Monica looked round and said, "I'll be all right. He's taken care of me. I can't go with him – I won't leave my mother. I must see her decently buried ... and I must have Masses said for her soul."

Fifi made a tongue-clicking noise of

extreme exasperation. "Masses! He could have waited a few days, then; that's all it'll take. He's just like your other ones. I warned you but you haven't learned anything, have you?"

Ignoring her, Stevie and Monica turned back and hugged each other tightly, but not as lovers who are being torn apart do. They had slipped into the role of friends saddened by the inevitable parting of their ways.

"Goodbye, Steven," she said, holding his face between her hands.

He kissed her, saying, "Goodbye, Monica." Then she got out and stood waving while he started up the car and threw it into reverse, scattering dust and dead leaves as he drove away.

When the Jesuit father came down at last, they sent him back to the city in a taxi and then took turns to sit with the dying woman. Bernadette hung on to life till three o'clock the next morning and when she did die, she slipped away imperceptibly and without pain, thanks to the morphine which Stevie had acquired for her. Monica sat by the bed till dawn broke, dry eyed and holding her mother's hand in hers. Only when the brilliant sun of India came bursting up over the horizon did her tears begin to flow in a magnificent release.

Nineteen

Apart from the servants, Dee was the first to rise the morning after the party and staggered through to the bath-room for a shower only to find a reveller asleep in the bath amid dregs of melted ice and empty beer bottles.

Yawning, she climbed to the bathroom upstairs, which was empty though through the open door of the terrace room she could see sleeping bodies stretched out on the chairs and on the sagging sofa.

Later, showered and dressed, she consulted her watch. It was half-past one. Recognising the impossibility of rousing Ben, who hadn't crawled into bed till nearly six a.m., she went in search of something to eat. Two members of the rugby team were sleeping on the verandah, sprawled on the chairs, but amazingly the house was extremely tidy, with little sign of the chaos of the night before. The servants must have been up for hours to restore it to normality.

Ali appeared noiselessly in the kitchen

door and said sympathetically, "Only coffee, memsahib."

What he meant, she realised, was that there was nothing else to eat. She wasn't too worried because it was the end of the month and tomorrow Ben's salary would be in the bank so they'd have money again. *This is what it means when people say they live hand to mouth*, she thought. A status-conscious, middle-class upbringing by people who prided themselves on paying bills by return hadn't prepared her for Bombay's way of life and, even after three years, it still worried her.

When Ali brought her a cup of coffee he also offered her a plate bearing a slice of succulent ripe papaya from one of their own trees. It tasted delicious and as she ate, her heart gave its usual twinge at the thought of having to leave this Eden where even the penniless needn't starve. Only a few days left before they must go. They were due to take over a small rented flat in the city at the end of the next week and she felt like Eve being punished for eating the tempting apple.

Two of the chummery boys, who had been sleeping in the upstairs room, came into the sitting room with their noses twitching at the smell of coffee. They were soon joined by some others, all swollen eyed and sallow faced, groaning and asking Ali for Alka

Seltzers. In spite of obviously spectacularly painful hangovers, however, there was an atmosphere of restrained jollity and it seemed as if the party might even begin again. All that prevented this happening was the absence of anything to drink except water or coffee.

They were laughing and discussing the happenings of the previous night, making light of the Bill and Stevie incident, when Ben appeared looking miraculously fresh and healthy, as he always managed to do even after the most massive debauches.

"God, was that some party!" he exclaimed, grabbing a cup of coffee and drinking it standing up.

Then he kissed the top of Dee's head and told her, "It was the best we've ever had. I said you didn't have to worry."

She smiled. "Yes, it was a good party. What a pity about Bill, though."

"Bill?" Ben had obviously forgotten the incident. "What happened to him?"

"Surely you remember! He cut himself on broken glass and Ralph took him off to hospital. He'd been fighting with Stevie."

Ben frowned but was obviously not over-concerned. "I remember a bit about it, but I was well away by that time," he said.

Some of the party stragglers drinking coffee with them gave their versions of the accident. "Anne deliberately shoved her husband's face into the glass," said one.

"No, old Stevie chopped him," said another. Nobody seemed much bothered either way.

"He's a pain in the neck. Always fighting over that wife of his," said Colin bitterly. In the past he'd had trouble with Bill after innocently asking Anne to dance.

"I wonder what happened in the hospital, though," said Dee, thinking about her friend, for Anne had looked dreadful when she was driven off.

I should have offered to go with her, she thought and wondered if she could persuade Ben to take her to Cuffe Parade to offer belated help now. *Don't worry*, she tried to tell herself, *Bill's probably been discharged by this time. A lot of blood doesn't always mean terrible injury.*

One by one the hungover revellers left and by five o'clock, when the buffalo camp women began to straggle down to the well for their evening water, the lane was finally emptied of parked cars. Life was almost normal again and on the lawn Birbal was dragging his hose about as usual, though he himself looked different because he had a pristine white cloth tied nonchalantly around his head. It gave him a very raffish air.

The Pathan doorman, rubbing his eyes, staggered out of his sentry box and leaned on his gate, looking for someone with whom he could discuss the events of the previous evening. Ali came out too and stood in the Gulmohurs' drive so that they could converse animatedly across the gap between the houses.

Dee heard their cheerful voices and thought, "For days to come every event of our party will be talked about over again and again by them and their friends." The thought brought the niggling worry about Anne back into her mind. She ought to go to see her and offer help of some sort. What if it was true that Anne had pushed Bill on to the glass? He'd kill her when he got home.

"There's nothing to eat in the house except papayas and I'm starving," she said to her husband as the sun began to sink.

"Papayas are good for you," he said.

"Let's go into town and get something to eat," she pleaded.

"We've no money," said her husband.

"They'll let us put it on the slate at the Ritz," she told him.

He laughed as he said, "You must be hungry." It was usually Dee who objected to them running up debts.

"Or we could go to see Anne and Bill. They'll give us dinner," she suggested.

As she suspected he would, Ben groaned. "God, I don't think I could stand another night of Bill going on about his gangland connections. And if he's really suffering, he'll be unbearable, especially since it was a wimp like Stevie that brought him down. How's a tough guy like him going to explain that one away?"

Dee said nothing, only gazed at him and he finished up with his last objection, "Anyway, the food in their house is always rotten. You're better off with papayas."

She laughed, remembering an occasion when dinner at Nirvana had been cold baked beans out of a can because the Connors' cook had quit.

"I quite fancy baked beans actually," she said, getting up and holding out her hand. "Come on, I want to find out what happened last night and Anne might need help. She looked ghastly when she left."

Ben grumbled a bit but good-naturedly went with her.

Dee could not explain why she was so apprehensive during the drive to town but she was certainly relieved to see lights blazing out of Nirvana's upper windows as they drove into the gravel parking space.

Gopal opened the door to them and Ben asked, "Is your sahib at home?"

"Sahib sick. In hospital," was the reply.

"Your memsahib?" asked Dee, suddenly very anxious again.

Gopal stood back and let them enter.

"Memsahib here," he said.

Calling out, "Anne, Anne!" Dee ran along the long passage towards the sitting room but before she reached it, a bedroom door that opened on to the corridor was thrown wide open and Anne stepped out. Her face was haggard and her hair in disarray. It seemed as if she'd aged at least ten years overnight.

She reached out and grabbed Dee round the shoulders, hugging her tight. "I'm going away. I'm leaving him. I can't stand any more of it," she gabbled. Behind her stood a scared little Liza clutching fearfully at her mother's skirt.

"Where are you going?" Dee asked.

"Australia. I'm going to Australia. It's a big country. He'll never find us there," Anne sobbed. Over her shoulder, Dee could see that the bedroom was in total disarray with clothes heaped on the floor and an open suitcase on the bed.

Ben, who was always good with children, bent down and picked up the terrified Liza, hoisting her on to his shoulder and saying, "Come on, chicken, let's go into the sitting room and I'll tell you a story. Leave your mummy with Auntie Dee just now."

Dee pushed Anne back into the chaotic bedroom and closed the door so that whatever was about to be said could not be overheard. "Where's Bill?" she asked.

"Still in hospital. Ralph's keeping him there for a couple of days. He's lost an awful lot of blood apparently. There was a twelve-inch gash in his throat. If Ralph hadn't been there he would have died. I've got to get away before he comes out. He's been saying he'll kill me when he gets his hands on me. He says I pushed him on to that bottle deliberately."

Dee looked frightened. This confirmed her worst fears. "Pushed him? You didn't, did you?" she asked.

Anne groaned, "I don't know. I can't remember. I think I had one of my attacks..."

"You'd better get away. What'll you do about money in Australia?" said Dee.

Anne sank on to the bed, nodding her golden head. "I've got money. I've been saving for ages. I'll take it out of the bank first thing tomorrow morning ... and we've our air tickets to Australia for Tuesday, but I can change them for tomorrow if they've any empty seats. His company got them for us as part of his pay-off, but he didn't want me to tell you we were going so soon. You know what he's like. The tickets are for Sydney but Qantas'll change them for me and I'll fly to Perth instead. The plane stops there first."

"Do you know anyone in Perth?" Dee asked.

"No." Anne looked completely distraught.

"What if he finds you?" was Dee's next question.

Anne rallied slightly. "He won't. I'll dye my hair. I'll change my name. Liza and I'll begin new lives. I don't care if I never see anyone I know ever again. If I'm still here when he comes out of hospital, he'll kill me. I know he will, Dee. I think he's quite mad." The tone of voice in which she spoke the last five words was suddenly much more rational and cold than any she'd used that night and it was obvious she meant what she said.

Dee felt her skin prickle with fright as she listened. She knew what Anne said was true. Bill had gone over the border of frustrated anger into irrational rage, and it was not a complete surprise – he'd always been strange and unpredictable. What was more disturbing was Anne's behaviour. The excerpt from the medical book came back into Dee's mind. Was it possible that Anne had deliberately pushed her husband on to the broken glass, perhaps with the intention of killing him? Well, even if she had, Dee's sympathies were with her.

"But what if he gets out of hospital before you leave here?" she asked.

"He won't. He was raving last night like I told you and Ralph gave him something to calm him down. He said Bill'll be out of action for several days. The loss of blood was really bad – he only just got a transfusion in time. I think Ralph's sorry for me ... he more or less told me to make a break while I could. He said I should go home but I can't because Bill would know where to look for me there."

"Have you seen him since he went into hospital? He's maybe calmed down a bit," suggested Dee.

Anne looked at her pityingly. "No, I haven't seen him and and I don't want to. It was three o'clock this morning before I got home and I'm not going back to that hospital. I've made up my mind what to do and I'm going to do it." She stood up and threw a pair of shoes and a dress into the tumbled suitcase.

Dee stood up too and said, "Can we help?"

Anne looked round. "Yes, you can. Will you and Ben stay the night with Liza and me, in case he does come back? You never know with him."

Surprisingly, Ben was agreeable to this idea but suggested that he drive to Breach Candy hospital to check that Bill was staying in. If there was any chance of him getting out, it would be better for them all to go back to Chembur.

He went first to Ralph's flat on the top floor of the hospital block and spoke to his friend who said of the patient, "He's very feeble; he lost several pints of blood. It was a horrible gash, and if it had been a little further over I wouldn't have been able to save him at all. As it is he won't be able to cause trouble for a while."

"Anne's in an awful state. She's terrified of him," said Ben.

"I told her to go home – and I meant to England, not to her flat. He's raving about her having an affair – with Stevie, of all people! He says he's going to kill them both. Has anybody seen Stevie today, by the way?"

Ben shrugged. "Oh, he'll be all right. He left the party with Monica not long after you went. It's Anne and little Liza that Dee and I are worried about."

"Tell her to clear out – fast. I'll keep him sedated for a couple of days but I can't keep him under for ever. Tell her to get away and stay away. I've had to report the accident but I said he'd fallen on glass and cut himself. I didn't mention the fight, so the police won't be involved," said Ralph.

"That's good, because she says he's blaming her for making him fall on the glass," Ben said.

Ralph nodded. "I know. I heard him. If she did, I can't say I blame her."

On his way out of the hospital, Ben stuck his head into the room where Bill was lying – asleep, mercifully, so Ben didn't have to speak to him. His face was chalk white and so gaunt and stubbled that he looked like a disreputable character from a Dickens novel – Bill Sykes, perhaps. Wasn't it Bill Sykes, Ben thought, casting his mind back to his schoolboy reading, who murdered his girlfriend Nancy?

Twenty

The Carmichaels slept the night in Nirvana and next morning, when they got up, they found that Anne had dyed her lovely hair a dense shade of black. It changed her completely, taking away her air of aristocracy, and she was certainly hard to recognise.

Because it was Monday morning, Ben went off to work wearing a neatly pressed khaki bush shirt and trousers of Bill's while Dee took charge of Liza so that Anne could go to the bank in Hornby Road.

She was back within an hour, looking feverish and clutching a large manila envelope. "I've got it. Three thousand nine hundred rupees. Bill's hidden money in the house too and I'll use some of that to pay the servants. Then I'm going to the airport. Gopal, fetch me another taxi!"

Words came tumbling out of her in a torrent and she seemed to be on the verge of hysteria.

"I'll drive you to Santa Cruz," said Dee but Anne turned fiercely on her.

"No, no, you can't come with me. I don't

want you to see me off. I just want to *go*! That way if Bill asks you questions you won't know the answers."

She walked out of her flat and her marriage, leaving behind everything she owned except a few clothes in a battered case. Dee leaned out of the window and sadly watched as her closest friend lifted her daughter into the black and yellow cab and drove off without a backward glance.

Goodbye, Anne. I don't think I'll ever see you again, she thought sadly.

At half-past two that afternoon, as Dee was drinking tea and eating anchovy toast in the Gym while she waited for Ben, a gaunt man on a bicycle was pedalling painfully up the lane past her house in Chembur. She did not know his name but would have recognised him because he went by on the first Monday of every month and she'd seen him many times – a shabby old Parsee clad in a fraying white European-style suit and a battered solar topee.

By this time, the solar topee had ceased to be a status symbol as it had been in the days of the Raj when no European would venture into the sunshine without one, but the Parsee clung to his because he thought it it marked him out from the ordinary pedlars who tried to sell their wares among the isolated bungalows of Bombay island. The goods he had for sale would have marked him out anyway: strung along the handle-bars of his bike, and sticking out of a basket behind him, were immensely long, bright pink salami sausages.

He produced those unattractive-looking comestibles in a kitchen down near the Taj and on the days when he was boiling up his sausages the entire street stank. Muslims and Hindus alike avoided the place like the plague because he offended both their religious taboos but even when he wasn't making sausages, he was shunned because the smell of salami hung around him like an invisible cloud.

When Dee first arrived in the Gulmohurs he had turned up and tried to persuade her to buy his wares but the look of them – and of him – was highly unappealing, especially since he tried to ingratiate himself by insisting that Indians couldn't govern themselves and the British should "come back". She had turned him away and the rejection displeased him; he had gone off muttering that she was only an ignorant woman, and in any case he didn't need her patronage because he already had a good customer in the lane – Herr Gelhorn took two salamis off him every month.

On the afternoon she was waiting in the Gym, he was delivering his monthly order to Gelhorn as usual.

Raj Kapoor's scornful Pathan pretended

314

not to see him, and the impish children of the buffalo camp jeered at him labouring up the lane. He propped his laden bicycle against the German's gate before pulling the string of the hanging bell which clanged out, shattering the brooding stillness.

Down at the end of the drive he could see the roof of the white Mercedes so he knew his customer was at home, as he usually was on this day, but there was no response to his ring. He pulled the string again but still there was no sign of life from the house – not even a glimpse of the horrible dog. Irritated at having come so far and so painfully for nothing, he gave the gate a shove and to his surprise it swung open. The padlock chain had been neatly cut through.

Cautiously he pushed his bike in, looking fearfully around for the dog. Everywhere there was a strange waiting stillness. Nothing moved. He went on a bit further, down a slight hollow and there, beneath a clump of cacti and a blossom-covered hibiscus bush, he saw something that stopped him in his tracks.

The German's dog was lying stretched out and rigid with its mouth slightly open and a foam of what looked like dried shaving soap round its jaws. A million flies were crawling on its tongue and in its eye hollows. Some predator had tried to tear lumps of flesh from its body and bits of fur were scattered around but the vultures, who would normally have picked it clean, had not been able to get at it because of the prickly cactus under which it had taken refuge before it died.

The Parsee stared appalled at the corpse, wondering what he should do. Continue on down to the bungalow, or go for help?

Fearful of what he might find in the house, he chose the latter course of action, got back on the bike and pedalled quickly back up the drive to the gate of the buffalo camp. Summoned by his shouts, a trio of men came out and listened to his tale with hostile expressions on their faces.

"So the dog's dead," they said. "It's no loss, and what business is it of ours?"

"I think something's wrong in the house. There's no sign of Gelhorn but his car's there. Come with me to see if he's ill or something," said the old Parsee.

The buffalo men looked at each other. One of them suggested that it would be best to send a runner for the police but the other two, who disliked policemen with a terrible loathing because of their illicit liquor making, were not in favour of that.

They should take care, said the first one, for if they went into the house and something was missing they could be accused of taking it. It would be worse for them if the German was lying dead down there, he added. They might be accused of killing him.

Curiosity – a prevailing passion with Indian peasants – won out, however. They decided to go with the Parsee down to the house and take a quick look around. Headed by the camp's belligerent ancient with his bandook at the ready, they went through the gate and down the drive in a party, all looking around in apprehension.

The house was very still, as if it was waiting for them. Though the front door was locked it was easy to gain access by climbing over the verandah rail and in through the sitting room window which was half open. Two of the younger men went in while the other waited outside with the Parsee and the ancient. Soon there was a shout and one of them came back.

"He's dead too!" he said in a tone of some satisfaction.

They all rushed excitedly inside and crowded into the bedroom. Hans Gelhorn was lying sprawled on his bed wearing only his underwear. The upper part of his skull was a bloody pulp and one arm was hanging down to the ground with the fingers curled. Beneath the hand a gleaming revolver lay on the marble floor. A blood-soaked pillow lay beside him but the rest of the room was strangely unmarked by bloodstains which meant that he had been shot close up and the pillow put around his head to muffle the shot.

The old Parsee was horribly shocked and shaken but the other men stood around in a chattering group – not horrified, not appalled, nor feeling any pity for the body on the bed, only very interested. After a cursory search among the dead man's portable possessions, they decided someone had better go down to the village and fetch the police.

Ben left his office early that afternoon because his delayed hangover had begun to kick in and he was feeling very fragile. He and Dee drove back to the Gulmohurs in a mood of anti-climax.

Organising the party had kept their minds off their final departure from the house but now they were faced with it, and also with their imminent departure from India, since Ben's company could not be pressed into a definite commitment to increase his salary by any appreciable amount.

Unless they gave him an substantial rise, he'd said, he was not prepared to sign on for another contract, especially now that he'd have a child to support as well as a wife. His threat had not worked, however. The company thought he was bluffing and said they were prepared to let him go. The Carmichaels' days of happy insolvency in India

318

were therefore coming to an end, but although they had no idea what was going to happen to them next they were buoyed up with youthful optimism and by Ben's confidence that everything would turn out well.

They talked only desultorily on the homeward drive for they were both tired and longing to go to sleep but as the car drew up outside the Gulmohurs, Ali came running across the gravel drive, his eyes rolling in his head, to open the car door and gasp at Ben, "The police are here, sahib."

With one leg out of the car, Ben groaned, "What the hell for?" It occurred to him that either their party had broken the prohibition laws or there had been some repercussions from Bill's injury.

"It's the German sahib," croaked Ali. "He's dead."

"He's got nothing to do with us," snapped Ben and ran quickly up the steps into the sitting room with Dee following at his back. Her heart was racing with excitement and she felt as she used to do when she worked as a newspaper reporter and a story that might lead to a scoop popped up. Her editor used to say that good reporters could smell out big stories and she could certainly smell this one. In fact she'd smelled it from the time she went into Gelhorn's house – and now he was dead. How?

An armed constable in faded blue guarded their sitting room doorway and a tall, elegant police officer in an immaculately pressed khaki suit with a swagger-stick stuck under his arm was prowling the room, examining the art postcards Dee had stuck on the walls.

"I like that one," he said in a very polished English accent, pointing his stick at Van Gogh's bedroom chair.

Dee and Ben, neither of them affected emotionally by their neighbour's demise, stared at him in questioning silence as he advanced towards Ben with his hand held out, saying, "Inspector Mascarenas from Chembur Police Station."

Ben shook it. "Ben Carmichael," he said, and, indicating Dee, "My wife ... Deborah."

Inspector Mascarenas gave her a brilliant smile. "A very nice name."

"Thank you. But I'm usually called Dee."

"You should use your real name," said the inspector. His teeth sparkled like a Binaca toothpaste advertisement and he had a neatly clipped, very narrow moustache like the one worn by the film star Don Ameche. It suited him.

They waited in silence till he spoke again. "Have you heard about your neighbour?"

"The boy told us he's dead. That's all," replied Ben.

"Yes, he's been shot – either by his own

hand or by someone else's. We're not sure yet."

Ben and Dee sat down side by side on the divan beneath the window. "Shot! That's awful," she said.

"Any idea why?" asked Ben.

"Who knows? He'd plenty of money in the house but it wasn't taken and he left no note. Someone must have broken in, though, because the padlock on his gate was cut with strong cutters ... that's odd, isn't it?" said the inspector in a pleasant tone.

They both nodded and then Ben asked, "How can we help, exactly?"

"The doctor says he probably died early on Sunday morning. You were having a party then, weren't you? Who was at the party? Did you see anyone acting strangely?"

Ben shrugged. "Most of them acted strangely! There were at least a hundred and twenty people here at any one time but I didn't notice anything odder than usual going on."

The inspector sat down too and tugged at his trouser legs so as not to spoil the crease. "Let's start with their names," he said and took a notebook out of his jacket pocket.

"I've a guest list if that'll help," offered Dee, getting up to go to her desk. The inspector favoured her with a smile as he accepted the sheet of paper.

"Tell me everything you remember about your party," he said, pocketing her list.

Dee and Ben talked in turn, trying to remember who had gone home early and who had still been in the house the following morning. Neither of them mentioned Bill's accident or the fact that he'd been carted off to hospital by Ralph. Dee wondered why they felt constrained to keep that information to themselves but decided that it didn't have anything to do with the matter in hand and therefore it didn't matter. There was no point muddying the water.

The inspector was thorough. He wanted to know about the servants, about where the food and drink had come from, even where they had bought their ice. Finally he asked if they knew the German well, and why he was not at their party.

"We asked him," said Ben. "But he didn't come. He's been asked to other parties in the past but he's never come to any of them either."

"Was he polite when he refused? Did he make an excuse, did he say someone was coming to call on him or anything like that?" asked Mascarenas.

Dee spoke up. "I was the one who asked him. He said he might come but I knew quite well from his tone of voice that he wouldn't."

"He was not impolite? He made no excuse? He didn't appear to be depressed or suicidal?"

"No, not at all." She was quite definite about that.

"When did you invite him to the party?"

"A few days ago. I went up to his house and asked him. I wanted to borrow his bearer but he said he has no servants..." *Should I use the past or the present tense about Gelhorn now?* she wondered.

Mascarenas nodded. "We know his servant went off about six weeks ago. He was living alone. You went into his house? What did you think of it?"

"I was surprised to see so many guns on the walls ... and I thought the smell was awful because he was burning a buffalo's skull in his bedroom to frighten away snakes on the day I was there."

This piece of information did not appear to interest the inspector much. "He would have been better to frighten away burglars," he said standing up and closing his notebook.

"But he had the dog," said Dee. "It would never let anyone across the gate or near the house. How could anyone get near him with it prowling around?"

"The dog's dead too. It was poisoned," said the inspector.

This affected Dee more than the news of

the German's death. She remembered the snarling dog with the golden eyes. "Poor thing," she said, and slipped back against her husband in a faint.

Twenty-One

A terrible feeling of depression weighed Dee down when she opened her eyes the next morning. All she wanted to do was weep. Ben had already left for work and when she rose from the bed her legs felt as if the calves were filled with cotton wool. For the first time since she had arrived in India she felt like an alien in a strange, cruel land.

It was the first of November and outside the sun was blazing down as it would do every day till next June. At home it was probably wet or cold and the hunting season would be starting. Nostalgia swept over her as she recalled the thrill of sitting on a galloping horse with snow blowing into her face.

She dozed in bed for a while but eventually, wearing shorts and a cotton shirt, she walked out into the garden and sat down in a deckchair beneath the trees where Ali soon saw her and brought out coffee, the smell of which slightly revived her.

"The policeman is here again," he told her as he handed over the cup.

She groaned. "Tell him I don't know anything about the German," she said.

"But he wants to speak to memsahib," said Ali. Faced with the dilemma of defying his employer's wife or the police inspector, he would defy the wife.

"Oh, all right!" she snapped.

Mascarenas was even more dapper than he had been the day before. There was not a crease out of place in his uniform and his leather belt shone like silk. He was carrying his cap under his arm and his hair looked as if every strand of it had been polished.

"I hope you're feeling better this morning," he said as he came across the grass.

She frowned, suddenly worried in case he thought her faint had been brought about by a guilty conscience, though by this stage her pregnancy was fairly obvious. "I was tired last night. I'm having a baby. That's why I fainted."

A police constable brought him out a cane chair and he sat down beside her, saying, "I thought you were upset about Herr Gelhorn."

"No, why should I be? I hardly knew him."

"But you were neighbours. You must have seen him many times." His tone was smooth and she had a sudden suspicion that he suspected she had some sort of liaison with

Gelhorn. The idea was horrifying.

"Yes, I have seen him often and what I saw wasn't very pleasant. I thought he was sinister, in fact." She was determined to put a stop to his wild imaginings.

The word obviously intrigued him. "Sinister? Why?"

"Burning that buffalo head for one thing. He was so pleased when he saw how it upset me..."

She shivered slightly and Mascarenas leaned forward to ask, "You never saw any of his women?"

She stared at him in surprise. "Women? No."

He leaned back. "He used to bring women home and beat them – badly. We have had several complaints. You know one of the girls he attacked. She was at your party and she's a relative of the girl who used to live here with you."

She shivered at the realisation that this man knew a lot more about what went on in her house than she did herself. "I don't know who you're talking about," she said.

"You know Monica Fernandes and her cousin Carole, don't you?"

"Yes."

"Your neighbour beat Monica Fernandes so badly six years ago that he nearly killed her. She wouldn't lay charges against him, however, because she was too afraid. Didn't she tell you that?"

"No."

"Monica Fernandes was at your party. Who was she with?"

He probably knows the answer to that as well, she thought, so she said, "An American called Stevie Stone."

The inspector nodded. "Yes, a feeble sort of man. He went back to America by Air India on Sunday."

"Did he? I didn't know that. I don't think Stevie had anything to do with the German dying. He had his arm in a sling, you see," said Dee, remembering how hampered Stevie had been by his bound-up arm when he had been helping Anne in the dining room. Then she wondered how he'd managed to steer her friend around the dance floor expertly enough to incite Bill's ire. And he hadn't been wearing the sling when they fought, had he? She said nothing to Mascarenas about this, though.

"When did he and Monica Fernandes go home?" asked the inspector.

Dee shook her head. "I've no idea. About one o'clock I think. I was terribly tired and my memory's a bit muddled..."

"Were you there when the injured man was taken to hospital?" asked the inspector sharply.

"Yes, I was." So he knew about the fight

too. Who had told him? The servants, probably.

"You didn't mention that last night."

"It didn't seem relevant. Anyway, you can
go and speak to the man involved yourself.
He's in Breach Candy hospital."

"I've already been there this morning.
He'd got himself discharged by the time I
left. He told me he tripped and cut himself
on some broken glass. But that is not what
really happened, is it?"

"I don't know. I didn't see the fight." Her
mind was racing. *So Bill's out of hospital.
He'll have discovered Anne and Liza are
missing by now. I hope she's reached Perth –
how long does it take to fly there? Oh, God, I
hope he doesn't come here looking for her!*

It was as if Mascarenas could read her
mind. "I believe that Mrs Connor and her
child flew out of Santa Cruz yesterday," he
said mildly.

Dee blurted out, "Please don't tell him
where she's gone."

Mascarenas raised his eyebrows. "I think
he'll guess she flew to England."

Dee managed to conceal her surprise that
for once his information was incorrect. *If he
thinks Anne's gone to England when she's really
flown to Australia, I won't correct him*, she
thought. Anyway, Anne's flight had nothing
to do with the death of the German.

Inspector Mascarenas seemed ready to

take his ease in the garden for the day. Smiling serenely he accepted a cup of coffee from the obsequious Ali and looked around with definite appreciation. "It's very beautiful and peaceful here. You don't expect murder to happen in a place like this," he said.

She bristled. "It didn't happen here – and are you sure it was murder? You said last night that it might be suicide."

"But why would he poison his dog first – and why was the gate padlock cut? The night of your party was a good time to pick for a shooting, with firecrackers going off all over the place and lots of strangers wandering about ... The person who did it might have planned to kill him while your party was going on." Mascarenas sounded as if he was talking about some petty thief taking windscreen wipers off cars in the monsoon.

"Do you think the killer came from here? He might just as well be some business associate of Gelhorn's or have come from the buffalo camp. Have you thought of that?"

"Yes, I have. It's all being followed up." He seemed pleased that he had nettled her into a sharp response. Standing up, he bowed and thanked her for his coffee before he left the garden.

From the Gulmohurs he walked up the lane to the dead man's house where he wandered through the rooms, tapping the barrels of the prominently displayed guns with the end of his stick. They were all well looked after, polished and gleaming with oil. One of the weapons, a long-barrelled shotgun, hung lightly askew as if it had been hurriedly put back in place. Wrapping his hands in a sheet, the inspector lifted it off the wall, tied the sheet round it and took it away.

In the afternoon he emerged from the police station again and set out for the house of Monica Fernandes' aunt.

Two weeping women in black were sitting in the downstairs room when his jeep drew up at the door. Fifi recognised the inspector from the time she'd called in the police about the beating Monica had suffered.

"What do you want, Mascarenas?" she asked curtly. She did not like policemen even when they were on her side.

"Is your niece here?" he asked.

"Yes." They were talking about Monica as if she was deaf and blind though she was sitting by the window staring at them.

"Does she know that Hans Gelhorn was killed on Saturday night or Sunday morning?"

"Why should she know that?" asked Fifi.

They both stared at the girl who was sitting huddled in her chair. She shook her head and said vehemently, "I don't care if he

331

has been killed. I hate him."

"I remembered that," said the Inspector. "You were at the party held at the next-door property the night he died. You might have seen something, you might know something. Who apart from you hated him, for instance?"

"Lots of people. Other women he ill used. His old servant. People he worked with in the city, people he cheated. The Pathans he sold guns to," she said.

"You obviously know something about his business dealings," said Mascarenas.

"I read his papers when I was shut up alone in his house," she said dully.

"I want you to come to the station with me and make a statement." His voice was hard.

Fifi flew at him, screeching, "Leave her alone. She's just buried her mother. My sister died yesterday. If that man's dead my niece had nothing to do with it."

He was impervious to their pleas, however, and Monica was forced to go with him in the jeep and give a statement of what she knew about Hans Gelhorn and what she had been doing the night he died. When she finally returned to her aunt's house she was shaking with fright.

"I told them I know nothing about what happened to that man. I hadn't anything to do with it – but I'm so scared! What if they try to blame me?"

Fifi held her tight, patting her shaking back. "Of course they won't. They'll find the person responsible soon enough. It was probably one of the men from the buffalo camp. They hated him because he set his dog on one of their children once; didn't you tell the policeman about that?"

"I forgot. Should I go back there and tell him now?" sobbed Monica.

"No, stay out of the way. He'll find out for himself quick enough, I'm sure," said her aunt.

Later in the day, when it was cooler, Dee realised she ought to take her daily walk but could not face going up the lane. Instead, she decided, she'd only walk as far as the well. It wasn't very far but it would stretch her legs a bit.

As she was walking under the huge arch of purple bougainvillaea that branched over their gate she was startled to hear a voice coming from the roots of the hedge near her feet. Jumping back, she stared down into the sharp face of a filthy beggar who was crouched on the ground with his hand stuck out towards her. A trident-shaped yellow caste-mark was painted on his forehead and his waist-length hair was matted and tangled so thickly that it would have been impossible to pull a comb through it. He was completely naked except for a string crossing his chest and his skin looked so dusty that he couldn't have washed for weeks.

"Baksheesh, memsahib, baksheesh," he whined in a high-pitched beggar voice. Though they were treated by the natives with great respect, farouche-looking men like him terrified her, and she always ran from them for she was mortally afraid of them trying to tell her fortune. For some reason which she could not analyse she did not want to hear it.

"Go away, go away," she gabbled as the man in the hedge reached out towards her. *If he touches me I'll faint again*, she thought. Fortunately he didn't touch her, only lifted a tin cup containing a few pebbles and rattled it at her.

"Baksheesh," was all he said.

"I haven't any money," she shouted and ran back into the house, calling for Ali.

When he appeared she was weeping. "There's one of those holy-men beggars at our gate. I can't go out while he's there. Tell him to go away. Give him some money. Get rid of him!"

Ali shook his head. "He won't go away, memsahib."

She was on the verge of hysteria. "What do you mean? He'll go away if we pay him enough. Take some of the cookbook money. I don't want him out there."

Ali shook his head again. "Memsahib, he is a policeman – a detective. He's watching the house."

"Oh, no," she shrieked. "Why are they watching us? We haven't done anything. And what good is he doing out there? Everybody in the lane knows he's an undercover policeman except me! It's pointless."

Ali shrugged. "He's a policeman, memsahib. He'll stay there till they catch whoever killed the German sahib."

Twenty-Two

By the Friday of that week the festivities of
Divali were well and truly over and the
world had resumed its old routine. The
news of Gelhorn's death made surprisingly
little impact. It went the rounds and quickly
became an old story for no one was
sufficiently concerned about him to care
whether he was dead or alive.

Ben drove off to the city as usual every
morning; the buffalo camp men ran down
the lane with their milk cans on their heads;
the undercover detective slept in the hedge
and shook his collecting can at Dee whenever she showed her face. She could tell he
enjoyed annoying her.

In the Ritz, Nigel got up before dawn and
dressed very quietly so as not to disturb
Bernice.

The first thing that he discovered from the
malik when he arrived at his site at half-past
seven was that there was a problem with the
jetty foundations and a dive would have to
be made to examine them. He sent one of

his Goan foremen off in a jeep to the docks to alert the diving crew and was waiting on the pier with his hands on his hips when the divers' boat come round the point. There were only two men in it.

It dropped its anchor by a floating work platform and Jean-Paul leaned across with his hands up to his mouth to call, "What's the trouble?"

Nigel pointed to the end of the concrete barrier that would one day be the jetty. "The men say it's subsiding."

The Frenchman cursed. "It looks all right to me but I'll go down and look," he said.

Usually two men dived together but Jean-Paul's mate was still sick and so he had to go down alone. It was not a difficult job, though, just a drop of about twenty-five feet to examine the jetty base which was probably undamaged. Budgeon listened to his men and they were all scaremongers, Jean-Paul thought. Nevertheless he enjoyed strutting around in his heavy diving suit, lording it over the Indians.

"Send a couple of men out to help with the pump," he called to Nigel. The man driving the dinghy was a fat, easygoing, grey-haired Frenchman who breakfasted on pastis and was not keen on heavy work like hauling up a diver in his massive, weighty suit and metal helmet or watching the air pump.

Mehmet Ali appeared at Nigel's elbow. "I will go," said the tall Pathan.

He raised an arm to gesture to another hard-faced, beaky-nosed man, and the boy Yusuf came running over as well, calling out, "Take me, take me too..."

"All right," shrugged the malik and the three of them climbed into a little rowing boat to be taken over to the wooden platform where the air pump was set up and the dinghy was anchored. Already Jean-Paul was pulling his shirt over his head, displaying his golden chest and flexing spectacular biceps.

Neither of the older Pathans looked at him when they climbed on to the platform but immediately set about starting up the air pump's engine while Yusuf was detailed to help Jean-Paul into his suit. That morning, as if overcome by the weight of his unusual responsibility, the boy seemed unable to coordinate his movements and kept dropping bits and pieces of the diving kit.

The creek that morning was like shot silk with an oily glitter on the top of the scarcely moving water. Gallic oaths rent the air, however, and could be heard from the shore as Jean-Paul fulminated against Yusuf's clumsiness. Nothing the boy did seemed to please him and that of course only flustered Yusuf more. Mehmet Ali paused in his work with a peculiar expression on his face and shrugged scornfully but who or what he was scorning was not easy to pinpoint.

Jean-Paul, sitting on the platform, shouted down at the boy in the boat, "That! That! Give me that!" and pointed at the voluminous rubber suit that lay collapsed like a crumpled giant in the gunnels of the dinghy.

It was held up for him to step into. When his body was encased, he stood upright in enormous, weighted boots and pointed at the diving helmet. All three Pathans had to lend a hand to put it on his head and tighten the screws that secured it to his suit. He looked like a creature from another planet when he sat down again to allow the air pipe to be connected.

As he was slowly lowered overboard his French co-worker sat smoking a cigarette and spat vehemently. He did not like Jean-Paul. All the older man did was wander over to check that the air pump was working properly. Then he gestured to tell the Pathans to look after it, clapping the boy Yusuf on the back in a friendly way to make up for Jean-Paul's abuse, and ambled back to his seat at the tiller of the dinghy. Prepared for a wait, he pulled a bottle out of his pocket, unscrewed it, held it to his lips and took a generous swig before closing his eyes and tilting the brim of his straw hat down over his face as he prepared to go to sleep.

Down, down, down went Jean-Paul, the heavy boots pulling him towards the bottom. After him snaked his air tube, like an umbilical cord connecting him to life. At the other end of it Yusuf stood with his body obscuring the other Frenchman's view of what was going on while Mehmet Ali deftly twisted the point of a knife into the air tube. Then the three Pathans squatted down and waited in silence.

It took several minutes before Jean Paul realised he was choking to death – and then no amount of yanking on the line could bring any response. Above him, the Pathans sat impassively, watching the tube twisting and jerking frantically in Mehmet Ali's strong hands. He held it very tightly so that the other Frenchman suspected nothing and in the dreamy silence slept on.

They waited half an hour before they hauled Jean-Paul back up again. As he pulled on the rope Mehmet Ali said in Pushtu, "My regret is that we were not able to tell him why he had to die."

When the grotesquely lifelike diving suit had been brought up to the platform, it lay in an inert heap. Alarmed, the old Frenchman came bustling over and helped take off the helmet. The man inside was very dead.

In the excitement and shouting that followed, Mehmet Ali and the other Pathan simply melted away, but Yusuf stayed, cuddling his white puppy and watching the useless attempts to resuscitate Jean-Paul with wide-eyed amazement.

The old Frenchman walked up and down, saying over and over again, "Why didn't he give us a signal that he was in trouble? He should have pulled on the tube. It's not my fault. He must have passed out."

Inspector Mascarenas, immaculate as ever, headed the posse of police that turned up in a jeep and a big wagon with wire covers over all its windows from which jumped ten constables all carrying rifles. The police never took chances when something happened in which Pathans were involved. They covered the crowd while the inspector was rowed out to the work platform.

Jean-Paul was laid on the wooden boards and covered with a blanket from the work camp. Nigel, distraught, paced up and down beside the body. The French dinghy driver began his plaint all over again. "Why didn't he let us know he was in trouble? It's not my fault."

Mascarenas lifted a corner of the blanket and looked at the dead man, still beautiful in death. "Handsome fellow – or at least he was before this happened to him," he said.

Then he turned to inspect the diver's helmet and lifted the air tube, feeling it with his fingers as it passed through his hands.

The cut, quite large and very obvious, was about three feet along from the pump.

"Who was here when it happened?" he asked.

Nigel pointed at Yusuf and the Frenchman. Then he looked round for his malik. "Where's Mehmet Ali?" he asked Yusuf who rolled his eyes and shrugged. He seemed to be more distracted and half witted than usual.

"I can't understand it. My malik Mehmet Ali's disappeared, and so has the other man," Nigel said to Mascarenas, who sighed.

"Then your malik killed him, I'm afraid."

Nigel shook his head in disbelief, "Why?" he asked.

Another shrug. "Those Pathans don't always need a logical reason for killing. But this is the second murder of a white man in a week. There might be a connection."

Nigel looked blank. He'd heard from the Pathans about Gelhorn's death but couldn't think of any link between the two men.

Mascarenas yelled an order to his sergeant who turned and grabbed Yusuf. The boy began gibbering with fright as he was thrown roughly to the ground.

"He'll tell us," said the inspector to Nigel. "He was on the platform when it was done. Come here, boy."

He lifted his swagger stick to hit Yusuf but

Nigel jumped across and caught his arm, shouting, "Don't do that. Don't hit him. He's a simpleton. He doesn't know anything about it."

"Even simpletons can talk," said the police sergeant unfeelingly, but Nigel's grip on the inspector's arm tightened. "Don't hit him. Let me speak to him. He'll tell me what happened," he said.

He hunkered down beside the weeping boy on the ground and handed him the white puppy. "You're all right. Here's your dog," he said in his fragmentary Pushtu. "Hold it. I won't let them beat you."

Yusuf sank his face into the puppy's fur and wept. "You a good man, sahib, a very good man. They said you had to be avenged. They kill him for you."

Nigel leaned forward and asked softly, "For *me*? Why?" He was very conscious of Mascarenas standing at his back.

Yusuf whispered, "Because of your woman. Mehmet Ali was very angry." With a grimace he enacted the act of sticking a knife in the air pipe and twisting it round. "For your honour," he repeated.

Nigel looked up and saw some of his work gang standing round him like bodyguards. They'd heard what was said and their faces were impassive. One of the older men nodded and said, "Mehmet Ali has gone, sahib."

Though his legs were shaking Nigel stood up quickly and walked across to the police inspector. "You heard him say he saw Mehmet Ali slash the air pipe. He had some idea that the Frenchman was involved with my wife. It's nonsense of course."

"Will your wife give us a statement?" asked Mascarenas sharply.

"I don't want you bothering her. She's pregnant and not at all well, very nervous. I assure you there's been nothing between her and that man." He pointed at the body as he spoke.

"I'd like to speak to her later but I think that there's some connection between this death and Herr Gelhorn's. You see, we know he was running guns to the Pathans and he was very untrustworthy as far as money was concerned ... He probably double-crossed them, and this man could have been in on it too. Guns are taken off ships in the bay by dinghies like that one ... We'll take the boy to the station and get a statement out of him before I go to speak to your wife. Just a formality. You can tell her I'm coming tonight." Mascarenas seemed pleased that everything had been tied up to his satisfaction so neatly but there was pity in his eyes as he looked at Nigel.

Nigel's face had settled into deep, very tired folds and wrinkles. "I'll come with Yusuf to the station first. I don't want you to beat him. If you hurt him I'll kick up a hell of a row."

All work on the site had stopped. Nigel told the older Frenchman, "Stay here till the ambulance comes. Then your head office will have to inform his family."

The Frenchman nodded and launched into his protestations about not being to blame again but Nigel held up a weary hand. "Nobody thinks it's your fault. Don't worry," he said.

It was seven o'clock and almost dark when he tottered into the Ritz. As soon as his key turned in their suite door, Bernice, in a dark red cocktail dress that showed the tops of her magnificent white breasts, came running up to meet him – but not with a kiss.

"Where have you been?" she demanded angrily. "You know we're going to drinks at the Taj with Jean-Paul at six o'clock! He'll have been waiting there for an hour and it's his birthday!"

He looked at her out of weary, pouched eyes and walked towards the coffee table where a bottle of gin stood. Very carefully he poured himself out a glass and swallowed it straight.

Astonished, Bernice walked behind him, still scolding loudly. "You're so thoughtless ... Poor Jean-Paul ... his birthday ... it's so rude ... you never think of anyone but yourself."

At that Nigel turned quickly on his heels like the old fighter that he was and for a second she flinched for it looked at if he was about to hit her.

"Poor Jean-Paul isn't waiting at the Taj. He isn't waiting anywhere. He's dead, Bernice, and in half an hour a police officer is coming here to ask you if you had an affair with him," he shouted.

She gazed at him for a second without speaking, then she opened her mouth and screamed a long, terrible, blood-curdling scream. *"Dead!* Oooooooooh, ooooooooh, *nooooooooo..."*

Nigel grabbed her outflung hands and said in a cold, precise voice, "He drowned when he was diving at my site today."

She threw back her head and the carefully pinned-up hair escaped to tumble down her back. "No, no, no," she repeated over and over again. "Not Jean-Paul, not my darling."

Nigel pushed his red, battered face into hers. "He was murdered. My Pathans killed him because he'd been sleeping with you. That's true, isn't it? It's all your fault."

Her face contorted into a mask of hatred. "Yes, I love him. He was ten times the man you are, Nigel. Did you have him killed? If you did I'll see you hanged for it."

"No, I didn't kill him. But one of the boys told me they did it for me. Whose baby is it, Bernice?"

346

"His, of course. You're sterile. Nine years of marriage and not even a miscarriage. Didn't you realise it was your fault? Only a few times with Jean-Paul and I was pregnant."

Nigel suddenly became very calm and stepped back from her. "When the inspector comes you'd better not tell him any of that. You'd better pretend to be a virtuous wife."

"For your sake?" she jeered. She was so incandescent with rage and hatred that she was quite unafraid of him.

"No, for your own sake," he said and with his shoulders drooping like an old man walked towards the bathroom. Though she ran after him, pulling at the back of his shirt, he shook her off and went in, locking the door against her.

For a while she stood outside hammering her fists against the door panel, shouting and weeping bitterly, but after a while she gave up and ran back into the bedroom to pour another gin for herself and flop down on to the bed, wetting the pillow with her tears.

Inspector Mascarenas was late. More than an hour passed before he tapped on Bernice's door. She sat up, pinned back her hair, and shouted for Nigel to come out of the bathroom. There was no reply, however, so she had to answer the persistent tapping herself.

The police inspector came in and asked, "Where is your husband?"

She nodded towards the bathroom. "In there."

Mascarenas rattled the handle but failed to rouse Nigel either. In the end he put his shoulder to the flimsy door.

The first thing that met their horrified eyes was the corpse of Nigel Budgeon swinging from the shower rail with his leather belt buckled round his neck.

Twenty-Three

New York, 1995

By the time they were in mid-Atlantic, all the passengers on the *Selbridge Delta* were on friendly terms and Stevie – Dee could not think of him as Saul – was behaving in a courtly fashion, treating the women to pre-dinner cocktails in his cabin from time to time and chatting most pleasantly whenever they encountered each other on deck or at the swimming pool, which was where they usually congregated during the day. He showed no inclination to spend more time with Dee than with the other two women, and it was as if their long-ago acquaintance-ship had not survived the time gap.

Since her Bombay days she had not enjoyed so many days of unbroken, brilliant sunshine and so many staggering sunsets. With a stab of nostalgia she remembered her younger self throwing back the curtains in the Gulmohurs and annoying Ben by exclaiming every morning, "It's going to be another lovely day!"

Seeing Stevie again had brought the past back so forcefully that the memories which flooded into her mind seemed more immediate than what was actually happening on the ship. She did little serious work and as day after slothful day went past, she remembered more and more, and questions flooded into her mind – most of them unanswerable.

Where was Anne? Had she managed to disappear in Australia? For a long time Dee had hoped for a letter but none came. After a while she realised that they had moved around so much no letter could now reach her.

With less sympathy she wondered what had happened to Bill, and how Bernice's baby grew up. Blonde and beautiful or squat and pugilistic looking?

And Monica? How had life treated her? Seeing Stevie again had brought back vivid memories of the tall, dark girl. With sympathy she remembered Monica weeping about her dying mother, and seeing the girl on the terrace of the flat on Malabar Hill when she went with Anne and Liza to borrow Vijay. Monica had been as delighted as a child about her new circumstances, pirouetting on her high heels and swirling her full skirts. She was always so pretty, so ultra feminine, and would never have dreamt of wearing trousers.

After the party Monica had simply disappeared. No one brought her to parties any more, or knew anything definite about her, though it was rumoured she'd gone to join her cousin Carole in Calcutta. Dee had hoped that story was untrue; Carole was an air head who'd be a drag on Monica. What she'd hoped was that Monica went to America, maybe even married Stevie.

Before she'd returned to Britain, Dee had driven, with her new baby daughter lying on the front seat of the car beside her, to take a last sad look at the Gulmohurs. It had not been re-let and seemed very forlorn, locked up and empty, the garden already over-grown with a few surviving cannas strug-gling to raise their colourful spears to the sky.

She didn't go on up the lane to look at the house where Gelhorn was murdered because to her it had become a place of horror. Inspector Mascarenas had contin-ued to call at the Gulmohurs till she and Ben finally moved out and on his last visit told them that the police were satisfied Gelhorn was running guns to the Pathans and it was probably them who'd arranged his murder as well as that of Jean-Paul. Any-one who had dealings with them got their fingers burned sooner or later, he'd said.

No charges had been brought against

Yusuf, the simple-minded boy, who'd openly admitted that he had seen Mehmet Ali cut the Frenchman's air line, though the significance of that act seemed to escape him. Mehmet Ali had vanished like a wraith and, as soon as he was released, Yusuf did the same. Nigel Budgeon's distraught widow had categorically denied having any sort of liaison with Jean-Paul though it was decided that her husband had probably killed himself when he heard the story.

All the Pathans were deeply upset by Nigel's suicide, so upset that the police decided he too might have been involved with Gelhorn. "They could all been in the gun-running business together," Mascarenas told Dee.

She thought he was wrong but said nothing. What caused so many violent deaths, one after another in their isolated paradise, she had no idea.

She and Ben had attended Nigel's funeral in the little church on the top of Malabar Hill and solemnly shook hands with a veiled and weeping Bernice after the ceremony. The grieving widow had flown home the next day and no one heard anything from her again.

On the second-last day of the voyage Dee's mind was teeming with all the memories as she padded down the stairs to the ship's swimming pool and found Stevie sitting on a white plastic chair beside the cerulean water, assiduously rubbing sunblock on to his arms and chest. The enormous watch had been taken off to allow him to complete this operation properly and it lay on the floor beside his feet.

She looked down at it and smiled. "That's a magnificent timepiece," she said.

"It's a Jaeger Le Coultre," he said proudly, expecting her to be impressed by the name. Though she did not know how prestigious that watchmaker was, she reacted in a suitably admiring fashion.

"You always wore such big watches. How can you bear carrying such a weight around on your wrist?" she asked.

Something unfathomable flashed in his eyes when he looked up, as if he'd made a sudden decision. Instead of speaking he held out his naked wrist towards her and slowly turned it so she could see the inside where thick blue veins clustered. Tattooed in smudged black was a four-digit number – 9516.

At once she recognised its significance and knew what he was telling her by showing it. They looked at each other in silence till she sank into another chair by the poolside and said, "Oh, God, Stevie, how awful. I never guessed."

"Why should you? It wasn't something I

wanted people to know about me," he said quietly.

"Did Monica know?"

"Yes, I told her."

"Where were you?" she asked.

"Auschwitz-Birkenau." His voice was cold and matter of fact.

"How old were you?" she whispered.

"Fourteen when I went in. Eighteen going on seventy when I came out."

"How did you survive?" she asked.

"Luck. I was the right age and able to work ... But I used to think it would have been better to have died, like the other people in my family." His voice was cold and precise, the voice of a man with an overriding purpose and determination. A man whose personality had been forged in steel.

She stared at him in horrified silence as he went on. "We went into hiding in Berlin for a while but a neighbour informed on us and they came for us in the middle of the night. My parents were killed the day after we arrived at the camp. My sister Miriam and I were kept for the workforce – she was a year older than me and beautiful, even in prison rags. We looked after each other but one day a new SS officer arrived. He raped her and when she cursed him, he dragged her out into the exercise yard and shot her through the head.

"She was sixteen. I was in the yard when he did it and he made me strip her body and throw it in a cart. I swore then that if I survived and got out of that place I'd hunt him down and kill him."

"That's terrible," she said softly.

He was strapping on the watch again as she asked him, "So you wear that to hide the numbers?"

"I did at one time, but not any more. It doesn't matter who sees them now because I've settled my account. I took vengeance."

Her face showed that she was beginning to understand. It was as if someone had drawn back a curtain and let in daylight after ages in the dark. "You mean Hans Gelhorn, don't you?" she asked and he nodded.

"Gelhorn ... Erich von Reifstadt ... the SS man who liked killing Jews, who had no pity for the sick and old or the young and innocent."

"Oh." She sat back in the chair and stared at him. "How did you know where he was?"

"When I got to America, I told my uncle what had happened in the camp. He hired people to find von Reifstadt because he'd got away when the camp was liberated. I was sick with typhoid or I'd have killed him then but he'd gone by the time I recovered. Our contact heard that he'd gone to South America but that proved to be wrong and then we found out he was in India dealing in guns. When word came through that he'd been spotted in Bombay, I decided to go there and find him. We could have hired someone to do that for us but it was my wish to kill him and I wanted him to know who'd done it before he died.

"My uncle's company had offices in India and he arranged for me to go out for a bit ... I had to pretend to be a bit of a fool so's no one would guess what I was really doing. Looking back I realise that playing the fool wasn't too difficult for me." He gave a rueful laugh and then went on, "But Bombay's a big city and if a man's hiding there he's not easy to locate. Other people than me were tracking him and I was afraid one of them'd get him first, but I was lucky. That first day we went out to your house and I saw him, I knew him immediately. After that it was only a matter of finding a way to kill him. Your party was the perfect opportunity ... and my guilt made me determined."

"*Your* guilt?" she queried.

He grimaced. "Yes, mine. I felt guilty for having survived, and because I co-operated to save my skin in the camp. I sold my soul to the devil. I informed on other people, I told the Nazis who had money or jewellery and where they'd hidden it. I told them who was plotting and what they were saying..."

He put his hands over his face and groaned. "I did it to protect myself, and Miriam while she was alive. I kept one of her shoes after he shot her to remind me I had to kill that bastard."

His face was haggard as he remembered Auschwitz. Always, in his memory, it seemed to be under a grim covering of snow – not soft, white, Alpine drifts, but a miserly scattering that showed bits of ground beneath the crusts of snow like a starving man's ribs showing beneath rags. He saw again the big stone gate arching over the bleak railway line that brought freight cars full of people to an unimaginable fate. He remembered the stench and the terrorised cries ... and shuddered.

Seeing his anguish Dee took his hand. "Gelhorn – von Reifstadt – was a horrible man. Even before I heard your story, I thought that," she said.

"He deserved to be killed, not just for what he did to Miriam but to other people in the camp as well. He was one of the worst for brutality. I saw him kick children to death several times and he jeered at poor naked women going into the gas chambers."

She nodded silently. *An eye for an eye*, she thought. *Biblical revenge.*

He shook his head. "I wanted to explain to you why I had to do it. I thought you'd guessed ... the way you talked about that time ... It's all past but I could still be charged with murder, I suppose."

She flushed. "Please, Stevie, I haven't any intention of informing on you. I wasn't trying to pump you. The Gelhorn case was closed long ago. The police decided he'd been double crossing the Pathans over guns ... and Jean-Paul was doing the same thing, they thought. The Pathan who killed him disappeared. No one was ever caught for it."

"I was questioned by the police in New York," said Stevie.

"What did you say?" she asked and he looked sharply at her.

"I told them that I'd been at the party with my girlfriend and that my arm was in a sling because I'd dislocated my shoulder so I couldn't have overpowered and killed a big man like Gelhorn."

Dee had a sudden memory of Birbal watering the garden on the day after the party with a square of white cloth tied round his head. *That was Stevie's sling,* she suddenly realised. "You left the sling behind in the garden," she told him.

"Who found it?" he asked sharply.

"Our mali, Birbal. He wore it tied round his head."

Stevie grimaced. "And not a soul would take a second look at it then," he said.

"How did you get into the German's bungalow?" she asked. "That place of his was like Fort Knox ... and he had that awful dog."

"When that fool of a man Bill attacked me, he couldn't have done me a bigger favour because he created a diversion. In the middle of it all, Monica went up to Reifstadt's gate and threw some poisoned meat to the dog – she'd laced the meat with some of the morphia I got for her mother. Then we waited ... I knew it would take about half an hour for the dog to die. Fortunately it died quietly. He'd have heard it if it barked or squealed. He was passed out on the bed when we got into the house."

"*We?*" she asked.

He nodded. "Me and Monica. She covered him with one of his guns while I woke him up. I wanted him to know what was happening, I wanted him to know who was going to kill him ... she felt the same way." His tone of voice was so cold that Dee felt her body chill in spite of the warmth of the blazing sun.

"Did he recognise you?" she whispered.

"Not till I reminded him. I expect we all looked the same in the camp. But he knew Monica. He beat her up so badly once that she's never been able to have children."

"How awful," said Dee again. She remembered being told something of the kind long ago, by Inspector Mascarenas.

Stevie showed no emotion, however. "When I'd told him why he had to die, I shot him," he said. "I'm glad I did. I don't feel the least bit of remorse about it. We dropped the gun by his hand but we didn't really care if they thought it was suicide or not."

"Suicide didn't explain the cut padlock chain and the dead dog," said Dee.

"I was gambling that I could get away before the body was found," said Stevie. "I'd booked the flight before the party and the police would be able to check that. They knew Monica had good reason to hate him but they wouldn't suspect a woman on her own. She was magnificent all the way through. I couldn't have done it without her."

"Did she know what you were going to do from the beginning?" Dee asked.

"Yes, almost from the time I really began to plan it."

And we all thought Stevie was a fool, thought Dee.

"Did you hear about Jean-Paul?" she asked.

Stevie nodded. "Yeah, I heard about him. Monica told me. I thought it was a coincidence that the two of them were killed at almost the same time."

Dee said, "It must have helped you because, as I told you, the police tied them together. Poor Nigel Budgeon killing himself was taken as proof that he was in it too. Everything was neatly tidied up and forgotten. I don't suppose there's anyone left mourning Gelhorn. It sounds to me as if he got what was coming to him."

"Yeah, that's what Monica thought," he said. The pupils of his eyes were huge and dark as if he was staring down a long tunnel into the past.

"Did you see Monica again after you left Bombay?" Dee asked him.

He nodded and said, "Oh, sure. She came over to New York. I'd got her a ticket at the same time as I got mine but she wouldn't come till her mother died and she'd done all the church things for her. It was December before she turned up."

At that moment came the sound of clattering sandals on the metal stairway and from the corner of her eye, Dee saw Lucy negotiating her way down with a tray of drinks. She had to ask the question now because she might not have another chance.

"Did you marry Monica, Stevie?" she whispered hurriedly. He shook his head and said, "No; she married another guy and they're very happy. I'll make sure you two get together in New York."

At least that's one long-standing question answered, thought Dee.

Twenty-Four

The next day was the last full day of the voyage for they were due to arrive in New York at seven o'clock the following morning. On the last evening the passengers and officers were invited to a party in Stevie's cabin. He'd bought six bottles of champagne from the captain's store and persuaded the Filipino cook to make up a tray of unadventurous canapés: curls of smoked salmon enclosing balls of cream cheese, pickled gherkins and little sausages skewered by toothpicks.

It had not been the sort of voyage where people dressed for dinner – even the officers, who were of several nationalities, went about in jeans and T-shirts all the time. Dee compared this informality with the pomp and ceremony of P&O liners on which she'd sailed to and from India in the 1950s and 60s. She'd enjoyed that at the time but nowadays preferred a more laid-back way of travelling.

For their disembarkation party, however,

she made an effort; washed her hair, made up her face and put on the only formal dress she'd brought with her – a black, full-length jersey tube with long sleeves and a flattering neckline. As she climbed the short flight of stairs to the top deck, she wondered if her path would ever cross Stevie's again after tomorrow. It had been strange meeting him after so many years but even more strange that he'd revealed to her his terrible secret. In retrospect she wondered why she hadn't worked it out before; now she knew the truth she realised there had been plenty of clues.

Halfway up the stairs her step faltered. Stevie was obviously a much tougher nut than anyone had ever guessed. If he was capable of shooting Gelhorn, what might he do to make sure that the murder remained a secret? How did he know he could trust her not to talk about it?

I'd better lock my cabin door tonight, she thought, and then she laughed aloud at herself. *Don't be such a wimp*, she told herself. *Why should I be afraid of Stevie? After all, he told me his story without any prompting. He obviously trusted me. Anyway, the case was closed long ago, and he knows it's unlikely I'd try to have it reopened, for I've no axe to grind on Gelhorn's behalf.*

She trusted Stevie too, but then, she thought with mild disquiet, she'd thought she knew what he was like in the old days and she'd been completely wrong about that, hadn't she? She gave herself a mental shake to drive away the doubts and went into the cabin with a confident smile on her face.

The London ladies, Lucy and Harriet, were already in Stevie's cabin, looking magnificent. Lucy was wearing black like Dee, but her dress was tight fitting and very short skirted with a plunging back – obviously a designer gown. Harriet was in a drift of pale green with the bodice stitched all over with tiny flowers. It looked like the sort of dress you saw pictured in *Vogue* and probably was. The lovely clothes gave the cabin a festive and sophisticated air.

The officers had made an effort too and were dressed in black trousers and white shirts with their insignia epaulettes glittering in gold braid. Everyone had champagne glasses in their hands and as soon as Dee stepped through the cabin door, Stevie filled one for her and presented it with a flourish.

"It's a long time since you and I were at a party together!" he said, chinking the rim of his glass against hers.

Sharp-eared Harriet turned round and said, "Have you two met before?"

Stevie laughed. "Indeed we have. We're old friends. How long since we last met, Dee?"

She looked at him over the brim of her glass. "More than thirty years," she said.

Lucy came across and asked, "Did you know you were going to meet up on board?" She scented a mystery.

Dee shook her head. "No, not at all. I was amazed when I recognised him. He was even more surprised than me when I introduced myself because he didn't remember me at all at first. I had to remind him we were in Bombay at the same time years and years ago."

This delighted the women who chorused, "How amazing! What a coincidence!" They both looked at Dee with new respect, obviously thinking that perhaps she wasn't just an eccentric old lady after all. Perhaps she would even have enough influence with her old friend to make him change his mind about the Pre-Raphaelite picture which Stevie had steadfastly refused to discuss with them.

"I never do business on holiday," he said if they brought up the subject. But they knew that was not true because he spent hours on the ship's radio telephone shouting terse commands to the person at the other end. The bill must have been monumental – almost enough to buy the picture, Lucy said.

After she'd had three glasses of champagne, she came across to Dee. "Do you think you could ask Mr Steindl to look at the transparencies of my Holman Hunt?" she whispered in her ear.

Dee shook her head. "I'm sorry, I can't. I haven't any influence with him at all. We were only acquaintances in Bombay."

Lucy took the refusal in good part, saying, "Never mind; I think the way you met again after so long is an amazing story."

If you only knew how amazing, thought Dee.

"Will you be seeing each other in New York?" asked Harriet.

"I don't think so. He's promised to put me in touch with another old friend – again an acquaintance to be more accurate – who's living there, but he'll probably only give me her phone number. She might not want to see me. When people meet again after such a long time, it's often impossible to pick up the friendship. You've both changed such a lot..."

"Has Mr Steindl changed?" asked Lucy, looking across the cabin at their host.

Dee laughed. "Indeed he has," she said. "Very much." Apart from everything else that was different about him, the old Stevie would almost certainly have been bullied into buying the Holman Hunt.

Though the canapés were wilting and tasteless, the champagne proved to be superior and by the time the six bottles had been consumed, everyone had become giggly and full of *bonhomie*. After dinner, Stevie announced that he was not going to bed but intended to sit out on deck and watch New York hove into view, for already faint lights from that city were twinkling on the horizon.

"Sailing up the Hudson early in the morning is an experience not to be missed," he said solemnly. "You ladies should stay up and watch too. We go past the Statue of Liberty and she'll be all lit up. The sight of her always makes me want to burst into tears."

He looked across at Dee when he said this and she wondered when and in what circumstances he'd had his first glimpse of the statue. No wonder it made him weep.

Harriet and Lucy didn't want to stay up but although Dee went to bed, she couldn't sleep. The champagne coursing in her blood made her restless and eager to start on the next phase of her holiday. She loved what she'd seen of New York on previous visits and was looking forward to renewing and extending her knowledge of the city. With rising excitement she mentally reviewed all the things she intended to do before flying home again in ten days' time. One of them was to visit her American publisher's office and try to sell her book on Queen Eleanor – surely that spirited and daring lady was exactly the sort of woman American readers would love.

Eventually she gave up on sleep and decided to take Stevie's tip and go on deck to be dazzled by the Statue of Liberty.

She saw him standing by the ship's rail on the deck above her when she stepped out into the balmy night but didn't intrude on him, turning to gaze at the panorama of lights spread out enticingly before her. There lay magnificent, enticing New York in all its variety with the famous skyscrapers reaching for the heavens – the Empire State, the Chrysler and Woolworth buildings as well as many others she could not identify. They were the epitome of ambition and infinite possibility.

A pilot boat, dwarfed by the huge hull of their ship, chugged along like a dog on a lead by its side, though in fact it was the tug that was doing the leading and not the other way round. The water was very still and glittered with rainbow colours from the reflection of lights on shore. The scene was like a vast Turner watercolour.

She brought her camera out of the pocket of her bathrobe and steadied it on the rail in readiness for taking a picture of the Statue of Liberty which loomed alongside, the blazing torch in the woman's hand pointing upwards.

Just as her finger pressed down on the

exposure button, she heard a step behind her and knew the picture would not come out because her hand had shaken uncontrollably. If Stevie was planning to get rid of her, he could do it now. She could disappear overboard with hardly a splash and without a soul to watch her go. *Why didn't I stay safely in my cabin?* she asked herself, but knew that in a way she'd come out to test Stevie. She was deliberately playing with fire.

When she turned to look at him she saw that his eyes were full of tears. Wiping them away with the back of his hand and pointing at Manhattan, he said, "Sorry about the emotion, but that sight always gets me in the gut."

"I can understand that," she said.

He walked up to stand beside her and gripped the top of the rail with both hands. "The rage I lived with before I killed that man was terrible. I felt reborn after he'd gone but I still get devastated when I think of the waste of all those lives ... My parents and my sister should have been able to see this too."

"I understand," said Dee again, very softly.

He turned towards her. "Don't worry. You have nothing to fear from me. If you decide to inform on me, that's your decision. I'll face that if it happens."

"I have no intention of informing on you. I told you that already. What you said to me is strictly between us. The only person I might ever have repeated it to was Ben and he's dead," she told him.

He turned back to the spectacular view as if what she'd said satisfied him. "Where are you staying in New York?" he asked.

"East Ninety-Seventh Street," she said. It was only a middle-class district, and she supposed Stevie would be used to a far wealthier area but her friend's flat was one of the most pleasant she'd been in – large and comfortable, the ideal place to live.

"Near Central Park?" he asked.

"Yes, that end," she told him and he seemed reassured. The Central Park end was the smartest.

"I'm being met at the docks by my limo," he said. "If you don't mind leaving the ship as soon as possible, I'll take you into Manhattan with me. Getting a hire car from Hoboken docks can be difficult."

She was pleased at this offer and accepted gratefully. "What time are you leaving?" she asked.

He consulted the massive watch. "In exactly four hours," he said. "We dock at seven and I want to be away by eight. Then I can have breakfast with my wife. She's not an early riser. I've sure missed her, but she doesn't like boats and flies everywhere. As soon as immigration clears us, I'm heading for home." He sounded like a happy man and she was glad for him. The old Stevie had never seemed happy even when at his most ebullient.

The limo waiting for them at the bottom of the gangway was the height of magnificent bad taste – white, ostentatiously long and low slung, with a fluorescent silver trim along its sides. She stared at it in amazement and hoped Stevie didn't see how appalled she was at the sight.

The passenger door, a huge distance from the driver's, was held open for her by a chauffeur in a black uniform and braided cap. The interior was like a bookmaker's drawing room with deep sofas upholstered in spotless cream leather, a gleaming cocktail cabinet and a recessed television set. You could have held a party in it and Dee wondered what Stevie would think if she ever offered him a lift in her little Renault with newspapers and auction-sale catalogues all over the floor and dog hairs on the seats.

As she settled into the deep cushions she asked him, "Gosh, is this car really yours?"

He beamed at how impressed she sounded and said, "Yeah. It's my wife's favourite. She likes the soft seating and the smoked glass."

"It's certainly comfortable," said Dee, stroking the seat.

They swept silently and smoothly through suburban streets and into the city by the George Washington Bridge with Stevie pointing out sights as they went. When the street numbers dropped to two digits and ninety-seven was near Dee said, "I hope I haven't taken you too far out of your way."

"Not at all, you're on my route. I'm going to Sutton Place," he said and she was even more impressed for she knew Sutton Place was an enclave of the very rich in a rich city.

At East 97th Street, Dee's two pieces of luggage and her precious computer were carried into the lobby by the chauffeur who pressed the lift button and handed her in as if she were a duchess.

Stevie stood beaming beneficently. Before they parted, he kissed her cheek and said, "It's been a real bit of luck meeting you again, Dee. I was glad to be able to talk about von Reifstadt and you've made me remember lots of other things – good things – about my time in India. I hope you can come to my place for dinner tomorrow night. I'll try to get Monica and her husband there as well. And tomorrow you'll meet my wife of course."

He never gives her a name, Dee thought. *It's as if he glories in having a wife at all and the title alone is a pleasure to him.* The Nat King Cole song "The Story of My Wife", which had always made Ben go sentimental at a certain stage of parties, came vividly back into her memory and she felt a tingle of unshed tears in her eyes.

Fortunately Stevie didn't notice. Backing out of the door, he said, "The car'll pick you up at six twenty; OK?"

"That'll be wonderful," she agreed.

Twenty-Five

The black dress came out again the next night for Stevie's dinner party. As always, Dee was surprised at how early Americans dined. *You'd never be invited for a six-thirty dinner at home*, she thought.

When she sat alone in the back, the limo seemed even more immense than it had on the previous day, and she stared through the smoked glass at people on the streets, thinking it rather sinister that she could see them but they couldn't see her. They were in a different world. If Eleanor of Aquitaine was alive today, would she be driven around in a stretch limo? she wondered, and decided she probably would because Eleanor liked her luxuries.

Unlike the car, the Sutton Place address was extremely discreet – a brass-ornamented front door, a deferential doorman, a marble hall and deeply carpeted lifts. The lift operator seemed to know where she was going without being told. "To the penthouse," he said as they sped upwards. She

374

smiled, thinking of Virginia Woolf's *To The Lighthouse*.

The lift door swished back to reveal a carpeted hall with huge vases of white lilies arranged on antique side tables beneath rococo mirrors. A double door at the end of the hall was thrown open when she stepped out and revealed Stevie in a burgundy-coloured velvet smoking jacket which gave him the look of one of the medieval Doges of Venice. Beaming broadly he advanced towards her with both hands outspread.

"Come in, come in," he said enthusiastically. "Monica and Mel are here. Monica's desperate to see you. My wife's just getting ready. She'll join us in a minute."

My wife again, thought Dee. *Hasn't the woman got a name?*

The room she stepped into was vast and incredibly luxurious. The expanse of beige carpet was soft beneath her feet and she walked, dazzled, towards an entire wall made of glass, through which could be seen a stretch of the East River with tourist boats cruising up it.

In the corners stood huge Chinese vases full of exotic, pale-coloured flowers, and the furniture was very modern, low slung and upholstered in beige-coloured suede. Lamps that twisted like snakes suspended translucent shades over the chairs and sofas and a gleaming grand piano stood in front of the window so that anyone playing it could look out at the river. The biggest television set Dee had ever seen extended itself along one wall but the other two walls displayed Impressionist canvases – one a large Monet showing the artist's garden at Givenchy and the other a smaller Renoir of ballet dancers putting on their shoes. If they were not copies – and they didn't look like copies – they were worth several million dollars each. There was no sign of any Pre-Raphaelite works, but then that style would not have fitted in with the colour scheme of this carefully devised decor.

Everything in the room seemed bigger than normal and that was intimidating to Dee who was barely five feet tall. It made her feel like Alice in Wonderland after she'd recklessly imbibed from the bottle labelled "Drink Me".

A couple standing by the window provided the only spot of bright colour. The man was wearing a plaid jacket and the woman was elegantly wrapped in a scarlet sari with a sparkling golden hem. She came running across the luscious carpet with her eyes alight and a brilliant smile on her face.

"Welcome!" she enthused and folded Dee in her arms.

Time had dealt kindly with Monica. Her skin was still smooth and ivory coloured, her hair glossy and black, her enormous eyes still arresting, even more than in the past because they were now rimmed with skillfully applied kohl – a fashion which, like the sari, the young Monica would never have adopted. Obviously her pretensions to Englishness had been cast aside and she was now proudly Indian.

She was genuinely delighted to see Dee. Taking both her hands she cried out, "How wonderful to meet you again. I've often thought about you and Ben and that party you gave … I've told my husband about it many times, haven't I, Mel?"

The man in the tartan jacket stuck out his hand and said, "Hi, I'm Mel Baumgarten. Monica *has* told me a lot about you and your party." He was a pleasant-looking, tubby chap with thinning fair-turning-to-grey hair and a kind smile.

Monica's eyes sparkled when she looked at Dee. "It was all so long ago. It's a miracle that you and Saul decided to cross the Atlantic on the same boat … We were so surprised when he rang to tell us who he'd met!"

So he's Saul to her now, thought Dee, and was about to say something when Monica turned to Stevie and asked, "Does she know about …?"

He cut her off with a shake of his head. "Not yet," he said and led Dee to a sofa chair, warning her, "You'd better sit down now. You're in for a big surprise."

She sank into it, looking bemused as he called out, "OK, you can come in now."

A skilfully concealed door behind the television opened and a blonde woman in black stepped through it. Tears were glittering in her eyes as she paused in the opening and said to Dee, "Don't you know me?"

The voice was unmistakable: low and sweetly modulated, though it now had an American intonation.

"Anne!" Dee gasped. It was Anne, still blonde, still regal looking but plump and motherly now. She'd become a comfortable, friendly, happy-looking woman, no longer haunted by the demons that had used to give her those terrifying blackouts.

"Anne! Is it really you?" said Dee again in total amazement. She was struggling to get out of the deep seat when Anne ran across and threw herself down to give her friend a huge hug. They were sobbing and giggling at the same time like children.

Anne said, "I wanted to take you by surprise. When Saul rang from the ship on the radio telephone I told him not to give anything away so we could spring it on you here. You didn't guess, did you?"

Dee shook her head. "No! I hadn't a clue. I never dreamt of it for a moment! But I did wonder why he didn't refer to his wife by name. He always just said 'my wife'. I thought at first that he might have married Monica ... but when I asked him he said he hadn't, so I was left wondering."

Monica laughed. "We were only friends – but he did bring me to New York and then I married his dentist!" She put an affectionate arm round her husband's waist and kissed his cheek.

He laughed too and said, "I'd never seen a woman with such perfect teeth. I had to marry her – what an advertisement for me!"

This defused the emotional atmosphere a bit and they all laughed.

Dee still stared slightly disbelievingly at Anne and said, "But I never guessed about you two. Not on the boat and not in Bombay. How did it happen?"

Anne replied, "I thought you did know because you were always so noticing ... but I couldn't tell you. You know what Bill was like ... We fell for each other the first time we met – in your garden – so you're the one we've got to thank for everything."

Dee remembered that afternoon at the Gulmohurs when she had first seen an exchange between Bernice and Jean-Paul. She'd been so busy watching them she'd not paid any attention to what was going on between Stevie and Anne.

"The first time you ever met!" she said in amazement.

"Yes, really – but we didn't do anything

about it until the night of the party ... when we were helping you with the food he said to me that he loved me, and I said I felt the same. It was wonderful. But even then I thought we had no chance of being together. I was so afraid of Bill."

"Bill! What happened to him?" Dee asked. *Did Stevie have him written off too,* she wondered?

Anne's face became solemn. "He's dead. He was killed in a shooting accident in London about five years after I left him. Oddly enough he was only a passer-by who was shot by an escaping bank robber. That was ironic, wasn't it?"

Dee nodded, remembering Bill's fascination with crime. "Did you go to Perth?" she asked.

Anne shook her head. "No; I'm sorry to have told you lies but I couldn't leave any clues. I wanted Bill to think I'd gone to Australia but in fact Liza and I flew out of Santa Cruz to London where this man here was waiting for me. He'd arranged everything ... then we flew to New York. He wasn't afraid of flying then," said Anne, looking lovingly at her husband.

So Mascarenas was right about where Anne flew to, thought Dee.

Saul was beaming at his wife and saying, "I was terrified of flying even then but I was more scared of the police and Bill catching up with us. Anyway, if I wasn't scared of flying I wouldn't have been on that boat and we wouldn't have met our old friend again."

"That's true," agreed Anne, holding Dee's hand. "You've no idea how often I've thought about you, Dee. And about that party. If you and Ben hadn't asked us to it I'd probably still be with Bill – or dead."

"Yeah, that party was good for all of us," said Stevie. He turned to his wife and friends to say, "It's all right. Dee knows about von Reifstadt."

To Dee he said, "Your party gave me the chance to revenge myself on Reifstadt ... I knew what I had to do and it provided the ideal opportunity."

Monica came over and sat on the sofa beside the other women. Her face became serious as she leant towards Dee to add, "Sometimes I still dream about that night though it was so long ago. I was terrified. We didn't know if he'd kill us first but we had to try. I'd promised to help Saul but I was so scared ... and my poor mother was dying. Do you remember coming to sit beside me and comfort me? I longed to tell you what we'd planned but I couldn't of course. I'm glad you know now. We all trust each other and the only other person I've ever told is Mel ... It was like a nightmare – but it all worked out in the end."

Dee shook her head in sympathy and took

Monica's hand. There were so many questions she wanted to ask, so many things she wanted to tell them but there was one big question that had to be answered first.

"Liza, what about Liza?" she asked Anne.

"When Bill died, my father read about the shooting in a newspaper and wrote to tell me, so we were able to get married and Saul adopted Liza. She's married now in Boston with two little girls and Monica's the godmother to Bernadette, the oldest. We have another two boys – they're grown up now of course – and they're great fellows. What about you?" Anne asked.

Dee told them about Ben dying and what had happened to her since the days at the Gulmohurs. Then she said, "And I've four children ... three girls and a boy."

"Trust old Ben!" laughed Stevie as he went across to ring a bell for the maid who was told, "Bring out the champagne. We're going to drink a toast to old friends."